# A Powerless World

## Book 2

# When the Peace is Gone

**P.A. Glaspy**

**PRESS**

Originally self-published by P.A. Glaspy in 2016

Published by Vulpine Press in the United Kingdom in 2017

Cover by Claire Townsend

ISBN: 978-1-910780-48-0

www.vulpine-press.com

For Jim, my husband, my confidante, my cheerleader, and my best friend. I could not have done this without you.

.

# Chapter 1

We'd made it. We were safe, for the time being. But how long would it last?

Our arrival at the farm was a bit frantic, with introductions to Millie and Monroe, moving the animals to the pens, and getting everyone fed and situated. We didn't really have a chance to talk about the encounter on the road with the couple that was killed, though there was no doubt it was on all of our minds. After eating we got settled in a bit; we needed to talk about what had happened. I could tell by the look on Russ's face it was weighing very heavily on his heart. It was on mine as well, so I knew it was the same for the rest of the group. We weren't soldiers, trained for that sort of thing. It takes a lot to kill another person, and it was not something any of us had ever done, with the exception of possibly Monroe and Mike. We hadn't spent enough time with Mike to know what his experience had been, and Monroe never talked about his time in the service of our country. If anyone mentioned war he just got really quiet and didn't offer any input. To me, that meant it was a subject that was very disconcerting for him. I think we kind of knew why now.

We sat in the living room with our after-dinner coffee in hand. Surprisingly, Mike spoke up first. "I know you are all freaked out over the encounter we had on the road today. As a former Marine, I have had to shoot and kill people—people who were attacking me or my team. It is not an easy thing to do, to take a life. I hate that it had to happen, but I'm glad you were ready to do what you had to do to protect yourselves, as well as your loved ones, in a dangerous situation. When a gun is fired everyone in the vicinity is in danger. You have to be ready to take out whatever threat that may be present to protect those you love. Your reflexes were excellent. I just want everyone to know you did what you had to do, what you needed to do, for all of our safety."

Mike looked around the room. I'm sure he saw a myriad of emotions: sadness, anger, guilt, just to name a few, and quite possibly all of those on my face alone. He went on.

"I don't know what anyone else's skillset is, but I would like to offer my services for security training. While I am a machinist by trade, I have extensive experience with firearms and safety protocols. I was a range officer for a gun range a few years ago. I have handled just about every type of gun out there. I think we all need to be prepared for any kind of confrontation, and I can help with that. The last thing I want to say is this: none of you should feel guilty for what happened. Those people set themselves up for what transpired when they pulled guns on us. Never point a gun at anything you aren't willing to shoot. I know you won't get past it overnight, but it will pass. Sadly, I don't think this will be a solitary incident. We will have to defend what we have from those less fortunate, less prepared, and more desperate, as well as those who are just too damn lazy to earn anything and choose to use force to take what others have. I for one am very glad to be here and will do whatever you need done to pay my way. That's all I have to say."

Wow—I was surprised at the display of passion from a guy we'd just met a few hours ago. He was a keeper, no doubt about it.

Monroe addressed the group from his recliner. "We are definitely going to need everybody armed and ready to defend this place. We don't have a lot of neighbors, but we have a few. I'm thinking we should probably get out to all of them in the next day or so, to see how they're doing, what their plans are, maybe even bring them in here. We have plenty of room to set up tents, campers, whatever we need to put folks in. The more the merrier, as long as none of them try to take my bed." He looked down at his seat. "Or this here chair of mine. As long as they understand that, let's build up our little community and its security team."

There were giggles at Monroe's possessive furniture remarks, but we agreed with both men. Security was going to be one of our top priorities in the next couple of days and for the foreseeable future. As we were settling down again, Russ looked at our boys.

"Rusty, Ben, I need to know that you guys are okay. Fifteen-year-old boys should not have to deal with what we had to do today. Hell, thirty-something-year-old parents shouldn't, for that matter. I know it shook me up bad. How are you doing after what happened?"

The boys looked at Russ, then at each other. They had been quiet since it all happened, but honestly I was so freaked myself that I think I tuned it all out. My mind was telling me, Just get to the farm, and everything will be okay. Now that we were there I could see we had all compartmentalized it. The shock and awe of the bizarre circumstances were coming home to everyone. We'd taken lives. For the first time since this whole mess started, we had personally ended two people's existence. The more I thought about that, the more it upset me. I started crying, and of course when Janet saw that, she started crying as well. That's what best friends do: if one of us cries, we both cry.

Russ saw me bawling and wrapped his arms around me. Rusty came over and joined the family comfort hug, which of course made me cry even harder, only then it was because I was pissed off. My baby was having to deal with this shit. Rusty pulled back and looked at his dad and me.

"Honestly, Dad, it scared the hell ... er, heck out of me when that gun went off." Russ hid a grin at the cuss word, while I raised an eyebrow at my son, thinking, Watch it, buster. You ain't grown yet.

"Then, when I heard all the other guns going off, I jumped out of the truck. By the time I got out, the two people were already down. I didn't shoot, Dad. It was over before I even pulled my pistol out of the holster."

I breathed a huge sigh of relief, as did Russ. Ben was nodding from his mother's arms, where he had headed when he saw her crying.

"Me either, Uncle Russ. I was too far away. I didn't even really see anything until it was over."

Janet hugged her son and Bob ruffled his hair. Okay, they had been exposed to the ugliness that was our current world, but they had not been directly involved. Maybe we could maintain their innocence for a little while longer, though I wasn't sure how long that would be. Russ stood up and addressed the room.

"I think we should try to get some rest, folks. We'll crash wherever we can tonight, and get everyone more settled in the morning. I'll take first security watch with …" He looked around the room, and Mike's hand shot up. "With Mike. Who wants second watch with Bob?"

Brian raised his hand. "I don't think you should subject the new recruits to Bob yet. I'll take it."

Bob jumped up from the sofa, and Brian made a beeline for the kitchen. We all enjoyed their antics, which were some much-needed comic relief. We would not forget what had happened, but we had to focus on settling in for the long run. Now that we were there, it seemed a little safer, more secure, and less exposed. But how long would that hold true?

# Chapter 2

I woke up to the sound of a rooster crowing really loud. Geez, was the bastard on the window sill? I jumped out of bed, ready to shoo him away or wring his neck, since it was about 4:30 in the morning. I made my way to the window, which was not that easy—the floor of our bedroom at the farm was covered with … stuff. It was pretty late by the time we finally got settled in bed. Everyone was hyped up about the trip, getting here in one piece, and the new people seeing the farm for the first time. We talked well into the evening about the encounter on the road, as well as some elementary security measures. We had a lot of work to do and probably not a lot of time to get it done. We were not on an island, so we wouldn't stay hidden from the scumbags for long.

We brought a few loads in from the truck and trailer, but we were so exhausted from the tension of the day—hell, the week was more like it—we just couldn't get more done. We dropped supplies everywhere, dug out sleeping bags, cots, and blankets, and got everybody a place to sleep. We were crowded, but everyone had a bed for the night. To make as much room as possible we had Rusty on the floor in our room, and Ben was in with Bob and Janet, which freed up another bedroom with two sets of long bunk beds. We put people in the living room, in the basement, and I think a couple of the guys might have slept out in the cars.

What had started out as the six of us—our family and the Hoppers—had become close to twenty by the time we got to the farm. With Monroe and Millie already there, plus a couple of local boys who had been staying with them since the pulse, we were now over two dozen. Good thing the house was big. Even at that, we would still have to come up with some more permanent accommodations for the new additions. We couldn't keep two dozen people in a six-bedroom house without constantly invading each other's privacy, not that there would be a lot of that now anyway. We would have to address living arrangements pretty fast. If we were going to make it together, we needed everyone as comfortable as we could get them.

The guilty rooster was not on the window sill or even that close to the house. The lack of any other noise made him seem a lot louder than he was. Or maybe he had always been that loud, but the background noise of a modern electric world had dulled the sound somewhat. When we'd been here in the past there had been fans, air conditioning, and the hum of electronics everywhere— sounds we took for granted and paid no attention to in our daily lives. The sounds of progress were no longer there. It had been about two weeks since the pulse had taken out the power grid and everything electrical had ceased to work. We had a few electronic items that we had protected in Faraday cages at the house and there were some here on the farm as well. Everything else was toast. No electricity meant no lights, no fans, no a/c—that was going to suck really bad in Tennessee, really soon—as well as no late-model cars, no cell phones, tablets, computers—if it had been plugged in at the time the pulse hit, or had a computer chip in it, it was a paperweight now. Some appliances that were strictly mechanical still worked, as long as they hadn't been connected to the power grid when it happened, but that was about it.

I swore at the rooster and gave it a rude hand gesture. I figured I might as well get downstairs and get some coffee going since we had a full day ahead of us. I felt my way around the edge of the bed so I wouldn't step on Rusty, who was still sleeping soundly despite the way-too-early wake-up call from Sir Crows-A-Lot. Kids can sleep through anything. Russ was already up and gone, so I needed to check on him as well. I was not surprised, even though he had only gotten about three hours sleep after his security watch. He was extremely concerned about getting the place secured and getting everyone settled. Hmmm, maybe he already had the coffee going. That would be awesome. I grabbed some clothes from a bag on the floor, threw them on, and headed down to the kitchen.

As soon as I reached the top of the stairs, I smelled it: the delicious aroma of coffee. I love coffee just about any way you can create it. I'd had the means to make coffee no less than six different ways before the lights went out. The pulse only took out one of those—the pod coffee maker. The rest were either stove top, drip, press, or instant. Oh, and open fire, which was my favorite way to make boiled coffee, or cowboy coffee as we called it. Since I smelled boiled coffee, I was pretty sure Russ was the one who had made it. He loved it as much as I did.

I walked into the kitchen with my nose slightly raised, trying to inhale every bit of the aroma. Russ was sitting at the table with Monroe, Millie, Brian, and Bob. They grinned at my expression and Millie started to get up to get me a cup. I stopped her.

"No, ma'am, you stay right where you are. I can get my own coffee. I think we're all going to have plenty to do today. Save your energy."

I went to the counter, opened a cupboard beside the sink, and pulled out a coffee mug. After I had my coffee fixed up, I went to the table and grabbed a seat.

"I can't believe you guys are all up already. Was it the rooster for you, too?"

Monroe laughed. "Sugar, I get up at this time every day, even before the lights went out. A farm is a lot of work. It starts early and ends not too long after the sun goes down. I don't reckon that's gonna change."

Millie nodded. "Me too, but only because Monroe makes more racket than that rooster out there when he gets up."

Monroe winked at her. "You know I do that on purpose so you'll get up and make me a batch of your biscuits, right? I just can't start the day without my Millie's biscuits and gravy."

She smiled at her husband of fifty-odd years. "Of course I do. I snagged you with those biscuits when we were courtin'. Once you had the first one, you were mine, mister."

Monroe busted out laughing, and the rest of us joined in. Just then Janet walked in, followed by the Lawton brothers. Ryan yawned as he came into the room. "Man, y'all are having way too much fun for this early in the morning. Can we eat that damn rooster?"

That started us all laughing again. I stood up and headed for the counter. "No, because we need his sorry ass to make more chickens, or believe me, I'd stew him up in a heartbeat. You guys drink coffee? We've got a couple of pots already done."

Bill looked at me like I was an angel right there on Earth. "Oh my God, yes. We ran out of coffee a couple of days ago. Black, straight up."

Ryan was vigorously nodding his head next to his brother. I handed them both cups, then gave Janet hers. I knew how she drank her coffee: just like I did.

Russ looked at the group around the old, worn kitchen table. "We're going to need to get everything unloaded and stored away. I want to get those trailers out of the yard and tucked back in the old garage out of sight. They're like a billboard telling the world we hauled a bunch of stuff in here. Once that's done we can figure out where everyone is going to sleep on a more permanent basis."

He turned to Bill and Ryan. "Guys, sorry about the rooster, but I'm thinking we'll set up a big six-man tent for you single guys outside for now, but close to the house in case anything happens or we get a really bad storm. Once everyone decides if they want to stay or not, we can build a basic bunkhouse. That will put you two, Mike, and Brian in the tent. You think you can work with that?"

Ryan grinned at him. "Man, you saved us out there, probably saved our lives. You think we're gonna complain about a bed, food, and security, because of an early-rising chicken? We'll consider it a daily wake-up call. Besides, we usually get up by 5:00 a.m. anyway. Landscaping is hot work. You want to get it done early."

Russ nodded. "Ok, that's four. After Monroe and Millie, Bob and Janet, and Anne and I each take a bedroom, that leaves three more. We'll put Ben and Rusty, as well as … Monroe, what are those boys' names? I don't think I caught them last night, or I was so tired they didn't stick."

Monroe replied, "Matt and Nick Thompson. They live the next place over. Not a farm, just a homestead on about an acre or so of land. Their mom and dad were gone to Memphis to see her momma. No way they get back from there with no supplies. That place will be a war zone. The boys help us out here when we need extra hands, so we had them move in after the power went out. I don't know for sure their parents are gone, but I doubt they're getting back any time soon. That's 250 miles away."

Russ went on. "Okay then. Rusty, Ben, Matt, and Nick can take the room with the two sets of bunk beds. That's four bedrooms. One of the spare rooms has two double beds, so I think we should give that one to the Scanlins, if they decide to stay. They should fit in there fine. That leaves one bedroom, but we still have two families—the Raines and the Roushes. Both are three people. We'll also need a spot for Marietta. Suggestions, anybody?"

Millie said, "The attic has room for a few people, but Lord, it will be hotter than the fires of hell up there this summer. The basement seems a logical choice. Very temperate, not too hot and not too cold. We could move some of the items we have down there over to the barn or out to the yard. It's just old clothes, gardening tools, that kind of thing. You could possibly put one of those families down there, maybe string a curtain or sheets up to give them a little privacy, but it won't be much. But then, I don't guess beggars can be choosers now, can they?"

I chimed in. "We could put Marietta on a cot in the sewing room if that's alright with Millie. It's small, but it would give her some privacy as the only single woman. Would you be okay with that, Millie?"

Millie smiled. "Of course, child. That's a wonderful idea. Not like I'm going to be spending a lot of time quilting for a while. We'll be too busy getting by."

Bob looked at Russ. "You're talking like you think the Scanlins are staying. Do you think they won't want to go look for their friends … What was their name?"

"Luke and Casey Callen. Supposed to live out this way somewhere."

Monroe's head snapped up. "Luke Callen? I know him. He lives about four or five miles from here. I see him at the CO-OP from time to time. Haven't seen any sign of them since it all went down. We should go check on them anyway."

Russ set his coffee cup down. "So, we'll take today to get everything unloaded and stowed. We'll get everyone situated in the spaces we have available in the way we've laid it out. If we have any time left, we can try to run over and check on the Callens and let the Scanlins see them. Then we can modify our setup if we need to. Does that sound good?" Nods all around brought the planning session to an end.

Millie stood up. "Well, since that's settled, if you girls will help me, we need to make breakfast for a bunch of folks. We're going to need the fuel for the day we have ahead of us."

I didn't doubt her one bit. It was going to be a busy day.

# Chapter 3

If you have never cooked for two dozen people at once, let me tell you, it is an experience. Even though Millie and Monroe had no children, Millie came from a large family. She easily mixed up four dozen of her mouthwatering biscuits, a stew pot of gravy, and fried eggs made to order. Since we didn't have room for everyone in the kitchen and dining room, we roused them in smaller groups. We fed the first of us that were already up after the first batch of biscuits was done. Then we got our boys, Brian and Marietta, Mike, and the Thompson boys next. Once they were done, we finished with the three families. We wanted the younger kids to be last, since sometimes they dawdle over their food, and we didn't want anyone having to wait for them to finish.

As each group came down and we took their egg orders—I almost got a pad of paper, and was wishing for a pencil to stick behind my ear and some gum to chew and pop—Russ explained the plan for the day. There seemed to be a wave of relief over the parents' faces when we laid out the sleeping arrangements. Had they thought we were going to take back the invitation to stay, or separate them from their kids? They didn't know us very well—yet.

Once everyone had fueled up on breakfast, the group headed for the door. I ran to the front, one hand on my hip, the other up in that traffic cop stop position. *Damn, I wish I had a whistle.*

"For my crew, you know better. Get out back to the pump house and get busy. To the new folks, take this as a friendly reminder: there are no doctors, dentists, nurses, or anything of that nature working these days. We cannot afford to not take care of our health, and that starts with brushing after every meal. We'll set up a station for everyone out back to save on the septic. I mean, who cares where you spit? Just keep it away from the livestock and the gardens. If anyone doesn't have a toothbrush or toothpaste, see me. We have a lot. Also, we will set up a wash station by the hand pump out back. Wash before every meal and after *every* bathroom trip, no matter the reason. We can't afford for anyone to get a stomach bug or a cavity. Dismissed!"

The newbies looked a little scared, but my folks walked away snickering, so I guess the others took that as a sign I was serious but not issuing any public floggings for cleanliness infractions. They all headed out toward the back, except for Kate, who needed toothbrushes all around. They had been sharing one among them and had no toothpaste at all. We went out the front door to the trailer. I knew exactly where the stash of oral hygiene products was out there.

\*\*\*\*

Bob went over to Russ and Monroe. "You know, Anne got me thinking. With this many people we may put a hurt on the septic in the not-too-distant future. I think we might ought to think about some alternative toilet choices."

Mike walked up just then. "This sounds like a shitty conversation."

Bob almost choked on the coffee he was taking a drink of. It took him a minute and a few whacks on the back from Monroe to clear his airway.

"Damn, fella, give a man a head's up before you say shit like that. That shit ain't funny. I got shit to do and I can't be chokin' and shit. There—is that enough shit talk for ya?" Bob laughed and slapped Mike on the back—a little too hard. Payback for getting him choked earlier.

Mike grinned at him. "Seriously, I can help y'all dig some latrines if you think we need them. I have a bit of experience there. Guess what privates do in a brand new outpost camp?"

Bob shot Mike a smirk. "I'm sooo gonna start calling you Sergeant Shitter, dude."

Mike started to protest but Russ cut him off, lowered his voice, and spoke directly to Bob. "If Janet or Anne hears that, especially around the kids, you'll be on latrine-digging duty for life. Fair warning, bubba."

Bob thought about it, then, with a grim expression, replied, "You're right. I'm only gonna call him that under my breath, in passing, so no one else hears but us. A man has to know where to draw the line, particularly when he has two wives—one in matrimony, the other in life friend mode. Anne's like a work wife when I'm not at work. She bosses me around as much as Janet."

Russ kind of snickered, and Mike heehawed.

Monroe looked thoughtful. "Ya know, we still have the old outhouse out back. It could probably use some TLC, might need to replace some wood, but after all this time I would guess everything down there has composted. We can use that for the guys. I think the gals should get the use of the inside facilities. We can also dig a pit latrine for the guys to use for taking a leak. For both of those, we'll throw wood ash in every day from the cook fires or whatever fire building we do. That should help keep the smell down. It's only been me and Millie for the most part using that big ole septic tank, except the weekends y'all came out, so it should hold up for a while. I also stocked up on the enzymes that help everything break down, so we'll make sure to add that at least once a month. I'm not worried too much, but I reckon we can make a few changes here at the start that we might really be thankful for later on."

Russ looked at Mike. "Mike, I do hope you take Bob's ribbing as a sign that you are very welcome to our group and this place. We'd love for you to stay."

Mike smiled at Russ. "I'm in. I see a lot of potential here, and with some pretty basic fortifications, I think we can make it defensible. I'd be more than happy to help with that—after the latrine work is done. And believe me, I can handle anything Bob dishes out."

Russ replied, "I don't think we can wait for the latrine to be done. We need to work on security first. We'll freshen up the outhouse for now."

Bob started chanting, low so that just the guys could hear. "Sergeant Shitter ... oh, Sergeant Shitterrrrrr ..."

They were all laughing so hard the folk out in the yard looked in, and Millie came to the door from the kitchen. "What in the world is going on in here? I see you fellas are having a grand time. Have you already gotten those trailers unloaded and stowed? Do you need something to do? I'm sure I can find something for you if you do."

The four of them made a beeline for the front door, Monroe calling over his shoulder, "No, dear, we have plenty to work on. See ya later!"

**\*\*\*\***

With all the extra hands, we were able to get the trailers and trucks unloaded by noon, and after lunch the guys stowed them in the old garage. We then set to work sorting and putting up everything we had brought. Remembering it all nice and organized on the shelves at home, this disarray was grating on my nerves. My slight OCD was flaring up again. I had to resign myself to the fact that three households of preps were not going to fit nice and neat anywhere.

We put what we could in the root cellar, trying to keep the same organization Millie had already established, adding like items to the same shelf. We got most of the food in there, but it was packed so tight we basically had a path in, and that was it. There was no spare room for anything else. The rest of the supplies were stacked as orderly as we could get them in the part of the basement we weren't going to use for one of the new families. We tried to keep duplicate items together and not bury anything. Supplies are no good if you can't find them when you need them. We made a point of keeping first aid and sanitation items in the basement up front, closest to the door.

By the time we got everything organized and stored, it was the middle of the afternoon. Russ came up to me as I was coming out of the basement. "Babe, me, Bob, Mike, Brian, and Monroe are going to take a walk around, see if anything is out of place and try to get an idea of what kind of security measures we need to get set up."

He handed me one of the two-ways. "I'll have mine on me. If anything happens, just holler at me. If you and Janet can help get the new folks situated with the sleeping arrangements we talked about this morning, I think everyone will settle down. They seem to be a bit tense."

I nodded in agreement. "I'm sure it's the uncertainty of the circumstances. They don't know us—or each other, for that matter—all that well. They feel like outsiders, or that they're intruding, no matter how much we tell them they are welcome to stay. I'm sure we'd feel the same way in their place. I think we need to have a group meeting right after dinner tonight so we can assure them they *are* welcome and will become a vital part of this place."

He wrapped me in a big hug—you know, the kind that makes you feel warm and loved, and you want to just snuggle into for a week. He rested his chin on the top of my head for a second, then leaned back and looked me in the eyes.

"I don't think I could have done all this without you. I can't imagine how this would have turned out if it had happened an hour later. If you and Rusty had already left ..." He stopped, a pained look in his eye.

I reached my arms up around his neck. "But we hadn't left. As is his usual Monday ritual, your son was running late, thank goodness. Everything happens for a reason. We can wonder and stress about what could have been, or we can get busy living in the new now. It's going to be a ton of work, but we're together. We have our family, our friends, and some new friends; we have food, water, and shelter; we have protection and a plan. Let's get it in motion. I love you too, baby. Thank you for being so stubborn and making me see that something like this could happen. Now, enough of this mushy shit. We've got work to do."

I gave him a kiss, backed out of his embrace, and headed for the house. He went off to join the guys, with most of the dogs trailing him, but he stopped and turned back to me.

"Oh, Anne, I almost forgot. Can you tell the Scanlins it will probably be tomorrow before we can go look up their friends? We really need to get everyone settled and get some security set up today."

I smiled at him. "Of course. My guess is they will be okay with another day of rest here before they get back out there again."

He gave me a thumbs up and jogged to catch up to the guys. I headed for the house.

****

In the days following the pulse, I can't count the number of times I walked into a room and flipped the light switch out of reflex, or glanced at the microwave to see what time it was. Every time, I would think to myself, "Yeah, that doesn't work anymore." If there hadn't been so much to do in those early days, I could very easily have slipped into a deep depression over the loss of the conveniences of modern life. No more TV or internet, no more power to run pretty much every aspect of our lives that was maintained via electricity.

Now, walking into the shaded living room of the farmhouse, it seemed almost normal not to hear a television or radio playing, to be able to clearly hear voices all throughout the house, as there was no electrical hum of air conditioning or fans, or compressors on refrigerators or freezers. How quickly we humans adapt to our environment.

What I did notice was an enticing aroma emanating from the kitchen. I followed my nose in and found Millie and Janet working over the stove.

"I don't know what y'all are cooking but it smells awesome!"

Millie turned to me and smiled. "Kitchen Clean Out Soup is on the menu for tonight."

I guess my look was pretty dumb, because Janet started laughing. "Millie had a bunch of bits and pieces of meat and veggies from the past few days, not enough of anything for a crew this size, so we threw it all in a pot, along with a few jars of canned tomatoes, some potatoes and carrots, and some onions and celery, and we ended up with a pretty big pot of soup."

I looked at the pot on the gas stove. It looked like an industrial-size stainless steel pot, probably two- to two-and-a-half-gallon capacity, and it was pretty much full. Yep, that should feed two dozen people.

Millie leaned down to peer into the oven. I leaned over her shoulder. "And what tasty item do you have in there?"

She looked back at me with a grin. "Only the best cornbread made in the state of Tennessee."

She had a right to be cocky. She did make the best cornbread I had ever eaten. But I was curious about something. "How do you make cornbread for this many people at once? I've made two skillets for us and Janet and her crew, but I wouldn't think you could fit as many as we'll need in your oven at the same time. Eating breakfast in shifts this morning meant we were able to cook the biscuits in batches. We'll all be together for dinner. What's your secret?"

With a knowing smile and a crook of her finger, Millie started toward the screen porch. Once we were through the door, I smelled cornbread cooking out there as well. I'd forgotten she had a wood cook stove on the back porch. It was very old, from before gas or electric, but it still had burners and an oven. There was a pipe through the wall that vented outside. It was in pristine condition, which I was sure was due in no small part to Monroe's ministrations.

Millie went to the oven door and opened it to show off three more skillets of cornbread baking there.

"Wow, Millie! I had no idea you knew how to cook on one of these. There must be a trick to it. I mean, getting the right amount of wood, so your temp is right, then keeping it as steady as possible. When did you learn how to do this?"

She shut the oven door. "I've worked with it over the past few years. There is definitely a trick to it and you have to keep an eye on it. But in this situation this stove may be our salvation. We have enough gas to last for quite a while for the kitchen stove, maybe a couple of years, but if this situation goes on longer than that, we have this stove for backup. It will never run out of fuel as long as we have trees. I'd say we're going to have some hungry folks in here soon. When did you want to eat this evening?"

I thought for a second. "Russ wants us to get everyone settled into their sleeping arrangements first. Can we give it about an hour?"

Millie went to the wood stove and closed the dampers. "I'll have to keep an eye on this one. I'm still not completely confident in my skill with it. Janet, go turn the other oven off and leave the door closed. The cornbread is almost done, so it will finish cooking and stay warm until we're ready to eat. What do we need to do to help everyone get settled?"

"I think we can gather the other women and get most of it done with just us gals. The men are all out doing ... whatever they're doing. I think Sara has been keeping the younger kids occupied with 'school' today"—I did the air quotes—"so we can set Ben and Rusty with babysitting duty so she can be a part of this task as well."

Janet raised an eyebrow. "School? What's she using for books?"

I smiled. "I think these classes were about our new way of life. She grabbed one of the Thompson boys—Matt, I believe—and took them to see all the livestock, the gardens, and I think she even had them checking out weeds in the gardens. Since she is a teacher, I'm sure she will want to set up classes for the kids, but they may not always be about reading, writing, and 'rithmetic."

Millie nodded. "Yes, there is a whole lot more to learn about living in this world than they teach kids in school these days. Kids don't know anything about where their food comes from. They think it magically appears at the grocery store. They don't know what it takes to actually grow your own food. They'll know now. They have no choice."

Janet had a look on her face that told me she had come up with something. "Anne, I have an idea. We are going to need every able hand to maintain and defend this place very soon. I think we should set up daily chores for all the kids. Feeding the livestock, gathering eggs, filling the outside basins, pulling weeds—there will be plenty for everyone to do. Maybe we could come up with some kind of reward for their hard work, or a competition. We should have a Mom Meeting as soon as we can to get everyone's input on it. The parents will know what their kids are able to handle. Lord knows there's no free ride for anyone anymore."

Millie said, "They have a roof over their heads and food in their bellies. That's their reward. When I was a kid you knew what your chores were and you did them without being told. You're right: there is no free ride anymore, and everybody in this world needs to learn that if you don't work, you don't eat."

I grinned at my friends. "That is an awesome idea. Mom Meeting in the morning, first thing. We'll get the word out."

She was right. We were going to need every able body doing their part to help us all survive, even down to the youngest. It hadn't been that long ago that every member of a family contributed every day to the existence of life on a farm. From hunting, cooking, laundry, and food preservation done by the oldest kids, to weed pulling in the garden, livestock care, and wood stacking done by the youngest, all the children in the family did chores every day.

Kids today had no idea what it was like to live as their grandparents and great-grandparents had. Ours were about to learn.

****

We spent the better part of an hour getting everyone settled into their new semi-permanent accommodations. As I said, most of them didn't have a lot. The Scanlins had lost almost all of their stuff in the fire; the rest hadn't brought all their clothes with them because they didn't have a way to carry them—not one they had considered, anyway. The station wagon we had "borrowed" from their old neighborhood could have been used to carry some more stuff had they thought about it before they left. I would talk to Russ about maybe going back and seeing about getting some more of their personal items. I knew any venturing outside the fences of the farm would be frowned upon, but if we didn't get more clothing for these people, they were going to be running around naked before winter. Clothes wear out, and if you only have a couple of outfits, they wear out really fast. We could share some things, but that meant less for all. We definitely didn't have anything that would fit the smaller kids.

The new folks seemed happy with their cramped areas. If you have a choice between one room for four people or sleeping outside under a tree, you tend to be less particular. I thought about our two-thousand-plus-square-foot house and how at times it had seemed cramped with just the three of us and all of our things. Circumstances have a way of changing your perspective. Right now, I was thankful for the space we had and that all of us were safe and out of harm's way.

By this time, the house was heating up with all the bodies in it, so we decided to have dinner outside. Russ and Bob had drafted Lee Roush and the Lawton brothers to put together some long tables and benches for our group to eat outside whenever possible. They had been hammering and sawing all day out back. I also heard the generator running, as well as at least a circular saw and a sander. They should have something by now we could use, at least temporarily. We had stacks of plywood Monroe and the guys had gotten from scrap yards that carried factory seconds, as well as piles of not-quite-straight two-by-fours and reclaimed deck boards—he had a big shed full of lumber. Along with the lumber, there were nails, screws, nuts and bolts, and pretty much any kind of fastener you could possibly need. They would also use these supplies to build the bunkhouse for the single guys. Monroe's need to keep everything that might someday be useful was turning out to be a blessing in disguise.

We checked the food, and it was ready to eat. The soup smelled like heaven, and my mouth watered as I thought about crumbling warm, soft cornbread up in it. I checked my mouth for drool, such was my salivation. We pulled out two dozen bowls and spoons, as well as paper plates for the cornbread. Millie had homemade butter she had been keeping in the root cellar. That woman was an angel right here on Earth. She hadn't used the churn to make it though. She had whipped it up with her stand mixer before the power went out. She assured us she did know how to do it with the churn as well. Oh, note to self: kids can help with butter churning.

Millie looked around and smiled at us all. "I guess we better go check out these new tables. I'm sure we'll need to cover them with something. I'm thinking some old flat sheets will do the trick. We may also have to cover the benches if the wood is too rough. Let's see what the men put together for us."

We paraded out back, and under the big oak were two beautiful tables with benches. I'm not talking just a piece of plywood with some legs slapped on it. They were smooth with rounded and sanded edges, and not a wobble to be found. The benches were the same. There was even a small table that would hold at least six kids. Yes, we would cover them with sheets, but that would be to protect them from spills, because they were gorgeous.

We stared in amazement at what had been done with some basic supplies and power tools that, thank goodness, had been protected from the pulse. Lee was bending over one of the tables, using a hand sander on a spot on top. He stood up when he heard us going on and on over the results.

"I'm not really done, but we can at least use these for tonight. I'll try to finish them up tomorrow."

We stood there in awe, and I finally found my voice. "Finish them? They're great just the way they are. They look amazing. I don't know about anyone else, but I wasn't expecting anything this nice. You did an awesome job, Lee! You too, Ryan and Bill!"

The Lawton brothers puffed out their chests, then Ryan slapped Lee on the back. "It was all him. We just did what he told us to do. He's a great carpenter."

The rest of the group agreed. Lee smiled. "Well, I'd like to get a coat of sealer on the wood to protect it from the elements, but yeah, for the most part, they should be good to go."

Millie looked at her niece and said, "Janet, go round up the men and kids. I'm going to get some sheets to cover these tables in case anything gets spilled. Let's eat!"

I was ready, but, more importantly, I wanted to know what the guys were going to say to the group. This night could change things for a lot of folks, right here, right now.

# Chapter 4

While work was being done on sleeping quarters and food, Russ and his crew were walking the property looking for vantage points and weak spots. Twenty acres was a lot of ground to cover, but since the back side was all woods and backed up to another piece of property that was wooded as well, they felt like they only had to worry about the front piece for the most part, which was the section that had road frontage. It would take a lot of work to get in from the back. Even on the front and the sides, there was a considerably thick tree line to get through everywhere but the gate. Four strands of barbed wire encircled the entire farm, as well as the areas that had been cross-fenced for the different livestock. While that wouldn't keep the determined out, it would slow them down some. They focused their attention on the gate area.

Mike walked the front section a couple of times, looking into the tree line and specifically the area surrounding the gate. He went outside the gate and looked, trying to see back in. He walked the road a few hundred feet in both directions. When he came back through the gate and locked it behind him, he had a pensive look on his face.

Bob said, "What's up, Sergeant Shi—er, Mike? Did we do something wrong? We tried to camouflage the gate as much as possible but still keep it light enough so that Monroe could open and close it by himself. If we need to re-do it, we can. Now that we're all out here, he won't have to do it alone. We could—"

Mike held his hand up to stop Bob. "I was actually thinking that, for a bunch of civilians, you guys did an awesome job at concealing the entrance to the place. If I didn't know where it was I'd have a hard time finding it. The only thing I would suggest is sinking some extra posts on both ends of the gate to reinforce it against someone trying to ram it. It won't stop a big truck like a semi, but it will give them a new design on their grill."

Monroe bowed up. "Who you callin' a civilian, jarhead? I served in Vietnam!" At his raised voice, a couple of the dogs who had been lying in the shade lifted their heads to see what the commotion was. When they didn't see anything exciting happening, they went back to sleep. They were good watch dogs; they just didn't have anything to watch right then.

Mike inclined his head toward Monroe. "Yes, sir. I figured that. I was actually referring to those guys." He motioned toward Russ, Brian, and Bob. He looked back at Monroe. "How'd you know I was a Marine?"

Monroe snorted. "You leathernecks got an air about ya. I knew it as soon as I met ya."

Mike laughed. "Yes, sir. I guess we do. I hope you don't hold that against me."

Monroe looked him up and down, huffed, and replied, "Well, I reckon if yer willin' to dig latrines, you ain't too uppity. I got my eye on you though."

Brian looked at Russ and Bob and whispered, "Did we just see Monroe pissin' on trees?"

Russ laughed out loud. Bob smirked. "Yeah, I think we did. Not bad for an old soldier."

Monroe's head snapped up. "Who you callin' old?"

They all laughed at Monroe's indignation, though they tried hard to cover it up with coughing and throat clearing.

Russ held his hand up. "Okay, can we get back to security? What do you two veterans think we need to add here? It's obvious this is the spot we need to put the most focus on. What will it be? Foxhole? Tree hide? Both?"

Mike nodded. "I think both would be good. Foxholes about a hundred feet back on both sides of the gate, and a hide …"

He stepped back, looked in the direction of the house, and pointed to a large sycamore tree between the gate and the house. "I think that big guy right there is just begging for a treehouse."

Monroe grinned. "Yeah, it was about five years ago, so we built one for Rusty and Benny. You can't see it now because it's all grown up. The boys haven't been up there in a couple of years. I don't know what kind of shape it's in, but I bet there's at least a platform we can start with. The view is great from up there. You can see a good bit past the road and a pretty wide perimeter of the property. Might have to trim some limbs out of the way for spottin', so do whatever you need to do. I forgot all about it until you pointed to the tree. I don't reckon I'll be climbing up to check it out, but you younger fellas can go on up there if ya want."

Mike smiled at the guys. "Then looks like we have a plan. Let's check out the treehouse and head back to the farmhouse. I got a feeling chow is soon. For tonight we can do a perimeter sweep around the house and, if there's a stable platform, set someone up in the overlook."

They headed to the treehouse to check it out. When they got there, Mike and Brian offered to go up and check it out.

Bob backed away. "You guys check to see if it's safe—you know, stable. If I got up there and fell out and broke my neck, Janet would kill me."

Russ looked at him. "You do realize that if you fell out, as high as that is now, you probably would break your neck and die, right? How could she kill you if you're already dead?"

Bob gave a slight shiver. "She'd find a way, believe me. Y'all think she's all sweet and quiet, but that woman is hell on wheels when she's pissed."

Monroe held up his pinky finger to Bob. "She's got you wrapped up on that finger tighter than a smoked sausage. Admit it, boy."

Bob looked down, then up at his uncle with a sheepish grin. "Yep, she does. Just like Millie has you wrapped. Ain't love a bitch?"

Monroe squinted at Bob, then laughed so hard he took to coughing. Now it was Bob's turn to smack him on the back.

While all the ribbing was going back and forth, Mike and Brian had made their way up into the treehouse. Mike looked around while Brian tried to tread on every available spot.

"Mike, I think this floor is pretty solid. I don't feel any soft spots at all. This tin roof probably helped a lot. Man, when these guys build a treehouse, they don't mess around. This thing is nicer than my first apartment."

Mike grinned and nodded. The treehouse had a solid wood floor, a tin roof, four walls, and a little landing out front with a railing. There were windows on three of the four walls and an open doorway.

"Yeah, when these guys build something they mean for it to last. It's weathered, but I think it will work great for what we need. I'll want to take out the whole front so the view isn't obstructed to the road, but I think the rest can stay. It will provide cover and some protection from Mother Nature. We'll need to cut out a few branches, but I don't want to take out too many. If we didn't know this was up here, then the cover is excellent. We need to keep as much of that intact as possible. This thing is damn near perfect!"

Mike looked down at the guys about twenty feet below them and gave them a thumb's up. The ground crew sent one back to them. Mike and Brian climbed back down.

"That will definitely work, Monroe," Mike said. "The only fixing up we'll need to do is the climb up. Some of those slats are pretty brittle. I'd suggest an aluminum ladder, or maybe a deer stand if you have one. Once we take off the front, there won't be much else to do."

Monroe thought for a moment. "Ya know, I may have a deer stand ladder in the shed. Found one in a junk shop. The seat part was pretty mangled, but the ladder looked okay. You fellas can put some camo paint on it to make it blend. I also have some ghillie material I got at an army surplus store a few years ago we can use for the front. Didn't have a need for it when I bought it, but you just never know when you might need something like that. I guess now is that time."

Bob looked at Monroe. "Is there anything you *don't* have in this place? Seems like everything someone needs, you've got."

Monroe smirked at Bob. "Being a hoarder ain't such a bad thing now, is it?"

Bob shook his head, the rest of the guys laughed, and they all headed for the house. Monroe was right though. Being a hoarder was a really good thing now.

****

Supper was great. There was a gentle breeze blowing across the lawn under the shade of the massive oak tree, which kept the bugs at bay and cooled us off enough to truly enjoy the soup and cornbread. The dogs were really happy to get the treats the kids were giving them under the table. Everyone went on and on about the food, as well as the tables and benches. When most of the folks had finished eating, Russ stood up and addressed the group.

"Gang, I think we have everybody situated with a place to sleep with some semblance of privacy, except for the single guys. They won't be staying in the tent forever—we're going to build a bunkhouse, probably right over there." He pointed to a spot just past the oak, right off the corner of the house. "We want a permanent structure that will stand up to the elements and possible marauder attacks."

At that comment everyone got really quiet. Russ continued. "I know no one wants to think about things like that, especially when we just got here and just got settled, but it is something we have to consider and prepare for. Those folks who are taking supplies from wherever and whoever they want will eventually run out of things in town, or even in areas like we all just fled. They will find their way out here. We have to get ready for that inevitability."

He paused, and I knew he was giving us a chance to let all that sink in. The joy from the meal was pretty much gone now. Way to go, baby. Debbie Downer in the house … er, yard.

He went on. "We are going to need every able body we have and possibly can get to defend this place. We have supplies to sustain us for at least a year, even at the numbers we have currently, and don't think for one second that this place and everything here wouldn't be a gold mine for some low-life POS and his buddies to try to get their hands on. With that said, we wanted to formally invite all of you to stay here with us. It will be work, and it will probably be dangerous, but that's going to be the case no matter where we are. I believe we can make a stand here and make a life for ourselves. We will pretty much be living like our great-grandparents did as far as amenities go. They did it, and I have faith we can do it too. So, we'd like to know how you all feel about our offer." Russ took a seat.

The newbies looked at each other, then Brian stood up. "As the first addition to this group, while we were still in our houses back home, I can tell you that these people are good folks. I mean, really good people. Hell, they're the best as far as I'm concerned. They had every reason to tell me to take a flying f—"

Brian looked over at the kids. The guys snickered. "Anyway, I showed up on their doorstep looking for someone to help me because it was all about me. They didn't have to, but Russ took the time to tell me what he thought was happening and what I needed to do to get ready for what was coming. When they decided I wasn't a total lost cause, they brought me into their home and into their family. We already had scavengers in our neighborhood before we left, and I have no doubt I would probably be dead right now for the peanut butter and saltines I had in my house if I had stayed.

"I was Mr. I-want-all-the-latest-gadgets guy. I grew up with nothing, so I thought that was what was most important: having the latest and greatest toys, and that mine had to be better than my neighbors', which happened to be these folks. When the power went off, all of those things became worthless. I was quickly humbled to understanding I was in no better shape than anyone else out there. All the money I had in the bank was gone—I had no way to get to it anyway. And what value does it have now? You can't eat it. You can't wear it.

"Russ laid it all out for me when he didn't have to take the time to do that, and I'm thankful I went to their door that first day. These are good people. The best. I keep repeating that because I mean it. When they invite you into their lives, it's not something they do lightly. They looked at me, and my reactions to the new now, and decided I was worth keeping around. What Russ did just now is the same thing, only for all of you. I for one am staying."

Brian sat down and Marietta wrapped an arm around him. She stood up next. "What Brian said, pretty much word for word. I showed up on their doorstep looking like a hot mess after walking for days to get to them. They took me in and I'll be forever grateful for that kindness."

She sat back down to a few chuckles. Short but sweet.

Mike and the Lawton brothers had been talking quietly. All three jumped up at the same time and said simultaneously, "We're in!" They sat back down to gentle laughter as they high fived each other.

Mike added, "I told you how I felt last night. I'm in." Russ nodded and smiled back.

Bill looked at his brother, then the rest of us. "We're landscapers by trade, but gun lovers and pretty avid hunters. We can help with security and food."

Lee Roush stood up next. "I don't know what I would have done without these guys." He motioned to the group from his neighborhood. "I have no way of knowing if Jackie is alive or not, but I fear the worst. She wasn't equipped to make it home alone in a situation like this. I do know she would want me to find a safe place for our kids."

He looked over at the kids' table. Aiden and Moira were looking at him with tears in their eyes.

"I can help build things like the bunkhouse you're talking about. The kids can help with any chores you deem necessary for all of our survival. I hope it's okay if I count on you ladies for help with them. We'd like to stay."

He started to sit back down, and I looked at him with tear-filled eyes. I jumped up, rushed over to him, and wrapped my arms around him.

"Of course we'll help with them. We are going to be one big family now. Your kids are our kids."

He hugged me back, smiled at everyone, and took his seat, wiping his eyes. I went back to my place between Russ and Janet, blubbering. I'm such a softie.

Pete was next to take the floor. "We feel the same way as Lee about wanting a safe place for our son. We're staying as well. I can drive any piece of equipment you've got or can find. I'm a fair mechanic, too. Sara wants to get a school schedule set up for the kids with a curriculum that is tailored to our new survival way of life. And of course, Tony can help with chores. Thank you for the offer. We really appreciate it."

He sat to a chorus of "yes, thank you" from the rest of the group.

The only ones left were the Scanlins. The Thompson boys didn't get a vote. Monroe would make them stay, not that they wanted to leave. I looked at Sean, who was looking around the table. Sean didn't stand, but he addressed the group, and Russ in particular.

"You know, when we first met you and Brian on the road that day, we had already been through hell. I think we were kind of shell-shocked over everything that had happened, and we were just hoping we could get to Luke and Casey's place. Even though we didn't know enough to stay off the road, we somehow knew we needed to get out of the city or anything remotely resembling it."

Russ and Brian shared a smile at the reference to them finding the small family on the road. Sean went on. "While we do still want to see about them, Kate and I have talked and we believe, as you all do, that there is safety in numbers. We'd like to stay and maybe we can talk Luke and Casey into joining us here, if that's okay. Their place is about five acres, but their house is nowhere near as big as this one. They also only have fencing to contain their few livestock, and their place is pretty visible from the road. I think this setup"— he motioned around us—"is much more suited to sustainability and security. The skills we can offer are that I know about home brewing. I work—well, worked—for a distilling company, and I have been making moonshine for years as a hobby. Kate's skill is even better. She's an LPN."

With this news there was a lot of conversation at the table. A nurse! We got a nurse and didn't even know it! And moonshine? We could use that for medicinal purposes … and relaxing purposes.

Monroe jumped up, full of excitement. "Sean, wait 'til you see what I got out in the shed! Got my hands on a nice-sized still a few years ago. Fella told me it was once used by Popcorn Sutton, but I don't reckon that was true. Why would Popcorn have let a perfectly good still go? I been dying to see it in action. Hot dog, we gonna make us some shine!"

The table erupted in laughter at Monroe's enthusiastic reaction, except for Millie, who just smiled and shook her head.

Russ stood again and addressed the group. "Then it's settled. Tomorrow we'll go check on the Callens, and of course they are welcome to come here and stay; we'll figure out where to put them. We'll start working on building the bunkhouse as well. Lee, with your skill set and the awesome job you did on these tables, you get that project. Mike and Monroe will be working on our defenses out by the gate. The rest of the guys will assist with both projects and any heavy lifting that needs to be done. Anything you ladies need the men to work on?" He looked at me, then Millie, then Janet.

I spoke up. "We are having a Moms' Meeting in the morning right after breakfast. We want to lay out a chore list for the kids and help Sara get the school curriculum set up. We'll take the responsibility for the livestock and the gardens, as well as cooking and cleaning. I'd like to suggest you guys work on some alternative energy sources. If we could get some power, we could make it more bearable this summer when the heat really kicks in. The ceiling fans will keep the air moving and maybe keep us all from melting. But the most important thing is electricity will turn the pump on for the well. Running water, fellas—hot showers. Toilets that flush on their own. If we could have those two things, this new lifestyle would be much more bearable."

Everyone was murmuring their agreement when Mike interrupted. "I saw you guys have solar panels. Did you protect the charge controllers and inverters? If you have some that didn't get fried, we might be able to rig up what we need for solar.

Bob replied, "Yeah, we kept most of the electrical parts in Faraday cages in a crawl space under the barn."

Mike grinned. "Great! Let's go check them out when we're finished here."

Russ looked around the table with a satisfied smile. "I'm happy you've all decided to stay. It will take all of us, and possibly even a few more, to protect and defend what we have here. I'm going to work out a patrol schedule this evening, and I want everyone else to get a good night's sleep. We have a big day ahead of us tomorrow."

Millie stood and issued orders. "Everyone take your dishes into the kitchen and set them on the counter. We'll collect them for washing. Kids, we have a bunch of board games in the attic. Ben and Rusty, you boys go bring them down. After you all have washed up and brushed your teeth, you can set up in the screen porch and play, if it's all right with your parents."

She looked the group over, and the grown-ups were all smiling and nodding. She went on. "You can play with any of them, just make sure you put everything back in its box when you're done, so we don't lose any pieces. And if I hear any fighting, it's bedtime for everyone. Understood?"

She was met with a chorus of "Yes, ma'am, Ms. Millie" from the kids. They rushed to the kitchen with their dishes, then out to the pump to get cleaned up.

Sara leaned over to Millie. "I hope we can get that kind of enthusiasm from them when 'school' starts."

Millie shook her head. "I wouldn't count on that unless you can figure out a way to make it into a game."

Sara smiled. "I'll work on that."

The men wandered off, some to scope out the spot for the bunkhouse, others to check out the parts for the solar power. The gals grabbed their dishes and headed for the kitchen. Thankfully there was a pump for the well in the kitchen mounted on the sink so we didn't have to haul water in. Janet got some water boiling, while Marietta and Kate scraped the bowls into the slop bucket that was kept by the back door, per Millie's instructions. Marietta asked what the bucket was for—that is, why they were scraping food scraps into it. Millie donned her teacher look. A new class was about to begin: Life on the Farm 101.

"Well, dear, on a farm nothing goes to waste. There has been a bucket by this door for the better part of fifty years. When it gets full, we'll give it to the hogs. They'll eat pretty much anything you give them, even food that's gone bad. Saves us a bit on feed as well."

Marietta looked at the bucket, which had remnants of breakfast, lunch, and supper in it. She looked back at Millie and said, "I'm so glad I'm not a hog. That looks gross."

Millie giggled, as did the rest of us.

As we washed, dried, and put up the dishes together, talking and carrying on like women do, a thought crossed my mind. Even though we had lost the modern conveniences—electricity, running water, and all the things that go along with them—we had gained something else, something we didn't even realize we had lost. This is how it was "in the old days." This is how families lived. This is how they got so close and were so fiercely protective of each other. They were together all the time, working, talking, playing, living their lives. This is how they survived. I knew we could as well as long as we could defend what we had because, unlike the old days, there were people out there who didn't want to work for it. They wanted to just take it, or kill for it, if the person they were robbing didn't hand over their hard-earned supplies. Unfortunately, there were plenty of those types of people out there who were adapting to this situation in that way. Rather than working to create a life in this new world, they chose to try to take from others who had. Those were the people we were expecting, and we didn't think it would take them long to find us. Everything from here on out was about our survival and keeping the wolves at bay.

# Chapter 5

We finished the dishes and brewed up a few pots of coffee. It had been a long, hard day. We gathered the pots, cups, sugar, and cream and went out to the front porch to enjoy the mild night air. The porch was eight feet deep and ran the width of the house in front and the length on both sides, around to the screen porch out back. It was one of those real Southern homes with lots of chairs, including a few rockers. We do enjoy our porch-sitting in the South.

It was still April so the nights were very pleasant. That would be short-lived in Tennessee and could change as early as next month. Lord, I hoped the guys would be able to figure out how to get us some power. As I was contemplating that thought, the group that had gone to the barn came back with their arms full of parts. I'm guessing it was the controllers and inverters needed to convert the DC power collected in the solar panels to AC that we could then use in the house. I didn't know how it all worked but I knew that part. Okay, I pretty much knew only that part.

They walked up to the porch and unceremoniously dumped their loot on the bottom step. The dogs sleeping at our feet jumped up and barked at the unfamiliar sound. After a look around, they decided their protective services were still not needed and went back to their napping. Bob had a voltmeter in his hand and was grinning like the cat that ate the canary.

"Tested, and they're all good to go. You ladies will have hot running water in no time!"

To a chorus of "woo hoo!" from all of us, Millie clapped her hands together. "Well, that calls for a celebration. Would you gentlemen like to join us for some coffee?"

Monroe rushed up onto the porch. "You betcha, Millie darlin'. Did you bring out my 'special ingredient,' too?"

Millie rolled her eyes at her husband. "When have I not brought that out with the evening coffee?"

She reached into the pocket of the apron she wore pretty much all the time and pulled out a silver flask. Monroe's eyes lit up; he licked his lips and reached for the flask. Millie snatched it back. "Isn't there something you're supposed to do first?"

Monroe grinned at her, walked up, and planted a big kiss on her, full lip-lock. While he was doing that, he slid his hand down into her apron pocket and took out the flask.

He pulled back from the kiss, leered at his wife, and said, "Damn, woman, you still have the softest lips I've ever kissed."

She cocked an eyebrow. "And how many women have you kissed, pray tell?"

"Enough to know that when I kissed you I didn't need to kiss nobody else."

They looked at each other with love and laughter, and you couldn't help but be in awe of the devotion they had shared for so many years.

Bob broke the spell. "Get a room, will ya? No one's gonna need sugar in their coffee after all that sickening sweetness. C'mon, Monroe, pass that flask."

It was Janet's turn to roll her eyes. "My husband, the hopeless romantic."

Bob looked at her with a bit of a forlorn expression and lowered his voice. "I'm romantic, honey. I just prefer to keep that mushy stuff just between us. Can't have the guys thinking I'm wrapped or something."

Russ jabbed him with an elbow. "We don't think that, buddy. We know it."

With that, Monroe held up his pinky finger to Bob then went into a knee-slapping, laughing fit, which of course made the rest of us laugh even though we weren't in on the joke. I wished we could always be this carefree. I knew we couldn't, but I wished it just the same.

The other group of guys came walking around the corner. Lee was smiling, and the Lawton brothers made a beeline for the coffee.

"Well, I think we have the spot scoped out for the bunkhouse," Lee said. "Monroe, I'd like to get the corner posts set first thing in the morning. I saw some six-by-six beams in the lumber pile. I think those will make great corner posts. Then we can just use whatever lumber we have for the walls. I don't see us putting up insulation and drywall for this, but we'll need to figure some way of keeping the guys as warm as possible this winter. That's assuming we're still in this situation this winter. We may have to scavenge for lumber for the roof trusses. Are we okay to use whatever is available here?"

Monroe put his hand on Lee's shoulder. "Son, if it isn't already part of a building here, you are welcome to use it. I have collected wood, hardware, plumbing parts, machines—I'm not entirely sure what all we have anymore. I do have a lot more lumber in a shed about a half-mile from here. You can hook that flatbed trailer up to the tractor and bring it down. I didn't want too much wood too close to the house in case of a fire. I'm sure there are roof trusses there from a house that was being torn down a few miles from here about ten years ago. I've also got an old wood-burning stove in the barn you can use in there. That should keep the fellas warm. No insulation, but I have some old tar paper you can use for the walls. It will help keep some of the cold out. Got some sheet metal you can use for the roof, too. We should be able to fix it up pretty livable. How big you gonna make it?"

Lee thought for a moment. "I'm thinking fifteen by twenty should do it. That would give us three bunks along each wall about six-and-a-half feet long, then we can go two high, which would give us twelve bunks total. That should leave about nine feet in the center for the stove, and maybe a table and chairs, if we make the bunks three feet wide. What do you guys think?"

Russ replied, "Sounds perfect. How many helpers will you need? We can all work on it first thing in the morning if needed."

"Well, if we all worked together, we should be able to get the corner posts set pretty fast. Then I can probably do the rest with just me, Bill, and Ryan. Maybe one more guy if we can spare the men."

Monroe spoke up. "Use Matt and Nick. They're good-sized boys and one can do the gopher work. Will that do for ya?"

"That should do it. We'll get started right after breakfast then. I'm hoping we can have it done in a day or two."

Bob looked shocked. "Wow! You can build it that fast? How come it takes so long to build a house then?"

Monroe cackled. "Well it ain't like we gotta wait for the building inspector to come out, or the codes guy to inspect it now, do we, bubba?"

Bob grinned at his uncle. "Nah, I'm pretty sure those guys are trying to figure out how to cook the neighbor's cat right about now." That remark received a mixture of giggles and gags.

Russ sipped his coffee and looked at Mike. "What will you need for the treehouse and the foxholes, Mike? Hardware, supplies, man power?"

Mike replied, "A claw hammer, or a crow bar would be even better, to take out the front wall. Nails, or something to attach the ghillie material to the roof. I'm not sure how you want to dig the foxholes, but I'm hoping it's not with shovels."

Monroe snorted. "Hell no, we ain't using shovels. We're using the bucket on my tractor. Pete can drive it."

Pete perked up at that. "I've been listening to this whole conversation, just waiting for you guys to talk about something I could help with. I mean, yeah, I can use a hammer and a saw, but my thing is definitely machinery. If it's got a motor and wheels, I can drive it."

Monroe looked him over. "I hope that's not just limited to modern vehicles. My tractor is older than you, son, and as ornery as me."

Bob chimed in. "That's pretty ornery, dude. You sure you can handle it?" Monroe made to swat Bob, but he ducked out of the way.

Pete grinned. "Yes, sir, I can handle it. Just lead me to it."

Russ nodded and said, "We'll work on that in the morning, after we get the bunkhouse started. Brian and I will take first patrol tonight, then Bob and Mike will take second. It's already dark and pretty quiet, so I think we can do it in two shifts tonight. Tomorrow, we'll work out a schedule for two- to three-hour rotations, twenty-four hours a day. We can't think just because it's daylight we won't be attacked. I at least want someone in the treehouse at all times. We might be able to utilize the younger boys for that duty."

I started to protest, but I stopped myself. They weren't little boys anymore. They needed to know how to protect and defend us and themselves in this environment just as much as everyone else. I just wasn't ready to admit my "little boy" was almost a man now.

Instead of protest I offered a suggestion. "I think we should have some kind of training for them first, as well as anyone else who isn't familiar with or comfortable handling a firearm. In fact, I think everybody should go through some drills, just to make sure they know what they're doing and we know they know what they're doing. We don't need any accidents with no doctors or emergency rooms to go to. You guys can rig up a course or something, and everybody has to pass the initial test or get training. What do you think?"

They were all nodding in the affirmative. Brian spoke up. "I think that is a great idea, Anne. We could set it up similar to what we had to go through to get our carry permits, except tailor it to each person's sidearm. Just make sure they know how to load and unload, put the safety on and off, and see how they handle the gun. We should also set up a cleaning station, maybe in the barn, and teach everybody how to break them down and clean them. A clean gun is a reliable gun."

Russ was grinning at me. "I knew there was a reason I kept you around besides your cooking. You're a pretty smart gal. That's a great idea, all of it, yours included, Brian. We'll get started on that tomorrow as well. Wow, looks like we have a big day ahead of us. Better start getting kids in beds and getting some sleep, gang."

As we got up to gather the kids, I noticed Sara and Pete both had strange looks on their faces. It was like a mixture of pain, fear, and confusion. I went up to Sara.

"Sara? What's wrong? Are you worried about something?"

She looked down, then back up at me. "Anne, I don't know anything about handling a gun. I've never held one in my life because I never had a reason to. Does everybody have to be armed? Honestly, they scare me."

Russ overheard and walked up to us. "Is that what's bothering you, too, Pete?"

Pete nodded. "I'm not scared of them, but I know nothing about guns. Never shot one, never even held one."

Russ looked at them both. "Well, we're not going to force anyone to do anything that makes them uncomfortable, but I will tell you that you need to learn how to use a gun. Those people we ran into on the road are just a sample of the kind of folks we are going to be dealing with. They will kill you for the clothes on your back, let alone the food in your home. If you don't want to be on guard duty, that's fine—we'll find some other ways for you to help out. You both have skills we need. I will ask that you at least watch the training so that, if something happens, you will be able to pick one up to defend this place if needed."

Pete put his arm around Sara and nodded. "We will, Russ. Thank you for understanding. We'll try to help out however we can."

Monroe stuck his head around Russ. "Where y'all from? I mean before Tennessee, cuz I can tell by the way you talk you ain't natives."

Sara replied, "We moved here a couple of years ago from New York. We grew up in the Northeast. Pete got transferred down here for his job."

Monroe backed up. "That explains it. Nazi York. Telling people guns are evil and no one needs one, except that the politicians who are saying it are surrounded by their armed bodyguards."

Sara and Pete looked a bit shocked. Bob snorted in laughter while the rest of us hid our faces to try to cover up the smirks. Millie stood and walked over to her husband. "Come along, dear. It's late. We have a big day tomorrow."

Monroe grumbled all the way into the house, though all I caught was "damn Yankee liberals."

Bob grinned at the Raines. "I'd apologize for him, but it wouldn't do any good. Besides, I agree with him. Welcome to Tennessee! We have lots of guns. We love to shoot our guns. We'd be more than happy to teach you to do the same. Try it, you might like it." With that, he headed toward the back of the house.

"Bedtime, kiddos! Wrap them games up and don't forget to put all the pieces back in the boxes. You don't want Ms. Millie on your case, believe me."

We followed behind him to make sure they did just that. We couldn't afford to lose game pieces. It's not like we could run to the dollar store and buy new games to replace them.

I linked my arm in my husband's. "Baby, do you think it's really going to get that bad? That people will come storming in here, shooting the place up?"

Russ stopped, turned me to him, and with the most serious look I think I have ever seen on him, said, "Yes, honey, I do. I think it's already gotten that bad. The scavengers back in the neighborhood, the people on the road by the mall? What do you think would have happened if we had stopped to try to help them? You saw how desperate they looked."

I nodded, sadly acknowledging that what he was saying was true. He went on. "And let's not forget the 'road block'"—he actually did the air quotes—"and the trap right before we got here. Those people were absolutely ready to kill us or, at the very least, hurt us bad, to get our supplies. Those men would have taken you and Janet, possibly the boys, and done things that make my blood boil just thinking about. So again, yes, it's bad, and it's going to get worse. Count on it."

Well, didn't that just suck?

# Chapter 6

After the long, busy day before, I had hoped to sleep in just a bit longer the next morning, but the rooster reported for duty right on time. Who needs an alarm clock when you're on a farm? I got up quietly, as Russ was still sleeping from his watch duty the previous night, did my business in the bathroom that we shared with the folks upstairs, and headed down to get what sounded like it would be a busy day started.

The early morning crew was assembling in the kitchen—that would be those of us who couldn't sleep through the rooster alarm. Millie was at the stove, putting a second pot of coffee on to boil. Monroe was talking to the Lawton brothers and Lee, who must have been excited about getting the bunkhouse started. Janet was pulling out coffee cups; she turned to Millie.

"Aunt Millie, I know that you think of this place as ours—all of us, not just you and Uncle Monroe—but we kind of defer to you when it comes to cooking. I don't want you to think you have to bear all the burden of deciding what we're eating, plus do all the cooking for this many people. We ended up with a lot more folks than we originally planned on, at least for the beginning of something like what has happened. If you want to handle it, that's fine; but if we need to help, or take it over, we'll do it, no problem. I don't want you to wear yourself out trying to do all this for everyone all the time."

Oh, didn't I feel like shit. I hadn't even thought about that. Millie had pretty much handled all the food prep yesterday while we were getting everything unloaded and put up. But we needn't have worried. She smiled at Janet and shook her head.

"It's not a burden, dear. I grew up in a big family—there were eight kids. I learned early how to cook for a bunch and how to make enough out of a little. I feel like I'm getting to use my skills again. Monroe will eat anything I put in front of him."

At the sound of his name, he looked up at Millie and blew her a kiss. She smiled serenely at him and went on. "Right now, outside of helping with putting up stuff from the garden, with all these people to do the chores, I won't have much else to worry about. This is how I can contribute. You know me. If I need any help or to take a break, I'll let you know."

Janet walked over and hugged her aunt, then held her at arm's length. "Alright then, did you have anything in mind for breakfast, because I think with all the projects we have planned for today we need to make it something quick. I was thinking a big batch of oatmeal with some of those late strawberries, and some honey and cinnamon. How does that sound?"

Millie nodded, still smiling. "I think that sounds like a delicious plan; and if you will work on that I can get some bread started for lunch. I think we'll be on sandwiches for lunch until further notice. Peanut butter and jelly, or tuna, are quick, easy, and full of the protein everyone will need for the chores they'll be doing. I would like to chat with you gals in the mornings for ideas about supper each day. Two dozen folks are a lot to cook for on that meal. The good thing is there aren't usually a lot of leftovers to contend with, what with no refrigeration now. I was thinking maybe beef and noodles tonight. We've got a bunch of canned beef chunks and cases of egg noodles. That with some French-style bread should make a good meal. We should add a veggie though. How about green beans?"

My mouth was watering just listening to her. "Yes, ma'am, all of that sounds amazing. Just let us know what you need help with."

She waved a hand at me. "This one will be easy. I'll make the bread after lunch. The green beans will need about an hour. The rest is fast. If you can get someone to bring the stuff up from the basement, that's all the help I need right now."

This was TEOTWAWKI, right? I had a feeling with Millie around we wouldn't notice it that much, at least not from an eating standpoint. I couldn't wait for supper now.

\*\*\*\*

It took about an hour to get everyone up and fed once breakfast was ready. Like I said, two dozen people is a bunch to run through the kitchen. We did shifts again, which helped. After the last bunch were done, we sent the kids out to the screen porch and shooed the men out back to their building project. It was time for the Mom Meeting.

We all sat down at the kitchen table. Even though she wasn't a mom, we included Marietta. This meeting would lay out chores for the women as well. Janet had a pad and pen. She started by making a list of all the kids and their ages, then listed the women folk. The youngest was Moira, at six years old. The oldest was Matt, at seventeen. He could technically be grouped in with the single men, but we'd keep him with us for now. She handed the list to me. I looked it over and started the meeting.

"Okay, ladies, here's what we have. Four kids under twelve. They can take care of weed pulling in the gardens. We'll need to make sure they know the difference between a weed and food. At six Moira may be too young even for that. We may give her feeding the rabbits, ducks, and chickens with Tara and Katlyn. We'll definitely start teaching her the difference in weeds and good plants, along with the rest of the kids."

I checked the list. "Tara, Katlyn, Aiden, and Tony can definitely pull weed duty. I think we can have Tony work with Ben and Rusty on feeding the larger animals as well. Rusty, Ben, Matt, and Nick will be responsible for chopping wood for the wood stoves.

The younger kids can stack and carry. Those four boys will also take turns mowing the yard. They will pull sentry duty as well, probably with one of the men. We'll have the girls gather eggs each morning, and the younger boys can haul the milk from the cows and goats once they've been milked. They can also keep the outside wash stand in water. Am I forgetting anything?"

Sara and Kate looked at each other, then back to us. Sara commented, "Wow. That's a lot of chores. I had no idea there was that much to do each day. Will we have time for school as well? Sounds like their day is full of other things."

She seemed a bit disheartened. I tried to reassure her. "It sounds like a lot because it takes a lot of work to keep a farm going. Most people have no idea where their food comes from. Farmers do not get the respect they deserve for providing pretty much everything we eat. It is hard work to take care of crops and livestock. We also have some extra challenges with the power being gone, so we have added work to make up for that. We will be washing clothes by hand, for instance. That means pumping and heating water. The good thing is, with this many people, it won't take long to do the daily chores.

"In the beginning, the kids will be slow because they are learning how to do the tasks. As they learn, they'll get faster. I would say they can have all the livestock feeding and collecting done in thirty minutes to an hour. That will be their first priority. Then, garden duty and wood chopping and stacking are next. We want them to be done with that before the heat of the day. I think they can do that in one to two hours each day. They should finish right around lunchtime. After lunch, I would think two to three, maybe four hours of the three Rs would suffice, wouldn't you?"

Sara didn't look any less concerned. "Anne, I really think we need to make sure they don't fall behind in their studies. When the power comes back on, schools will open back up; and they will be playing catch up with the other kids. Is there not a way to devote the majority of the day to studies?"

I looked at her incredulously. "Sara, who do you think these other kids are that are going to get ahead of our kids, who, by the way, just happen to have a teacher with them? What is your estimation of how long this will last? If this is as widespread as we think it is, it will probably take years to get back to any semblance of normal. This is not a glitch or a hiccup. This is a major reset of our way of life. You have to stop thinking of this as a temporary situation. If our theories are correct, your son will be a legal adult before we see anything even remotely resembling what we had and lost two weeks ago. Honestly, it could take a decade or more to recover, and it may never again be what it was.

"The most important things in everyone's lives right now are water, shelter, food, and security—pretty much in that order. All those other kids, if they make it, will not be trying to keep up their studies. They will be trying to exist. As I said, you can have their afternoon time. Their mornings are going to be full."

Even in our current reality, some people just couldn't fathom that life as we knew it was over. I didn't want to sound like a bitch, but I couldn't think of any other way to get her to understand that all that crap that was important before, meant little to nothing now.

She stared at me, and I could almost see the light go on in her head while tears formed in her eyes. "I'm sorry, Anne. It's so hard to think of this whole situation as the way it's going to be now. We had computers and a world of knowledge at our fingertips on the internet. I still can't believe I can't go to my phone and look up 'how to distinguish weeds from edible plants' anymore. That's something that would be really helpful right now, since I have no idea which is which either. I can see you all put a lot of thought into how to survive if something like this happened. I'm just kind of lost right now. Surviving, shooting, scavenging—these are not things I know how to do. I just hope you all will have some patience with me while I learn. I really want to know how to live in this new, old world."

I softened my tone a bit. "I understand, Sara. I was like you once. I didn't believe anything like this could happen. But I planned for when it did. I have some really good books on some e-readers that we protected from the pulse that will help you with things like plant identification. You also have us, our guys, Monroe and Millie, even the Thompson boys, who all know the difference between a weed and food. Although, truth be told, you can eat some of the weeds, too. You've been killing food in your yard for years."

She looked at me wide-eyed. "Seriously? Like what?"

"Dandelions, for one. The flowers, leaves, and roots are all edible and actually good for you. They have potassium, antioxidants, and vitamins A and C. Chickweed is another edible 'pest' plant. Clover is edible but not tasty, although you can make jelly out of the flowers. The point is that we are all in school now. We are all going to be learning how to survive and thrive without what we had before. How about if we have our school in the morning, while the kids are doing chores? We can go through the e-readers, find stuff we want to learn more about or how to do, and then you can share what they need to know with the kids as part of your curriculum in the afternoon? We don't have school books, so this is all going to be pretty primitive anyway. We'll call our mornings Laundry and Learning, since I'm pretty sure we'll be doing laundry every day now."

They giggled at my joke, and everyone seemed to calm down but, more importantly, get on board. We needed all of them to understand what the priorities in life were now.

Janet stood up. "I think we have a plan for now. I'll take the little ones out to take care of the small animals and show them how to handle them, as well as how to get in and out of the pens without letting any loose. Anne, you can take the bigger kids out to the barn to feed the pigs, goats, cows, and horses. I'd love to know if we have any hidden talents in the milking department, but I'm sure Uncle Monroe has already handled that this morning. We'll check with him about letting them watch, and possibly participate, this evening. Then we'll take them all to the garden for Weeds versus Food Level One: Know the Difference."

We all got up and got ready to head out. I took in all the ladies at the table. "It will take all of us to make this work. You are all important to the success of this place. We don't know each other that well yet, but we will figure it all out. I'm a hugger, so if you don't want one you better back up."

There were big grins, small smiles, and a few giggles as I made my way around and hugged them all. No one backed up; in fact they hugged each other as well.

I gave them all an encouraging smile. "Ladies, let's get to work!"

Sara and Kate followed Janet while Marietta followed me, as we all went out to gather kids and get busy. School was in session.

# Chapter 7

While the gals were laying out the schedule for the kids, the guys were setting the corner posts for the bunkhouse in the ground. Lee was a great carpenter and was meticulous in his work. That was clear from the tables he had built. He made sure the posts were exactly level, and he measured the distance between them multiple times as they were going in the holes. With so many of the men to handle the big beams, it didn't take them long to get the corners set and ready.

Monroe walked up, looked the setup over, and paid particular attention to the point where the post disappeared into the ground. He questioned Lee. "How'd you set the posts without any concrete? I know I don't have any of that. It doesn't keep well if you can't keep it dry all the time. Too much humidity here for that to be possible. What'd you use?"

Lee came over to him and leaned on the closest post. It didn't budge. Monroe was impressed. "Damn fine work, young man."

Lee smiled. "I've done research on lots of different ways to build lots of different things. I came across an article a few years ago that described how to sink a post without using concrete. In fact, the author explained it was better not to use concrete. Basically, you dig the hole as close to the size of the post as you can, burying up to a third of the post in the hole. We went with as deep as we could dig with the auger attached to the tractor, which ended up about four feet deep. Next, you drop a rock in the hole for the post to rest on. That keeps the bottom out of the damp soil. We went with a few to get us to about nine feet of pole to work with. Then you brace the post up level and fill in the hole with a mix of dirt and smaller rocks, tamping it down every few inches. When you get to the top of the hole, you leave a little mound so the rain will run away from the post to keep it from rotting. That left us with what should be enough pole to build out walls and brace for the roof. I'd like to build the floor off the ground a bit in case we get any heavy rains; that way the water will run under the building instead of through it, so we'll need a little bit of post to attach that to as well. I think the guys did a great job, don't you?"

Monroe eyed the posts, holding his hand up to the rest of them with his index finger and thumb forming a right angle. He closed his left eye and moved his hand down until his thumb lay on the horizon. He moved from post to post, checking each one. He dropped his hand, sniffed, and said, "I guess they look pretty level. Glad you fellas thought to use the tractor. It would have taken you hours to dig those holes by hand."

Pete was grinning at him. "Love that old machine, Mr. Warren. She runs like a champ. Knocked those holes out in no time."

Monroe squinted at him. "Name's Monroe. Only folks that call me Mr. Warren are people I probably don't want to talk to. Doctors, lawyers, government alphabet assholes, those kind of people. I'm glad you like the tractor. She's never let me down in forty years. I reckon we'll be finding all kinds of uses for her now. If Lee is done with her, we can run out to the gate and see if they're ready to dig some foxholes."

Pete laughed and nodded, then looked to Lee. Lee waved him off. "We need to hook up to the trailer and haul lumber down from the other shed, but we can do that with one of the trucks, if that's okay with everybody. I think both tasks are important, so if we can do both at the same time, that's probably the best option."

Russ had walked up to them by now, mopping sweat from his face. "Good idea. Use my truck. It's closest to the door. Keys are under the floor mat on the passenger side. I'm going to head out to the gate with these guys, unless you still need me."

Lee shook his head. "Nah, we're good. We'll be gathering materials for a while, and I think we'll put the roof on first so we can get it somewhat in the dry in case it rains. We might need some extra hands this afternoon getting the trusses set; but, like I said, I want to gather all the materials here first. Me, the Lawton brothers, and the Thompson boys can handle it for now. I'll let you know when we're ready for the next building phase."

Russ clapped him on the shoulder. "Thanks for the hard work, Lee. We're really glad you're here. You guys don't forget to stop and get some water in you before you head out to the other shed."

Russ, Monroe, and Pete headed to the tractor. Pete deferred to Monroe to drive, but Monroe climbed on back. "You brought her out this morning; you might as well keep on handlin' her. I'm just along for the ride."

Pete grinned at him and climbed into the driver's seat. He cranked the tractor up, and they headed down the driveway toward the gate to find the security crew. They would find more than that when they got there.

****

Mike, Brian, and Bob had left the bunkhouse building site as soon as the last post was in its hole. They didn't need everybody to fill and tamp holes once they got the things in the ground. They had stopped by one of Monroe's junk sheds to pick up the tree stand and ghillie material for the treehouse, now officially being called the Bird's Nest. Bob had named it, trying to be funny, but everyone liked it and he had been strutting around like a peacock ever since. As Bob knew where most of the supplies were, he grabbed the crowbar, hammer, and nails.

"Can you guys think of anything else we might need for this thing? Straw, mud, hair? Get it? Bird's Nest?"

He grinned at his own joke while Mike and Brian just shook their heads. Mike looked at him and said, "Dude, you ain't right."

Bob pushed his chest out. "Yep, but ya gotta love me."

Brian replied, "The only person who's 'gotta love you' is Janet, poor woman. The rest of us tolerate you, mostly. Sort of. Somewhat."

Mike snorted a laugh. Bob cut his eyes at him. "Something funny, Sergeant Shitter? You finding all this amusing?"

Mike, who was quickly getting used to Bob and his ways, laughed out loud. "Extremely funny. By the way, there will be an equally annoying nickname for you in the not-too-distant future, bubba. Count on it."

Bob tried a menacing look, but couldn't pull it off. He grinned again. "Looking forward to it, Sergeant."

They grabbed their supplies and headed for the treehouse. When they got to the tree, they dropped everything and took another look at the steps leading up. Brian took the tree stand and leaned it up against the trunk.

"Looks like we're going to be damn near perfect reaching the platform with this rig, and this is much sturdier than what's there now."

Mike looked it over, nodding. "Yeah, this ladder is going to save us a ton of work. Didn't Monroe say he had some paint we could camo this thing with? We should do that first."

"I know where it is. Be right back." Bob headed for the house.

Mike turned to Brian. "In the meantime, let's start pulling these steps off as far up as we can reach them. Set aside any you think we can re-use for something else. I'm pretty sure nothing gets thrown away around here."

Brian laughed as Mike handed him the claw hammer and took the crowbar for himself. They worked together, one pulling the steps off, the other pulling the nails out. They had most of the ones they could reach down by the time Bob got back with the paint. Mike immediately gave him a hard time.

"Damn, man, I was about to come looking for you; thought you got lost. We were running out of things to do. What took you so long?"

Bob was agitated. "You've seen Monroe's storage sheds, right? Do any of them look organized to you? I had to dig through about four boxes of shit before I found them."

He held up three cans of spray paint: black, brown, and green. Mike took the brown and green. He started shaking them and turned to Brian. "Lay that ladder on the ground. I hope Monroe doesn't get pissed if we get paint on the grass."

Bob was shaking the black can. "Nah, he hates the lawn. Said he'd plow it under if Millie would let him. What can I do?"

"Come in behind me with the black. No pattern, just random spots. It's supposed to look like the forest, which has black spots caused by shadows. The hope is that no one will see this when they look through the trees from the road."

They went to work, covering the old paint on the ladder. When they were satisfied with the results and it had dried, they set it up against the tree.

"I think that will work. Let's figure out how to get this thing attached." Mike grabbed the ladder and laid it back down.

"Since the premise of a tree stand is to be able to climb up to a perch, it's supposed to be set away from the tree, usually the distance of the platform at the top. This one still has the platform; it's the seat that's gone. We don't have any of the cabling that would have come with it originally, but I think we can come up with something, hopefully even sturdier than the original setup."

He looked at the tree stand, then back at the tree. "Let's go see what Monroe has in the way of scrap metal. If I can find the material to make a brace for this about a third of the way up, that should work fine."

They headed out to the shed beside the barn. Monroe was not an organized man by any means, but he at least kept like materials together. They went to the scrap metal pile. Brian reached for a piece on top, but abruptly dropped it and yelled out.

"Damn it! That thing cut me!" He stuck his hand in his mouth and sucked on the spot.

Mike shook his head at him. "Buddy, metal can and will cut you as quick as glass. You better go get Kate to clean that up for you."

Brian pulled his hand down and looked at it. "Nah, it's alright. Let's finish this, then I'll get her to look at it." He was already wrapping it in a rag he had found nearby.

Bob looked at the cut over his shoulder. "You know we don't have any tetanus shots now, right? If you get lock jaw, don't come crying to me. Oh wait ..."

Mike grinned at Bob's joke, but then donned a more serious expression. "He's joking, but it's a concern. I'd feel better if you'd go get that looked at, get a clean bandage and some antibiotic ointment on it. We can handle this. Go see Kate."

Brian grumbled, but headed toward the house. Bob looked at Mike. "Our first injury. Hope there aren't too many of those, but I'm sure there will be. Let's get this thing mounted. Did you find what you need to do it?"

Mike held up a piece of threaded rod about three feet long. He also had a bracket with three holes in it—one on each end and a threaded hole in the center. Lastly, he showed Bob a U-bolt bracket.

"If you guys can get me something to drill with, I can use this stuff. We'll mount the flat bracket on the tree with some long screws. We can then thread the rod into the threaded hole in the center. If I can get my hands on a drill, I can drill a hole for the other end of the rod to go through the U-bolt bracket. We wrap the U-bolt around one of the rungs, and we have some stability, then we tighten everything down. Oh, I'll also need a hacksaw, to cut the rod to length."

"You know something, Sergeant Shitter? You're kind of handy to have around. Let's get those tools. I can't wait to see this put together."

"Why thank you, Pinky."

Bob jerked his head in Mike's direction. "Pinky? What the hell you gonna call me that for?"

Mike held up his pinky finger and grinned. "You can thank Monroe for that one."

"Son of a bitch."

\*\*\*\*

Brian was walking up to the porch when we saw him. Kate clocked the blood and immediately headed his way. "What happened? Is anyone else hurt?"

Brian shook his head. "No, just me. I was attacked by a jagged piece of metal. Mike wouldn't let me help anymore, said I had to have you look at it."

Kate was pulling the rag away to get a look at it. The cut was jagged, but not too deep. It was oozing blood, but still bleeding. "Good thing he did. This rag is filthy. We need to get this cleaned up and get a fresh dressing on it. Anne, you have medical supplies, I'm sure."

"I do. Come on in the house. We'll clean him up in the kitchen."

We all went inside. Medical supplies were something I had prepped heavy because, as I kept telling everyone, there were no doctors to run to now. I went to the basement and pulled out a box labeled "Simple First Aid." This was alcohol and alcohol wipes, antibiotic ointment, Band-Aids, bandages, and tape—the things we'd need for minor cuts and scrapes. We had bottles of over-the-counter pain meds and fever reducers, as well as fish antibiotics in another box marked "Meds." The veterinary versions are almost the exact same thing as what is dispensed for humans, but you don't need a prescription for them. We had other boxes with different types of first aid items in them, including sutures and IV kits. Janet and I had both taken some extensive first aid training, but I was relieved to have an actual nurse here. Kate took charge of her patient.

"Come over to the table, Brian. Janet, can we get a light source over here?"

Janet grabbed a flashlight and held it over Brian's hand. Marietta was hovering, worried about Brian, so Kate set her to work as a distraction.

"Marietta, can you get me a pan of water at the sink? Something shallow we can get his hand in."

Millie was in the kitchen when we came in and was already pulling out small towels that looked like tea towels. She had also pulled out a small metal dishpan, which she handed to Marietta.

"Here you go, dear. This should work fine."

Marietta took the pan to the pump and started filling it. Millie took the towels to Kate. "Do you need hot water? I can have some heated in a jiffy."

Kate was peering at Brian's hand. "Let's see how clean we can get it with alcohol first. Oh, Millie, these towels look fancy. Are you sure you want me to use them for this?"

Millie placed them in her hand. "Yes, dear, I'm sure. I can't think of a better use for them. They've been sitting in that drawer for years."

Kate took the towels and set them on the table. She took one from the top and dipped it in the basin Marietta had brought to her. She started to clean the grime from around the wound and

Brian winced. She looked at him, smiled, and continued with her task.

"Sorry, I know this is not going to be pleasant, but an infection will be a lot worse. It doesn't look deep, but it is pretty jagged. I think our best bet is to clean it out, load it up with antibiotic ointment, and wrap the whole thing. You are officially off any kind of work detail that involves dirt or anything that will irritate this wound."

Brian started to protest, but Kate was firm. "Brian, do you want to risk losing your hand, or your life? We can't take any chances right now. You could get a staph infection, which could kill you. No. You're grounded, mister."

We hid our smirks by turning away to find something else to look at. Kate was vying for my Betty Badass status. I loved it. She cleaned the wound, then poured alcohol over it. After Brian stopped dancing around and hollering from that, she put the ointment on, followed by a large gauze pad held in place by a gauze wrap and surgical tape. She leaned back and surveyed her work.

"I wish we could give you a tetanus shot, but that's obviously out of the question. Keep this clean and dry. I want to see it three times a day until I say otherwise. Understand?"

Brian nodded, looked at his hand, and got up from the table. "Bob is going to give me so much shit for this."

Janet and I completely lost it then. She caught her breath long enough to say, "Oh yes, he most definitely will. Sorry about that."

"Well, I might as well get it over with. Thanks for patching me up, Kate. Later, ladies."

Brian headed out the door. We were still laughing as we gathered supplies. Kate looked at me with a handful of them. "Anne, maybe we should set up a first aid station somewhere. Is there a space we can use? I'd love to be able to have everything readily available if we need it. If that had been worse, we would have wanted the supplies within immediate reach."

"Great idea, Kate. Let's see what we can set up in the basement. That probably offers us the most usable space right now." I loved hearing Kate talk about setting up more permanent areas. I really wanted them to stay. It sounded like that was what they wanted too. We were heading down the stairs to the basement when we heard the gunshots.

# Chapter 8

While we were still at home after the pulse, we had all taken to wearing our pistols all the time. That hadn't changed since we had arrived at the farm. The new folks didn't all have sidearms, but those who did—Mike, the Lawton brothers, and Sean—wore theirs as well. Kate carried their 38 Special in her pocket. Lee didn't have a gun, so he had been given the .357 from the man on the road. We had extras, but he had requested that one. His reason was they had tried to use it to hurt us, so he would use it to protect us. Sound reasoning, if you asked me.

We hadn't really developed a plan for who would go where and do what if something happened here. We hadn't gotten that far yet. There was so much to do to get everyone settled in and get our defenses set up that we hadn't addressed it. Consequently, there was chaos when the shots were heard. Kids were running toward their parents, parents were looking for their kids, the dogs were running around everyone barking, and most of the men were heading toward the shots. Fortunately, the kids were all in the immediate area—some in the gardens, some in the barn—so I walked out on the porch and yelled for them.

"Kids! In the house! *Now!*"

They ran to my voice, and Millie was there to herd them all inside, along with Kate, Sara, and Marietta. I turned to Millie and said, "Get them down to the basement. Keep them there until one of us comes to get you."

She had a shotgun in her hand and nodded at me. "Anybody gets this far, they're gonna have to get through me to get to these babies. Be careful, darlin'."

I quickly hugged her and ran down the steps with Janet on my heels. Ben and Rusty were standing in the yard with their guns drawn, looking around. The Thompson boys were there as well, with pistols at the ready, scanning for anybody who wasn't supposed to be there. I got to them just as they were heading down toward the gate, where we thought the shots had come from.

"Guys, hold up. We need you to protect the kids and the house. Most of our supplies are in that house and the root cellar. We can't afford to lose them. If you'll each take a side, the four of you can pretty much cover the whole yard. Go inside the house, get upstairs, and find a spot you can see the furthest from. Keep your heads down. If you see anyone you don't know out there, shoot in their vicinity. Hopefully you can keep them occupied until we get more bodies to wherever they are. But if they get in the house, shoot them. Don't hesitate. Stay in there until we get back here, understand?"

The boys nodded, and with a group "Yes, ma'am" headed for the house. I wasn't the security expert here, but in their absence, I tried to make sure the kids were as safe as possible, while still helping to secure the place. I was pretty sure Russ and the guys would agree with me on that one.

Janet and I ran toward the road. That was where it sounded like the shots had been fired and that was the direction the guys had headed. Pete had gotten as far as the treehouse on the tractor. When they heard the shots, Russ yelled for Pete to stop the tractor; he and Monroe jumped off, pulled their guns, and grouped up with Mike and Bob. Brian had already been headed that direction, so he had caught up as well, pulling his pistol with his good hand. As Lee and the Lawton brothers had a head start on us, the guys were all there when we arrived. Mike hadn't quite finished attaching the deer stand to the tree yet, but with the help of a couple of them holding it steady, someone could climb up and get a look. Russ saw me coming and met me on the way.

"Anne, run back to the house and get my binoculars. Take Janet with you. Grab the tactical shotgun and the .308. Hurry."

Mike added, "Grab at least two more rifles, Anne. Whatever you've got that has a magazine. If it's got a scope, all the better. Do you guys have ARs? Mine's in the house with the rest of my gear, waiting for the bunkhouse. Behind the couch in the living room. Grab it."

Pete started our way. "I'll go with them, to help gather and carry the guns."

I turned around and ran back to the house, Pete and Janet on my heels. I was up the stairs faster than I knew I could run, pulling Russ's BOB out of the corner. They were never far away. I fished out his binoculars while Janet went across the hall and grabbed the long guns from their room. She came back with a 30.06 rifle and Bob's AR-15. I was draping the binoculars over my head when we met back up in the hallway, having slung both the .308 and the shotgun over my shoulders. We headed down the stairs to get back out to the guys. Pete was in the living room with Mike's bag slung across his back.

"This thing is full of guns and ammo. I didn't know what to grab, so I figured I'd just take the whole thing. I really need to learn more about guns, I guess. You ladies need any help?"

We shook our heads and headed for the door. Marietta met us in the doorway, hand resting on the pistol at her side. I'm sure we weren't quiet coming in and galloping up the stairs. She looked as scared as I felt.

"Do you know what's happening, Anne? Who was shooting?"

I paused long enough to lay a hand on her arm. "No, we don't know what's going on yet. Stay here and help keep the kids safe. Please."

There was a plea in my voice she must have heard, because she took on a determined stance at the door to the porch.

"You've got it. Be careful. Let us know when you can."

I gave her a quick hug and ran out with Janet and Pete. I was pulling the binoculars off as I ran up to Russ. He grabbed them and the rifle while Bob was getting his rifle from Janet. Pete handed Mike his bag. Mike immediately dug out the AR.

"Okay, girls, head back—"

I didn't let him finish. I was shaking my head, feet firmly planted where I stood. "No way. Millie, Marietta, and Kate are all armed in the house, and the kids are down in the basement. The older boys are watching all four sides of the house from upstairs just like we did at home when there were invaders. There are plenty of people in the house. We're here to help. Don't make me remind you that both of us out shoot you guys every time we go to the range."

Monroe snorted a laugh, but got serious again almost immediately. "This ain't a target, sweetheart. This is a person with a gun who can and will shoot back. Hell, they've already shot, and we don't even know who they are, how many there are of them, what they're after, or where they are right now. I just hope they're still outside the fence. Russ, you see anybody yet in them things?"

Russ had apparently decided not to argue with me right then. He was looking through his binoculars toward the gate. "I can't see anything from here. Mike, is that thing ready to use?"

Mike had stopped work on the ladder when the shots rang out. "It's not completely attached, but we can hold it steady enough for you to climb it to get a look. Better yet, you guys hold it and let me go up. I've got my minis on me."

He pulled out a small set of binoculars from the pack he had been carrying since we met him. We hadn't asked, but my guess was either a small BOB or an EDC pack—every day carry—he kept with him at all times. Gotta love vets. They know what's out there, and a lot of them are borderline preppers—at least from a semi-tactical standpoint.

Mike took his rifle, slung it across his back, and grabbed the ladder. Bob, Bill, and Ryan steadied it on both sides and the back. The platform was already resting on the landing of the treehouse. Mike climbed up and hopped out onto the landing. He pulled up his minis and looked toward the gate, as well as both sides of it.

"I see a couple of guys. They look pretty young, maybe eighteen or nineteen. No more than twenty. They are on the road close to the gate, looking this way. I don't think they've found the gate yet. I see long guns on both of them, but no scopes. Might be a shotgun on one, rifle on the other one. They seem to be waiting for something. No vehicles I can see, but they could have parked them and walked out here. We would have heard vehicles, which is probably why they didn't drive in. Not sure what their agenda is. Maybe we should go find out."

Russ looked up at him. "Are you sure there are only two of them? I don't want anyone walking into a trap."

"I can't be a hundred percent positive, but I don't see anyone else. You think they heard the tractor?"

Russ looked at Monroe; Monroe was slowly nodding. "That makes sense. They hear the tractor, can't tell exactly where it's coming from since they can't see in here, so they fire some shots to see who comes running. Then they know where we are. Question now is, do we let them know?"

Russ replied, "I think we should wait for now, to see what they do. Mike, keep an eye on them."

Mike gave a short nod in the affirmative and continued his surveillance.

Russ looked at the rest of us. "Just hang tight, guys. I'd rather not announce our location until we have no other choice, but we're not going to be able to stay hidden forever. At some point we will be located, and I doubt it will be by people who want to join forces with us. Let's wait a few minutes and see what their next move is."

We didn't have to wait long. The shots seemed to go off right over our heads. I jumped a foot and Janet stifled a scream. Monroe was hot and loud. He didn't care whether they knew where we were or not now.

"Damn fools! Bullets have to come down sometime! We got to get out there, Russ, before they hurt somebody!"

Russ nodded grimly. "Yep, we do. Monroe, if it's anyone from around here, they should know you, so you need to be with us. You, me, Bob, and Mike should be a good show of force. Take the biggest, baddest dogs, too. Lots of folks are afraid of big scary dogs. Everyone else stay here. We need someone in the Bird's Nest, watching for any surprises. Sean, can you go up?"

"Sure thing, Russ. Hand me your binoculars."

Russ passed them to Sean, who climbed up to the hide. He immediately scanned the area again, then looked down at us. "Still only the two guys that I can see. They are looking this direction. It's possible they heard us talking—or Monroe's, um, raised voice."

Monroe looked up at him. "You can say they heard me holler. I know I did, and I'd do it again. Idiots!"

Russ started toward the gate. "Alright, let's do this guns holstered, but keep your hands on them. If anything happens, we won't have time to decide whether or not to draw. The rest of you stay here. Sean, let them know if anything changes out there."

I ran up to him and hugged him fiercely. "Be safe. I love you." We had always made a point of telling each other that whenever we would be apart for any amount of time. I felt it was more important than ever now.

He hugged me back and said, "Ditto to you. I love you too." He then looked to the guys.

"Alright, let's go find out what these dumbasses are up to."

\*\*\*\*

Jay and Clay Glass lived a few miles from the farm. They were not known for their hard-working lifestyle. In fact, more often than not they could be found hanging around outside the old general store at the crossroads, smoking cigarettes, drinking beer that no one could figure out how they got since they were still under age, and telling tall tales about their "adventures." How many adventures could two high school drop-outs who lived in their momma's basement have had? They had never held a steady job, instead relying on their mother's disability check to keep them in their vices. No one knew what about their mother, Rhonda, was disabled, as she seemed perfectly capable of walking around, driving, or going to bingo or lunch with her friends. The Glass family lived off the government—a government that could very well be non-existent now. These were the kind of people who needed to be watched out for, and probably defended against. They didn't know how to find food that didn't come out of a grocery store. They would be looking for someone to "help" them get by, just until things got back to normal—which probably wasn't going to happen any time soon, if ever.

They were standing in the road, looking toward the gate that they still didn't know was there. Monroe unlocked it and Russ and Bob grabbed the gate and swung it open. Monroe and Mike were walking toward the Glass brothers, who looked like they had just seen the door to a magical portal open before their eyes. Russ and

Bob fell in behind them, and Monroe was ranting as he walked into the road to confront them.

"What the hell are you doing out here? Just shooting for the fun of it? You do know them bullets got to come down, right? Do you think they just stay up in the air once you shoot 'em? You gonna answer me, boy?"

The Glass brothers were backing away from Monroe's verbal assault, as well as the German Shepherd/Rottweiler mix dogs at his side with their hackles up and a low growl in their throats.

Clay spoke up. "Uh, we was … uh … hunting. Yeah, hunting for some rabbits, or sumthin' like that to eat. We been out of food for a couple of days now. The store's closed, said they ain't gettin' no more food, looks like, so Momma sent us out to try to find sumthin' we could eat. But we ain't seen no rabbits, squirrels, nothin'. Y'all got any spare food for a neighbor? We'd be much obliged, and we could replace it when the power comes back on and the store opens back up."

Monroe glared at him. "If you were huntin' rabbits, why were you shooting in the air, over my place? You seen some flying rabbits out here?"

Jay snorted to cover a laugh, then somberly replied, "Well, uh, to be honest we knew you lived out here somewheres, Mr. Monroe, and we was hopin' if we shot you'd come see who it was, then we'd know where you was, so you could help us out."

"And why would you think I'd help you out? You should go on and try to find them rabbits and squirrels. There's plenty out there. I got my own people to look after and tend to."

Jay went on. "Tell ya true, even if we got a rabbit or a squirrel we wouldn't know what to do with it. We ain't never hunted before. Our daddy ran off when we was little, so it was just Momma and us. We didn't have nobody to teach us stuff like that. What do we do with it if we get one?"

Monroe seemed to soften at the thought of these young men trying to provide for themselves and their mother. Then Clay opened his mouth and changed the mood of the gathering.

"Who cares? If y'all got food, you can share it with us. That's the right thing to do. As long as somebody's got food, everybody can eat, right?"

Bob stepped forward. "Wrong. *We* have food for *our* families, not yours. *You* need to go find something to eat somewhere that isn't here."

Jay seemed to sense the situation had taken a bad turn and tried to salvage it. "We'd work for it, whatever ya need. We can do all kinds of things. And it wouldn't be for long—just until everything comes back on."

Bob was shaking his head. "We don't need any help. We've got everything covered. By the way, just how long do you think this is going to last?"

Clay shrugged. "Dunno, maybe a month or so at the most. I mean, we're kinda off the main road a-ways, so it makes sense it'll take 'em longer to get our power back."

Bob looked at him incredulously. "Do you think this is just a power outage? Did you not notice that none of the new cars work, or cell phones? This is going to last a hell of a lot longer than a month. It could be years, which is why you fellas need to learn how to feed yourselves. I'd suggest you get going and get busy doing that."

Clay was getting agitated. "Didn't we just get done tellin' ya we don't know how to do any of that? We need help. You could give us enough to get by for a couple of days. That ain't askin' too much."

Russ stepped up to the assembled group. "Then what happens in a couple of days when that food is gone? Will you know how to feed yourselves then? No, you'll be right back here, wanting more. We can't help you. We have our own families to take care of. You need to leave, and don't come back."

Jay looked desperate. "But what do we do? What do we eat?"

Monroe reached down to the side of the road and pulled up a dandelion, root and all. He held it out to them. "You see this right here? This weed? You can eat every bit of it. There's all kinds of nuts, berries, and wild onions out in the fields you can eat. Go sit in the woods and wait for a squirrel. There's food all around you. You just have to do a little work to get it."

Jay was looking at the dandelion with renewed interest, but Clay was still trying to get something for nothing.

"Well, we ain't leavin' 'til you help us. We're gonna stay right here, maybe keep shootin' out over your trees there. Best hope we don't get a lucky shot in, where someone gets hurt."

Mike finally stepped in. He walked over and got right up in Clay's face. He spoke low and steady, with no emotion. "If there is one more shot fired toward this place, or even in this vicinity, it will be the last thing you ever do. You won't even know it's coming, because I saw you long before you saw us. You need to leave now, while you still can. This is the only warning you will get."

The dogs, sensing the change in the emotion level, started slowly toward the brothers, still growling, very aggressive.

Jay grabbed his brother's arm and started dragging him back down the road. "C'mon, Clay, they ain't gonna help us. Let's go."

Clay struggled against his brother's grasp and started to raise his rifle. It looked like a .22, but even that small caliber could kill if it hit you in the right spot. He'd barely got the barrel moving upward when all four men drew their sidearms and pointed them at the Glass boys. Mike was slowly shaking his head.

"You don't want to go there, fellas. You'll be dead before you can even get that gun raised up. Go home to your momma. Don't come back."

Clay stopped the movement of the gun, but couldn't keep his mouth shut. "This ain't over. Y'all can't just let people starve while you got food. Y'all need to learn to share. Y'all need to learn to help your neighbors. It ain't right to let folks starve while you eat high on the hog. This for sure ain't over."

The brothers turned to walk away while the guys stood there and watched to make sure they didn't change their minds. Never taking his eyes off them, Mike said, "You know that's the truth, right? This ain't over. They'll be back when they get desperate enough."

Russ nodded. "Unfortunately, yes. Security just became our number one priority. Let's get those foxholes dug."

# Chapter 9

With the Bird's Nest done and the Gopher Holes dug—Brian's naming contribution, apparently trying to outshine Bob—Russ consulted with Mike on any more security measures we should employ. Mike again suggested adding another post to each side of the gate to strengthen the hinge area, and added, "Maybe a good stout post in the middle of the gate, dropped in the ground. We wouldn't fill in the hole, so we could move it if we need to get out. With the camouflage on the gate, I think we could set it where no one could see it. They'd get a big surprise if they hit it, trying to break it down."

Everyone agreed those were really good ideas. Pete offered to take the tractor up and get the auger hooked up to it for the post drilling. Janet and I asked him for a ride back to the house so we could bring the kids and the rest of our people back out.

When we got back by the house, we jumped off, waved at Pete, and hustled inside. Marietta was still by the front door, watching for anybody who didn't belong. We let her know the danger was passed, for now, and headed in to tell the rest of our folks. Janet went up after the boys, and I headed to the back of the house to get the rest of the crew.

Marietta was curious, wanting to know what had happened, so I let her know we'd tell everyone when we got them all out again. We sent the kids out to the screen porch, and we women and the bigger boys went to the living room.

"First off, everyone is fine. The shots you heard were not aimed at anyone. We had some visitors who were, quite frankly, looking for us. Millie, you might know them. Jay and Clay Glass?"

Millie nodded grimly. "Yes, unfortunately. They are not what I consider 'good people.' They abuse the system to get a free ride. Well, I guess that would be used to abuse now, wouldn't it?"

"Correct, and those are the kinds of people who will cause us the most problems. They've been living off the government teat for years and either don't want to take care of themselves, or don't know how to do it. I think the Glass brothers fall into both categories. One of them, Jay, seems to want to know how to make it without assistance, but the other one, Clay, is looking for someone to take care of them. We don't think we've seen the last of them. The guys are finishing up the reinforcements out front by the gate. After dinner tonight, we'll be having a sit-down to set up some protocols for what to do when something like this happens. All other projects are on hold for the rest of the day, until the new security measures are in place. We want this place to be as safe as we can make it. All that said, everyone did very well today for not having a plan in place yet. We don't have to walk around on egg shells; we just need to be ready to act and react when we need to, and quickly. Is there anything else we need to discuss?"

Kate spoke up. "You'll be happy to know we put our time down there to good use today. We have a mini clinic set up, including a couple of cots. We grabbed an empty rolling tool chest Monroe had down there and added the supplies for easy access. We even set up an old floor lamp to use for an IV stand. We finished it off with a shower curtain for privacy if we need it. It turned out pretty well. You ladies did a phenomenal job of collecting supplies, by the way. There isn't much we're lacking, outside of a doctor and a sterile environment."

She grinned at the end. We all knew we had about as sterile an environment as we were going to achieve for now.

"Thanks, Kate. Prepping is all about trying to think of what you would need if you couldn't go to the store and buy it or didn't have the skill to make it. Medical supplies fall into that category, although we have quite a few medicinal herbs growing here, along with bolts of white cotton cloth to use for bandages if needed. We can show you that stuff when things calm down a bit.

"Speaking of things we can't buy or make, we are going to need more clothes, a lot more, for all of you and your kids. I know Kate and Sean lost everything in the fire. If we can make a run back to your neighborhood, can you help find clothes for the Scanlin kids, Sara? I'm sure we can get Lee's kids' stuff from their house.

I'm more worried about Tara and Katlyn. While we can make clothes, it will take a bit to create patterns, and we'll have to tear down existing pieces for that. Millie has an old treadle sewing machine we can use, and we have piles of material and notions, but we need to start somewhere."

Sara was nodding thoughtfully. "You know, Anne, there was a family that lived just a few doors down from us that had two young girls. I'm not sure exactly how old, but I know they were younger than Tony and older than Moira. That should put them in the right age range, or close anyway. I never saw them after the pulse, so we can only assume they were all on their way to work or school."

She shuddered at a thought that I'm pretty sure crossed all of our minds just then. Dear God, what had happened to those two little girls? For that matter, what had happened to all the kids who were already at school or on their way when the pulse hit? I said a quick prayer for people I didn't know and probably never would, and moved on. We had to make us the priority here.

"I think we need to suggest that this evening as well. We brought everything we had from our houses, but those won't last with everyone we need to clothe now, and we have nothing for the smaller kids. We really need to get back to your neighborhood and get clothes for all of you. And we need to do it soon. It's only going to get more dangerous out there as time goes on."

We were all in agreement that clothing was a top priority; we'd just add that to the ever-growing list. No matter how well you try to plan for whatever might happen, there's always something else you need.

Millie stood up and stretched her back. "Well, ladies, I don't think there's much else to do but get some supper ready. It looks like we are going to have another full evening. Might as well get to it."

****

Of course, the Glass brothers encounter was the hot topic of dinner conversation. We all felt we had definitely not seen or heard the last of them. Russ brought up setting up security details again. There was no doubt after today's events that he was right about needing to do it immediately. We decided we'd get that laid out after we finished eating.

The wind had picked up and some dark clouds were rolling in, so we hurried everyone to finish up so we could get everybody and everything inside before the rain that seemed to be on its way got to us. Since we didn't have a weather app to check the radar on anymore, we had to go back to actually looking at the sky to see if we could figure it out. It definitely looked, felt, and smelled like rain. That would be welcome, since we hadn't had any in a few days and young gardens need water. I hoped this wasn't a sign of a super dry summer coming. With no power, we would have to haul water to the gardens and the livestock, because we couldn't afford to lose any food source now. We had food stores, but we also had three times as many people now as we had when we prepped for this scenario. If we had food to feed eight people for a couple of years before, we now had food to feed twenty-four for eight months to a year. We could not take the chance anything we were growing or raising wouldn't make it.

We settled in on the screen porch to enjoy the breeze from the storm coming in. Russ spoke first. "Gang, those fellas today are just the beginning of who is out there looking for someone to 'help' get them through this. I know it's hard to think about other people out there hungry and helpless, but we can't help everyone. We have to take care of our people first."

Sara spoke up. "Couldn't we help a few of them? What if they have children? I don't know if I can, in good conscience, stay here warm, dry, and fed if there are children right outside this place starving."

Bob stared at her. "So, are you saying you would be willing to sacrifice food for your family, which includes your son, to feed someone else's kids? It wouldn't be a one-time deal, you know. Feed them once, and they'll keep coming back for more. You gonna let Tony go without so someone else's kid can eat?"

Sara looked indignant. "Of course I don't want my son to go hungry. But surely we have enough to help some of them. This place is covered in gardens and livestock, plus all the food stores in the root cellar. It seems like we should be able to help others less fortunate than us, to some degree, if only—"

Mike interrupted her. "Sara, we are those less fortunate people you are talking about. These folks brought us in here and offered us food and shelter. This place was set up and stocked for eight people. There are now twenty-four. What do you think that does to the food and water supplies that are available? How about that nice roof you have over your head? You want to share your room, too? If you want to go out and save the world, you go right ahead, but you can't do that from a place where you are a guest. I'd suggest you let the man finish what he was saying."

Sara seemed to go through a few different emotions during that diatribe. She went from shocked indignation, to anger, to perhaps contrition, and then finally to sullen acceptance. Russ was looking at her expectantly, but when she didn't have a rebuttal to Mike's awesome synopsis of the way things were, he continued.

"I understand your feelings, Sara, I really do. But as Bob told you, if you help them once they will keep coming back for more. And as Mike said, there are a limited number of resources here. I would have liked to have added a few more folks for security reasons, but I think we are probably at our maximum sustainability numbers for now. That's why it's so important that everyone does their part for our survival. That includes keeping out the people who want to take what we have. I hope you can accept that, because it's non-negotiable."

He paused to give her a chance to speak up. Pete did instead. "We're very thankful to be here, and we can accept those conditions, Russ. Please go on."

· Russ gave Pete a quick nod and continued. "We are going to have to have twenty-four-hour security details. We have ten men, counting Monroe, and four women, not counting Millie, who has offered to stay armed in the house at all times."

Millie nodded and smiled at Russ. "I'll guard the kitchen. An army travels on its stomach, you know. Besides, no one wants to mess with me and Gertrude here." She reached into her apron pocket and pulled out a 38 Special. I'd seen her shoot—I'd put her up against most of us for accuracy. She was bad to the bone with that little revolver.

Russ returned her smile and continued. "Then we have four teenagers who can help. That gives us eighteen people to cover twenty-four hours. I'd like for parents to not be on the same rotations as their spouse, so one of them is available to their children if needed. I'd love it if we could have four-man teams, but I don't see how we can do that and keep everything else done around here. So I'm going to suggest three per shift. That will give us six sets of folks on four-hour shifts. I think we can make that work. I'm going to ask for volunteers for the midnight to four shift and the four to eight shift. Those will be the hardest to do and stay

awake, although the rooster will do his part for the second one."
Everyone laughed.

Pete raised his hand. "I can take the midnight shift, Russ. As a trucker, I've driven many a mile while everyone else was asleep. I will need some training though. I know nothing about what I need to do."

Mike looked at Pete and replied, "We'll take care of that. Firearms safety training's first class is tomorrow morning. We'll cover security measures as well. Russ, I'll take over the security team scheduling for you. I'm sure you have plenty of other things to work on."

I saw my opening. "I have an urgent item we need to address. Clothing. We need to get back to their neighborhood and gather clothes for everyone from their houses and hopefully some vacant ones for the Scanlins. I know it's dangerous to leave, but this is not something we can put off. We have to have clothes for everyone. Seems to me the sooner we go get them, the sooner we can get back and lock this place down."

Russ sighed, but nodded in agreement. "You're right. We'll go first thing in the morning, before we do anything else. I would rather none of the women go, but I doubt I'm going to get my wish."

"I don't need to go, but I think Sara and Kate should both be in the group. One of the Lawtons, Lee, and Mike should be able to gather from their own homes, as well as keep an eye out for bad guys. This needs to be a grab everything, stuff it in bags, and go trip, so we should probably keep the body count down to make more room for clothes. I'm betting this will be a one-time trip, so get it all—clothes, shoes, coats, winter stuff—everything you can get your hands on quick. Oh, and bed linens, blankets, pillows, and sleeping bags if you have them."

Everyone agreed this was a priority. Frankly, the Scanlin kids were on a week or so of the clothes they'd left their burned-out home in, so they weren't fresh smelling at all, despite Kate's attempts to wash them out at night. Even then, wearing the same clothes every day, plus the constant daily washings, would wear them out pretty fast, especially with kids. We had come up with clothes for the grown-ups from our own stores, but those would dwindle as well. We needed more.

Mike worked out the security schedules so that Ben and Rusty were with their dads. I was still concerned about them working a security watch, but a bit less since they would have their fathers by their sides. Mike started on a setup for some solar panels to charge the two-way radios. Monroe had a set here that was linked to ours, so now we had four. Millie would monitor one in the house all day, and whoever was on duty would carry the others. Communication would be huge for quick responses to intruders.

Russ had offered to take the first shift that evening, so he, Rusty, and Kate started for the front gate. They took a scoped rifle, the tactical shotgun, the binoculars, and Russ's night vision monocular, along with their sidearms. They also grabbed some ponchos; the rain had arrived. It looked like our first full night of security would be a soggy one. We just hoped it would be a quiet one as well.

# Chapter 10

Since I would be awakened by the rooster at 4:30 or so anyway, I volunteered for the four to eight shift. That would get my security duty out of the way early so I could work on whatever else was needed for our daily lives. I heard Bob's SUV being started about seven. They were getting an early start. Good. The sooner they got the supplies, the sooner they could get back. I hated the thought of anyone leaving the relative security of the farm, but it had to be done.

They pulled up to the Bird's Nest and Mike stepped out. Bill Lawton was on security watch with me and Matt. Bill had been walking the front by the Gopher Holes and came jogging over when he heard the car. He looked in to his brother.

"Keep your eyes open, little brother. It's only been a few days, but a lot could have changed in that time. Don't take any chances and watch for traps. And don't forget my boots."

Ryan rolled his eyes at his brother. "Man, I ain't gonna forget your boots. You've only told me like five times since last night. Don't worry. We're gonna make this a smash-and-grab, as they say. We're gonna hit each house together so we can knock it out quick and we don't have to split up. We've got a radio, too, so if we get into any trouble we can call. It's only about ten miles. We'll be back in a few hours, right, Mike?"

Mike nodded at Ryan and looked up at me. "That's the plan. Anne, if you haven't heard from us by noon, there's trouble. I'm going to try to radio in on the hour, but don't get worried unless we go a couple of hours without contact. Probably just means we're busting a move to get the stuff gathered. We'll be back as quick as we can."

"Okay, but it's a waste of time for you to tell me not to worry. I'm going to worry the whole time you're gone. Hurry back."

He grinned at me and got back in the truck. Matt and Bill ran to close the gate behind them. I pulled up the binoculars and watched them until I couldn't see them anymore. They were outside our security area now. I prayed they stayed safe.

With about thirty minutes of my shift left, I saw Bob, Brian, and Ben coming down from the house. They were the eight to noon shift. I climbed down and met them on the ground.

"You guys are a little early. Anything wrong?"

Bob shook his head. "No, I just wanted to make sure everything was quiet this morning and that the clothing crew got out okay. Oh yeah, and Millie brought up weed pulling in the gardens. I didn't want to get drafted for that."

I laughed at him. "I think we've got enough kids to handle that particular chore. Since you guys are here I'll go back and get them together for the fun. The crew got out fine. They have a radio with them, so keep an ear out in case anything happens."

I handed him my radio and headed back to the house. Ah, weed pulling. What a great way to start the day. Sarcasm off.

****

Lee was driving, with Mike riding shotgun and the other three in the back seat. Mike was trying to watch everywhere for anything suspicious. There were no vehicles on the road that hadn't been there when they first drove to the farm, but, as they had discovered on the way, any vehicle could be an ambush point. Just being in a car that was running put a huge target on them.

They exited on the ramp off the highway that would take them to their neighborhood. As they started getting closer, they saw signs of activity that had not been there before. Houses that were broken into, doors and windows smashed. It looked as if someone had gone through and just busted into every house on the street. Mike tensed up and checked his pistol.

"Lee, slow down so we can check before we go in. Whoever did all this could still be here."

Lee gave a quick nod and let off the accelerator. As they turned down their street, Sara gasped. "Oh no. We're too late! Look at this place!"

The scene was shocking. Every house had its front door kicked in. There was clothing and trash strewn across the yards. It looked like every house had been hit. They were taking it all in when Mike saw a truck down the street he hadn't noticed before.

"There's somebody still here. Get us out of here. Now!"

Lee slammed on the brakes and threw the SUV into reverse. The street was still wet from the night before, so the tires spun loudly. As he was backing up, they saw three guys coming out of one of the houses close to where the truck was parked. The scavengers dropped what they were carrying and reached for their sidearms. Another stepped out of the pickup with a shotgun in hand. He raised it and fired at the SUV. While he wasn't close enough to do any damage, Mike did hear pellets hitting the front of the truck. Sara screamed. Everyone else pulled their guns. Lee reached the corner, turned, and headed back toward the highway.

Lee's hands were shaking on the steering wheel. "What do we do now? We can't go back empty handed. Hell, we can't go back to the farm period until we know they're gone. What if they followed us out there?"

Mike had the window down, trying to listen for the truck. He didn't hear it, but Bob's SUV wasn't really quiet either. He thought for a second.

"Keep going. Go past the highway. About a half-mile further is an old gravel farm road on the right. With the rain last night, it should be dust free. Turn in there. Go down that road and around the corner. We should be hidden from this street back in there and we can figure out what to do."

Lee found the road Mike was talking about and turned in. It was cut through a stand of trees and made a slight turn that kept them from being seen from the street. He found a wide spot and did a three-point turn to get the SUV pointed back in the direction they had come in. He turned the key off and looked at Mike.

"Now what? Sit and wait for them to leave? How will we know if or when they do from back here?"

Mike was pulling out the radio. "We're not waiting for them to leave. We're waiting for reinforcements."

\*\*\*\*

I was just finishing breakfast when I heard the radio crackle on the kitchen counter. It was such a shock to hear anything like that now that I think I jumped a foot at the sound. Millie grinned at me, whispered, "Me, too," and handed the radio to Russ, who was sitting at the table having a cup of coffee with me while I ate. We heard the tension in Mike's voice.

"Guys, are you there? We have a situation here."

Russ quickly responded. "We're here, Mike. What's going on?"

"We have some 'visitors' in the old neighborhood. They seem to be going through the houses looking for supplies. We saw them, they saw us, they shot at us, we got the hell out of there. It looked like there were only four of them. If we could get some backup, we might still be able to complete this mission."

We heard someone else keying in their radio, and Bob said, "They shot at you? Is anybody hit? Did you recognize them? What were they driving? Sons of bitches!"

Mike calmly replied, "They were too far away to do any damage with a shotgun. Some pellets hit your ride though. Sorry about that. No one got hit. They're driving an older pickup. I've never seen them before."

"I don't give a shit about the ride as long as you guys are alright. Describe the truck."

"Probably '70-model Ford. Rusted to hell, but was possibly black at one point. It had a crew cab, could have been one of the first ones made."

"Russ, does that sound familiar to you?" Bob asked.

"Yep, sounds like the crew that was in our area a week or so ago. They are obviously migrating away from town. Did they follow you, Mike?"

"No, most of them were grabbing things from houses when we turned down our street. We beat it out of there and got off the road. I haven't heard another vehicle, so I don't think they are looking for us. I'm not leaving without the stuff we came for. This is a perfect example of why we need to get this done and then hunker down at the farm. Can you send a few guys out here to back us up? I'd really like to run these assholes off or just get rid of them. It pisses me off when people shoot at me."

Russ laughed into the radio. "I hear ya, buddy. We'll get some guys together and head your way. Where are you exactly?"

Mike gave them directions to the spot they had holed up in. Russ, Bob, Bill, and Brian loaded up in the station wagon to head that way. A third of our people out there now? This was not going as planned—at all. Unfortunately, this was a mission that could not be abandoned. We *had* to have clothes and shoes for everyone. But at what price? Were those items more important than anyone's life? If anything happened to any of them, I didn't know if I could handle the guilt, since it had been my idea. I prayed for everyone's safety. There wasn't much else I could do.

****

Bill was driving. He said he knew exactly where Mike and the rest of them were. The other guys in the car were scanning the area for the dirtbags. While the guys hoped they wouldn't be headed in their direction, they were obviously working the whole area, so they could show up anywhere. When they got to the ramp, Russ had

Bill cut the engine so they could listen for other vehicles. They were all straining to hear, but it was quiet except for the birds and frogs; you could always hear the frogs after the rain.

When they verified there were no others close by, Bill started the car back up, turned right, and found the farm road.

Russ radioed Mike. "Mike, we're coming to you. Don't shoot."

"All clear. Come on in."

Bill drove back to the SUV and killed the engine. Everyone got out of both vehicles. Bob inspected his truck. There were a few dozen dents from the shotgun blast.

"Son of a bitch! I'm gonna kick somebody's ass for this!"

Mike was standing beside him. "Sorry, man. I kind of feel responsible."

Bob was shaking his head. "This ain't your fault. It's those scavenger assholes who did this. So, what's the plan? Because I'd just as soon go in there and beat the shit out of them."

Mike gave him a grim smile. "Me too, but we're not talking about a fist fight here. They've already shot at us. I think we should respond in like fashion."

Russ looked at him. "You have an idea?"

"Yep. I say we head back that way. Park maybe two blocks away and walk in. Problem is, with no other noise, they're going to hear us that close. There's no way we can be stealthy."

"Honestly, after your encounter, I'm sure they'll be expecting something. I think we should just go to the end of the street, park the SUV, have someone climb on top with this"—Russ held up the scoped .308 rifle—"and just wait. Either they'll come to us, they'll leave, or they'll start shooting. No matter which they choose, we'll be in a position to defend ourselves. I would suggest we leave the ladies here with Lee and the wagon, just in case. They can always come in when we give them the all clear."

There were general nods of agreement all around. Brian offered to stay with the SUV and act as sniper. "With my messed-up hand, I could be a liability up close and personal."

That met with the approval of the group as well. Now that they had a plan, it was time to enact it. Everyone who was going loaded up in the SUV. Russ turned to Lee, who was standing beside the wagon.

"Don't come in until we let you know it's clear. We'll radio you when it is. I'd suggest you wait inside the car, in case you need to make a run for it. Don't let the women out of your sight. They are a commodity right now. Call us if anyone shows up out here."

Lee nodded, shook Russ's hand, and got Kate and Sara inside the wagon. All they could do now was wait: wait to hear if it was all clear or all gone to hell.

# Chapter 11

Bill was driving slowly toward their abandoned homes. Mike was hanging out of the driver's side window with his minis, trying to get an advanced look at the scavengers. Late April in Tennessee meant all the trees were in bloom, so visibility was limited.

"I can't see a damn thing through all the pear tree blossoms. Stop as soon as you turn the corner, Bill." Mike pulled back inside the car. He put his minis in his pack and checked his pistol. He was carrying a Sig Sauer P220, a .45 caliber pistol touted as one of the most accurate .45s made. Paired with an ex-Marine, that was a force to be reckoned with. He had his AR slung in front of him at the ready.

Bill rounded the corner and stopped immediately. Brian climbed out the back and got on top with the rifle. He looked down the street through the scope.

"I see the four of them. They're looking this way. I see the guy holding the shotgun. It's that asshole that was driving the truck from over at our place. Two of the others were with him. I don't recognize the fourth guy. I don't see any other long guns, but they all have sidearms in hand. Looks like they're waiting for us to make the first move."

Russ gave out assignments. "Mike and Bill, step out so they can see you, then move to the back. The rest of us will climb out the back window. If they show force, we'll all come out. We have them outnumbered. Let's see if we can get them to choose a path."

The scavengers started walking slowly toward them. Russ called out, "Okay, let them see us." They all stepped out from behind the SUV, guns drawn. They moved to the front of the truck. And they waited.

They didn't have to wait long. The scavengers stopped, talked among themselves, then went back and loaded up in their pickup. They fired it up and headed down the street. They turned the next corner and were soon out of sight, although the guys could still hear the truck. After a minute or so the sound faded away. The men waited another five minutes, then loaded back up and headed down the street. Bill stopped in front of his house and got out, swearing.

"Those assholes kicked the front door in! There's side lights on both sides of it. They could have broken the glass, reached in and unlocked the damn thing. But nooooo—they had to destroy it. Animals!"

He went through the doorway and into the ransacked living room. The rest of the guys followed him in. The place was trashed. Furniture had been smashed and tossed aside. It didn't look like the scavengers had been looking for anything in there. They'd just ransacked the place for fun. Yes, because when the world goes to hell it's so much fun to tear up other people's hard-earned stuff.

Ryan had made his way to one of the bedrooms, and he hollered, "They took all the ammo that was out, but they couldn't get into the gun safe. And they left the clothes. We got clothes, people! Oh, and all the good guns." Turns out, the Lawton brothers were avid gun lovers. They had pistols in every caliber, revolvers, shotguns, and rifles. And a nice stash of ammo in the gun safe with them.

Mike looked in the safe. "I can't believe you guys left all those guns here."

Ryan had an indignant look on his face. "Dude, we didn't have a way to carry them all, with the other stuff we took. We figured we'd be walking for days. We always planned to try to get back here to get them. Guess what? We did!"

Russ chuckled. "Alright, I'm going to call Lee on the radio and get him and the girls here. We need to get everything loaded. Since we have two vehicles now, we should be able to get it all. Grab some bags, guys. Let's get busy."

****

After he got the call from Russ, Lee headed out with Kate and Sara. Russ had told them to keep an eye out for the scavengers, so

Lee had Sara driving while he and Kate watched for attackers. They didn't see or hear anyone else as they pulled in behind the SUV. They jumped out and rushed into the house. In the time it had taken them to get there, the guys had loaded up every bag they could find—suitcases, duffels, even trash bags—and were hauling them out to the SUV.

Lee went to Russ. "What do we need to do? Where do we start?"

"Head to your house. Start packing everything. Here, take some of these bags."

Russ handed him a box of industrial-sized garbage bags. As landscapers, the Lawtons did leaf removal in the fall, so they bought the large bags by the pallet. They had half of one of those pallets in their garage. Everyone had carried a couple of boxes each out to the SUV. Garbage bags wouldn't be needed again for a really long time.

Lee and the gals hurried across the lawn to the Roush home next door. As they were just about finished with the Lawtons' house, Mike and Brian went over with them.

The scene was a repeat of what they had seen at the Lawton home. Front door kicked in, furniture smashed and trashed, cupboards bare, with the dishes broken all over the kitchen floor. Lee stood in the center of what had once been a warm, comfortable living room, surveying the destruction. If Jackie did happen to make it home, this is what she would find. Everything they had worked so hard for destroyed. And for what reason? Why would people do this?

He asked the question out loud, his voice on the edge of hysteria. "Why? Why destroy everything? My God, someone has urinated in the corner! What kind of animals do something like that?"

Mike laid his hand on Lee's shoulder and said, "You answered your own question, Lee. Animals. There is no good reason for something like this"—he gestured around at the devastation—"other than just plain disregard for other people. My guess is they broke into our houses, found no food because we had eaten it all, and trashed the places in retribution. You can look at this from another perspective: what could have happened if we had still been here? What might these bastards have done to you, or worse, your kids? I for one am glad we were already gone. This is just stuff. In this new world, nice furniture and china are not important items. Clothes are. Let's go gather your family's clothes now."

Lee nodded, took one last look around, then headed down the hall. Kate and Sara were already back in Moira's room, stuffing clothes and shoes in bags. The state of the houses had given them all a sense of urgency to get done and get out. What if those guys came back, with more guys? Who knew how many dirtbags were in their "crew," holed up somewhere else?

With so many hands, they were able to get the items they were after loaded up pretty quickly. Within an hour, they had been through all their own houses, plus a couple that Lee and Sara knew had had smaller kids. Since the scavengers had already worked their way down the street, all the houses' doors were standing open. The ones owned by folks who were already gone and had never made it back were hard to go into. In one, food had spoiled in the refrigerator, which the scavengers had opened. The smell almost knocked them over when they entered. Ryan ran out to the yard and lost his breakfast. Lee and Sara followed suit.

"Oh my God, that's terrible! That's the most disgusting thing I have ever smelled! How are we going to be able to stand it long enough to get the clothes together?" Ryan was spitting the last remnants out as Bill brought him a bottle of water.

"I've got an idea, little brother. Hang on." Bill ran back down to their house, went into the garage, and grabbed a bag. He brought it back and set it down on the lawn. He pulled out a dust mask and handed it to his brother.

"It probably won't keep all the smell out, but it should help." To the group he said, "We use these when the pollen is high, or when it's rained a lot and the mold spore count goes up. Help yourselves."

Ryan put on one of the masks and started back to the house. When he got to the door he hesitated, sniffed a bit, then went inside. He immediately came back out, gagging.

"Nope, still smells almost as bad. What else can we try?"

Mike reached into his bag and pulled out a bandana. He handed it to Ryan. "Try it with this inside the mask."

Ryan stuck the bandana inside the mask and went back to the doorway. After a minute, he came back to the entrance with a thumbs up. "It doesn't mask all of the smell, but it helps. Stick something inside the masks, gang."

Needless to say, they moved through those houses quickly. When they had finished, both vehicles were crammed full of every kind of useful bag they had found, from backpacks to large suitcases, as well as lots of the big trash bags. There was just enough room for them left inside.

Russ, who had been standing watch with Bob, looked at the group. "Did we get everything? I don't want us to have to come back here. Were you able to find clothes for the Scanlins, especially the girls?"

Kate nodded. "I think what we found will fit them—if not perfectly, at least close. They may even get some growing room out of them. Thank you all so much for doing this for my family. I only wish the families who lived here had been able to get back home. Of course, if they had, we wouldn't have been able to get this stuff, so their misfortune became our blessing."

Sara stuck her toe up on that soapbox again. "This is why I don't understand why we can't help others as well. We are benefiting from these people's misfortune. Shouldn't we pay it forward, and help out others in need?"

Mike was shaking his head, the Lawton brothers groaning in unison, and Russ opened his mouth to speak, but Lee beat him to it.

"Sara, when are you going to understand—*we* are the others in need. You saw what those animals did to our homes. What do you think they would have done to us if we had still been here? Even if we were already gone, if Russ and his people hadn't offered to take us in, we could very easily have still been on the road trying to get to Sean and Kate's friends. How would that have played out with the couple we ran into that were killed on the way out to the farm? Yes, we're taking things that belonged to other people, but we have no choice. Those people are not here to offer it or for us to ask for it. This is the simplest way I can put it to you: if you and Pete had been at work, Tony at school, and hadn't made it home after the pulse, wouldn't you have wanted someone to use the things in your home you would never use again? Wouldn't you have wanted a family like the Scanlins, who lost everything through no fault of their own, to get some use out of those things?"

Sara looked at Lee and sighed. "Yes, of course I would. I'd want someone to use the things I'd left behind and wouldn't be back for. But what about the other people out there? What about the children?"

Russ shook his head. "Sara, there is no 'but.' We have told you that we do not have the resources to help everyone. If that's something you can't resolve yourself to understand, we may have to rethink our offer for you and your family to stay on the farm with us."

Sara, who had been maintaining a somewhat haughty expression as she chose to travel down one of those "let's save the world" paths, now had a look of sheer terror on her face.

"No! No! I'm sorry! I'm having a really hard time with this, especially where kids are involved, but no, please don't make us leave the farm!"

Russ folded his arms across his chest. "So you understand that you are in a very good place with us, right? I'd like for this to be the last time we have this discussion."

She was nodding vigorously. "Yes! Thank you for taking us in. Really, I'm so sorry. I won't bring it up again."

With that issue laid to rest, they were trying to decide who was going to ride back in which car when they heard a truck approaching. The scavengers were back.

# Chapter 12

Les was pissed. What should have been an easy day going through the houses they had busted into the day before had been interrupted by those assholes. That they may have been the legal owners of some of the homes meant nothing to him. They'd left, so anything they'd left behind was fair game. And he had claimed it. All of it.

There wasn't really much left in this area. It looked like most of these people had tried to ride it out, waiting for help to show up that never came. The further they got from civilization—or what he considered civilization—the leaner the pickings seemed to be. They had plenty of food and ammo to last him and his crew a good long while. Water was going to be a problem soon though. He still wasn't sure how they were going to handle that. Oh well—that was something to think about another day. Today was about getting more stuff.

They already had an impressive amount of supplies in their stash at the mall—food, water, guns, ammo, camping gear, some clothes—and they had recently added a couple of women for nighttime entertainment. It wasn't like they could watch cable or even videos—nothing worked anymore. The women weren't necessarily willing participants, but they liked eating, and nothing is free in this world. The rule was you stay, you play. Thing was, he was already getting tired of them, and they were starting to stink. They couldn't waste water on bathing, and he wasn't willing to share his stash of wet wipes with them. He'd need to find some new ones, maybe some cleaner ones. Then he'd cut those skank bitches loose.

He heard it before he saw it; there was no hiding a running vehicle these days. When the SUV turned the corner, he was already grabbing the shotgun on the seat beside him. He stepped out as Joe, Mac, and Dave walked out of the house across the street with some loot. They dropped their goods and reached for their pistols. Dave, who was a new addition to the scout team, got excited.

"Hey! Somebody's comin', Les!"

*No shit, Sherlock.* Les shook his head and looked back at Dave. "Do you think I can't see that, dumbass? Do you think I didn't *hear* it before it got here? Do you think I'm stupid or somethin'?"

Dave was shaking his head vigorously. "N-no, Les, n-no way, man. I just got taken by surprise, ya know? We ain't seen nobody else for a couple of days."

That was true. The last people they had seen had been a large group heading away from the burned-out street by the mall. They had stayed away from those people because Les and his guys had been severely outnumbered, and they didn't look like they had anything worth fighting for. They were dirty, skinny—pretty disgusting as far as he was concerned. They were carrying garbage bags and pushing grocery carts, and all of those looked pretty lean. Definitely not worth the trouble. Even the women didn't look appetizing. Les had a thing about dirty bodies, especially women. Since then, there had been nobody else out this way. Before that, those assholes on that sweet street had been the last they'd seen. They needed to get back over there. It had been a few days, and Les was betting they were either gone by now or were sitting on a huge stash of stuff. If they were gone, he wanted a look inside those houses. If they weren't … hell, he still wanted inside. Yeah, they'd go there next. First, he needed to get rid of those assholes who were trying to take his stuff. *This is my street now, dicks.*

Mac looked at Les. "What do you want to do, Les? Want us to shoot 'em?"

"Nah, I'll take care of it. Hell, look—they're already high-tailin' it outta here."

The SUV had slammed on its brakes and hit reverse, and was backing up to the cross street, tires spinning on the wet asphalt. Les knew he couldn't hurt any of them, but he was pissed they'd showed up, so he shot anyway. He was rewarded with the sound of pellets hitting the truck. The driver got turned around and headed out of sight. He turned to his men. They were laughing and slapping each other on the back, like they had done something. Les saw red. Those idiots didn't do anything but stand there and watch him. What were they so happy about?

"What the hell are you doing? Show's over! Get back to work!" They hurriedly picked up what they had dropped and carried it over to the truck, then headed for the next house.

Good help was damn hard to find, because these guys were morons. He climbed back into the truck and lit another joint.

****

When he heard the SUV again, he was livid. *That's it, I'm gonna kill these sumbitches.* He grabbed his shotgun as his men ran out of a house just down from where he was parked. They came together in the street, ready to get this over with.

"We got too much to do to keep dealing with these fuckers," he said. "When they get in range, take 'em out."

So far, they'd only killed a couple of people. That old couple that had had a shit ton of food and hadn't wanted to come up off it. The old man thought he could draw down on them. He was wrong. They killed the old lady because, hell, he was already gone, and she was wailing like a damn banshee, and Les just couldn't take it. So, it wasn't like they hadn't done it yet. Les was tired of these interruptions.

Joe and Mac had been with him for that one, but Dave hadn't, and he looked like he was either going to puke or piss on himself. *Yeah, you're a bad ass, Dave. Your "I killed a dude for looking at me wrong" was a punk ass lie, wasn't it?* Les smirked at him, then turned his attention back to the SUV. He saw them exit the truck and go to the back. *Putting the engine block between them and us. Not bad for a bunch of pencil pushers.* He caught sight of the guy on top with the scoped rifle. *Man, that looks sweet from here. I'm gonna keep that one for myself.*

While he was walking toward the SUV and daydreaming about getting his hands on the rifle, he was surprised to see a lot more men step out from behind the SUV than he had thought were there. *Those sneaky bastards. Must have climbed through the back window so we couldn't see how many there were of them.* Les was seething, but they were outnumbered, which meant out-gunned, and he didn't trust these idiots to shoot well enough to do much good. He needed more guns. He needed the rest of his crew.

He turned to his men. "Alright, I'm done playin' with these assholes. We're gonna get the rest of the boys. We're gonna finish this. C'mon, get in the truck."

They got in the truck and Les turned the key. "No more Mr. Nice Guy, boys. From now on, we take out anybody who gets anywhere near us or our stuff. There ain't enough to go around as it is. The more of them we get rid of, the more there is for us."

He put the truck in gear and headed out. *We're gonna finish this. Today.*

****

When they heard the pickup, everybody panicked. Could they get away? If they could, where would they go? They couldn't go back to the farm. What if these guys followed them there? Mike took charge and stared issuing orders.

"Everybody in a car. *Now!* One gal in each one. Everybody else, divvy up!"

They quickly headed for one of the cars, mostly the ones they had come out in, except for Kate and Bob. She went to the wagon, and Bob wanted to drive his SUV, so the Lawton brothers went together to the wagon, with Bill behind the wheel. All of this was negotiated in a matter of seconds, as they were running for the vehicles.

By the time they had gotten in and got the cars started, the truck had turned the corner. The driver let out a roar. "Oh, hell no! You ain't goin' *nowhere!* You been a pain in my ass all day, and that shit is *over!*"

He sped up and pulled his truck in front of the SUV, which Bob had just put into gear. Bob slammed on his brakes as a crowd of men jumped out of the truck. There were six of them, all pointing pistols or revolvers at the group. Mike shoved Sara down on the back floorboard. Kate crouched down in the wagon. Bob put the SUV in park and sat there, waiting. The scavengers were still outnumbered, but somehow they hadn't figured that out yet, even though there were now two vehicles. Unfortunately, they did have the advantage.

The man who was clearly their leader started issuing orders. "Alright, everybody out. Hands up, no sudden moves—my boys are just itchin' to shoot somebody today."

Mike looked down to Sara and whispered, "Stay in the truck. Stay down. Don't make a sound." She nodded, so scared her whole body was shaking. The guys climbed out and shut the doors, doing their best to shield Sara from the crew's sight. In the wagon, the other guys did the same for Kate.

The leader was strutting around like a rooster in front of Bob's ride. "Well, well, well. Look what we got here, boys. A bunch of cowboy wannabes. Y'all thought y'all had us outnumbered, didn't ya? Hell, looks like you do—but we got the upper hand now. So, we'll be taking both those rides, everything in 'em, and all your guns. If you don't cause us no trouble, we'll let you walk out of here." That wasn't going to happen, but no reason to get stupid here.

He looked at Russ. "Don't I know you from somewhere? Yeah, you're them guys from the other side of the mall. Drew down on us for no reason. We was just out lookin' around …"

Russ sneered at him. "You were looking for houses to break into and rob. We heard your men talking about it."

The man laughed. "We were collecting resources. Seems like that's what you've been doing here." He sneered at Russ, who didn't answer.

After a moment, the leader continued. "Joe, Mac, go see what they were so hell bent on getting in here to get."

"You got it, Les," one of the men said, and they started toward the SUV, which was the closest to them.

Mike stepped forward. "No." That was all he said. Les looked at him like he had lost his mind.

"What did you say? Did you just tell my men not to do what I told them to do? Are you insane, boy? Do you want to die?"

Mike looked him right in the eye. "No. Do you?"

Les laughed. "You *are* insane! How do you think you're gonna stop them?"

Mike calmly replied, "Like this."

With that, he pulled the knife from the sheath on his belt faster than anyone could see or believe, and threw it at one of Les's men; it buried in his chest. The man's eyes grew wide as he looked down at the hilt protruding from his shirt, blood seeping out around it. He dropped to his knees and fired his pistol as he was going down. The bullet hit the pavement and ricocheted into the SUV.

Everything happened really fast after that. Men were diving for cover on both sides, everyone but Mike. He pulled his pistol and shot the other man in the leg as he was backing up to take up a spot on the other side of the SUV's engine block. The man went down, but not without firing back at Mike. He grazed Mike's arm—not enough to stop him, but enough to piss him off even more. Mike shot him in the chest, and he went down for good. He swept to line Les up in his sights next.

For all his brazen talk, Les was already hiding behind his truck, yelling at his men before they were all there as well.

"Shoot those fuckers! They killed Joe and Mac! Take them out!"

The rest of his crew were behind the truck by now, firing wildly. Mike and his group were returning fire. One of the bullets hit a window on the SUV, causing Sara to scream. Les jerked around at the sound and stood up.

"Hold up! Stop shooting, you dipshits! They got women with them!"

The gunfire slowed to a stop. Les stood up behind the truck.

"Well now, y'all didn't say you had women with you. Tell ya what—you give us the women, and we'll let you take everything else. No reason to be greedy. Everybody wins."

Lee yelled back at him. "Touch them and you all die! They are not property to be traded. They are human beings! They're wives and mothers; they're people who matter a hell of a lot more than any of you!"

With that, Lee fired at Les. He missed, but he made Les duck back down behind the truck. Les's men started shooting again, and the guys returned fire. No one but Mike had any military training, and no matter what anyone tells you, Monroe was right: shooting at a paper target is not the same as shooting at a person who's shooting at you. Everybody mostly missed, although the vehicles took a lot of shots. Bob thought he winged one of them; Mike knew he got another in the leg. The marauder band climbed in their truck on the protected side, trying to stay down, with their guns above their heads, firing wild shots intended to distract. Les fired up the truck, threw it in gear, and took off. He was still crouched down in the seat, driving blindly since he couldn't really see where he was going. He took out several mailboxes before he got back on the road. As he sat up so he could see, the back window exploded around them all in the backseat; Brian had retrieved his rifle and opened fire on the retreating truck. He worked the bolt to load another round, but the truck had already disappeared around the corner.

With the action finally stopped, the guys came out from behind the SUV to survey the damage. Mike had been grazed on his left arm. Ryan had several cuts on his face from exploding glass. Bob had the worst injury; he had been shot in the top of the thigh. Nothing life threatening, but he was raising hell over it.

"Those bastards shot me! Look at this! It hurts like a son of a bitch! Janet's gonna kill me!"

Russ called for Kate, who came rushing over. She looked at Bob's leg, then ripped the bottom of her T-shirt off and wrapped it around his leg.

"It went all the way through. I see the exit wound. We need to get back so I can get it cleaned up. Let me see that arm, Mike."

"It's fine, Kate. He just winged me. Help me get this bandana tied around it. It'll keep 'til we get back to the farm. Check Ryan out. I think they might have messed up his pretty face."

Ryan jumped up and pulled the side view mirror out. He looked at his face and swore.

"Dammit! Look at that shit! We need to find those assholes and finish them, Russ! Look at my face! I'll never get a date for the dance now!"

The guys hesitated, then laughed at Ryan's antics when they saw his grin. Russ slapped him on the shoulder and started for the wagon.

"I'd love to think we've seen the last of these guys, but I doubt that's the case. Right now we need to get back to the farm and get our people seen to. Keep your eyes open. Stop at every intersection so we can listen for anyone who might be following us. The last thing we need is for these douchebags to know where the farm is. Let's get back."

They loaded up in the vehicles. Bill drove the SUV and Russ took the wagon. Lee was in the SUV with Sara. As they were heading out, she touched his arm to get his attention. He turned to her and saw tears flowing down her face.

"Thank you. I can't imagine what might have happened if those men had taken me and Kate."

Lee looked at her with the most serious and determined expression she had ever seen. "I can. I have imagined the absolute worst things that could have happened to Jackie. I have nightmares every night about what she might have gone through. I won't stand by and watch that happen to anyone else's wife, any other child's mother. That's my tribute to her. That will be her legacy."

Sara cried harder and leaned her head over to lay it on Lee's shoulder. He smiled and closed his eyes, remembering the many nights he and Jackie would sit on the couch watching movies and she would do the same thing. He cried silent tears at the memory as they made their way back to what was now their home. He was anxious to get there. He needed to hug his kids.

# Chapter 13

There was a lot of action when they got back to the farm. When we saw Bob and Mike with blood-wrapped appendages, and Ryan's face, everybody started asking questions at once.

"What happened?"

"Are you guys alright?"

"Oh my God, Bob, you're bleeding!"

Russ yelled above the din. "Calm down, everybody. We're all okay. We'll tell you all about it right after we get these guys cleaned up."

Kate herded Mike, Bob, and Ryan down to the basement, with Janet hot on their heels. I rushed to my husband, looking him over carefully.

"Are you hurt? Was it those guys from our neighborhood?"

"No, I'm fine, and yes, it was them. And the leader remembered me. It was bad, Anne."

I wrapped my arms around him and held him tight. I wanted more than anything to know what had transpired, but I knew he needed to process it, then tell everyone. I could wait. He needed this more than anything right now.

"I'm so glad you're home safe, baby. What can I do for you? You need anything?"

"A tall bourbon, but I'll settle for a glass of water right now."

"You've got it. Have a seat."

I went to the sink to pump up a fresh pitcher of water and pulled out a half dozen glasses. I was pretty sure they'd all need to hydrate after whatever they had just been through. I looked out the window and saw Lee sitting at the table with both his kids in his lap. They had their heads together, like they were having a private conversation. Lee was hugging them fiercely, as if he thought he might lose them—or possibly that they had come close to losing him. Yes, we definitely needed to hear this story.

As I was handing Russ the glass, Mike came up the stairs, followed by Ryan. Mike's shirt sleeve was gone; in its place was a bandage wrapped around his bicep. Ryan was complaining.

"I can't believe she can't do anything else for my face, besides dab it with alcohol, which hurt like a mutha. Now I have to walk around looking like I have a disease or something. Bob is already calling me Spot."

Mike turned to him. "Next time he does that, just reply, 'Whatever you say, Pinky.' He'll shut up."

"Why Pinky?"

"Private joke. He'll know what it means."

Ryan shrugged and walked over to the pitcher to pour himself a glass of water. Mike sat down beside Russ at the table. I fetched him a glass as well.

"Thanks, Anne. Russ, you got any idea where those jerks are holed up? Might be doing society a favor to go there and finish the job. They serve no good purpose to anyone."

Russ shook his head. "No, I don't. We've only interacted with them once, right before we left our homes, and we weren't on friendly terms. At the time, I just wanted them away from my family. We did see them several times on our street early on, so it could be they are in that area somewhere, but I have no idea where. I truly hope we've seen the last of them, because I don't want us venturing out of here toward 'civilization' again."

Mike nodded. "Agreed. The less we are exposed to the rest of the world, the better. I'm sure we'll have to deal with those Glass boys again at some point, but I hope it isn't soon. The Bird's Nest"—he paused and slowly shook his head at the name—"is done. We didn't get the foxholes finished, but we can do that tomorrow. I think we need to give everybody a break for the day, don't you? It's been a hell of a morning."

"Agreed. Lee is pretty shaken up; I think he just needs to be with his kids right now. No working on the bunkhouse. Let's get some tarps laid out in the barn, and we can pull all the clothes out so they can be sorted and washed, if needed. Anne, do we have any idea how we are going to wash clothes for this many people? If you try to do it with your little hand crank unit, you ladies will spend all day, every day, washing clothes, and probably still never get through all of what we brought back."

Monroe walked in with Millie. "I got something you can use."

Mike grinned. "Why am I not surprised?"

Monroe squinted at him, then continued. "Can it, Jarhead. Follow me."

We all traipsed out to one of Monroe's many storage sheds, all filled with things—most of which we had no idea what it was. He opened the door and walked through a path he had made through the stuff. He pulled a tarp off a machine and stood there, beaming.

Now it was Mike's turn to squint. "What is it?"

"It's a washing machine, ya idgit! Can't you see the wringer on it?"

Monroe was standing next to a gas-powered washing machine. It had a square tub; it did indeed have a wringer, and there was a motor under it that looked like it had come off of a lawn mower or a go-kart. Same thing.

"Does it work?" My turn to ask questions.

"No idea. Got it for nothin' from a guy tryin' to sell it. I fired it up right after I got it, but that was probably thirty years ago or more. I say we pull it out and see."

Russ and Mike went to pick it up. They grunted with the weight. Ryan stepped up to help.

"Holy shit, Monroe, how'd you get this in here? I know you didn't move it by yourself." Mike was straining, and I'm sure his injured arm wasn't happy about it.

Monroe laughed. "Hell no. The guy I got it from helped me. Never thought we'd see a time when something like this would be needed again. Now look at us."

"If you didn't see a need for it, why'd you keep it?"

Millie answered that one. "He keeps everything, dear. Somewhere in one of these buildings I'm sure we'll find the lost city of Atlantis—or at least some of their tools."

Everyone laughed, except Monroe. He huffed and said, "You see how much of it we're using now, don't ya? I knew it might come in handy one day. Every bit of it."

Millie held up the end of a big boat anchor. "Even this, dear? We're only, what, twenty or thirty miles from a lake or river? Oh, and we don't have a boat."

We were all rolling with laughter then. Everyone except Mike. "Actually, that anchor could have lead in it. We could use that to make bullets, if we can find the right equipment."

Monroe was beaming now and started to say it, but we all said it with him. In unison: "I got something you can use!"

Monroe shook his head and waved us off. "C'mon, get that thing outta here. I want to know if it works. Then I'll find those bullet molds."

Mike, Ryan, and Russ were still snickering as they carried the antique washing machine out of the shed and toward the backyard. This day was getting a little better, at least in the laundry department. I couldn't help but grin as we walked back to the house. A washing machine that might actually work! When I saw Lee and his kids still sitting at the table in each other's arms, I remembered we still didn't know what had happened that morning. We needed to hear that story. We needed to know what was out there.

****

After lunch, the guys filled us in on what had happened. Shock is a bit tame for what I felt. There were people out there now who would kill you just because you interrupted their pillaging—of your stuff. They would try to take what you had without even knowing if it was something they could, in fact, use. Worst of all, they would trade all that for women, to use in ways I did not want to imagine. Sara had been completely despondent since they had returned. She was almost catatonic, truth be told. After Russ told us about the talk they'd had, and then the near miss she had personally experienced, I doubted we would hear any more from her about "others less fortunate." It was a new, dangerous world out there, one that she was ill prepared for after the sheltered life she had led—sheltered from the standpoint that she believed everybody was good and would help each other in a crisis. Kind of like I used to be.

Pete was beside himself. "Thank you just doesn't seem to fit the response I should be giving you guys for saving Sara's life. First thing tomorrow, we are both going to be in firearms training class. We will help defend this place and all of you. You have my word."

Sara didn't say anything, but she nodded in agreement. It was too bad it took a situation like what had happened for her to understand that guns are only bad in the hands of bad people. In the hands of good people, they can save lives. In the end, what mattered was that they both understood now how ugly the world was becoming. No laws, because there was no one to enforce them; no decency, because people were reverting back to survival mode, where anything goes and it's every man for himself; no peace, because every day was going to be about surviving and defending what you had. I did say this was going to suck, didn't I?

Russ looked around the group. "I know we're all worried about who might be out there, or who might be gearing up to try to take this place or some of our people, but we can't live our lives in fear. We have to do whatever we can to fortify this place and protect our families, our supplies, and our home, but life is about more than that. We still have work to do here in those areas, but I think we need to take the rest of the day to just chill out a bit. I don't want anyone working on any projects this afternoon. We are going to take Sean and Kate to see their friends, the Callens, to see how they're doing, and if they'd like to join us. We'll find a spot for them if needed. The rest of you recoup if you need to from this morning, or maybe go through the stuff we brought back. Nothing big. We'll get back to it tomorrow. The very first thing in the morning is firearms training. It is very apparent after the last two days that everyone needs to know how to defend themselves and their loved ones. Make that our loved ones."

He stood up. "I need a couple of guys to ride shotgun on this short trip. Monroe will be going, since he knows them as well. Maybe one more should do it."

Bill started walking toward him. "I guess since we have so many wounded I'm up. I'll go."

Ryan looked at his brother. "I'm not wounded—well, not that bad. I can go."

"Bro, we're trying to gather troops, not scare them off. With that face, they'll run screaming. Then, when they get a load of those pock marks …"

Ryan jumped up and started for his brother. Bill took a boxing stance, ready for the assault.

Russ grinned at them. "You should stay here and rest up, Ryan. Bill should be plenty, but we'll be taking a radio at any rate. This is going to be a quick trip. How far away did you say they live, Monroe?"

"Maybe four miles or so. I've only been there once. No more than ten minutes to get there, if the road's clear."

"We'll be taking my truck, which should be able to clear the road if needed. As soon as Kate finishes checking Brian's hand, we'll get going."

Kate came up from the basement just as he said that, with Brian following her. "I'm done. He's doing okay, as long as he continues to keep it clean and dry. The sooner we get going, the sooner we get back. After this morning, I'm going to be more inclined to be a homebody."

Sean went to his wife. "Honey, I'd feel a whole lot better if you'd stay here and let me go. We don't know what the situation is over there. I don't want you in a position to get hurt—again."

Kate looked him in the eye. "No, we don't know what we will find over there. Someone may be hurt and need my help. I have a small bag ready. I'm going."

Russ nodded grimly. "Alright then, let's get on the road. This should be the last excursion we have to make out. I want to get this place locked down again. We're safer here."

For now, he was right about that. Question was, how much longer would that be the case?

# Chapter 14

As soon as Russ and his group left, we started sorting the clothes they had gathered. They had done really well, getting an assortment of kids' clothes and shoes. They might not fit them well but they would have something to wear. Marietta and I dug through until we found some things we thought would fit the Scanlin girls. Since their parents were gone, I called them to me and showed them what we had picked out. They squealed with glee, like it was Christmas morning. They immediately took off the clothes they had been wearing for the last couple of weeks and put on new ones. They were a little big, but the girls couldn't have cared less. Tara held the ones they had taken off out away from her, like they were diseased.

"Can we burn these, Miss Anne? I don't ever want to see them again."

I smiled at her. "I think that is a wonderful idea. We'll need to wait until dark though. For now, we'll leave them over there in the corner."

She nodded. "I remember. We can't have daytime fires, because the smoke can be seen from far away. I can wait until tonight."

Oh my goodness. Even the young ones were picking up on the new way we had to live. I didn't know whether to be sad or proud. I think I was a little of both. We found them some shoes that were a close fit, so they could at least swap out what they were wearing, and a couple more outfits. You would have thought we had taken them on a shopping spree, they were so proud of their new stuff.

They skipped off to put their "new" clothes away. I heard a sniffle and turned around to see Marietta crying.

"Are you alright, honey? What's wrong?"

"Oh, Anne, that is so sad. Those poor little girls, so happy to have the clothes that belonged to other little girls who never got home. Their misfortune is someone else's joy. Don't get me wrong—I'm very grateful to be here with all of you, for your gracious hospitality, for everything you've done for me. It just really stinks, what this world has become. If it weren't for all of you I'd probably be dead, like the people who owned these clothes are. We're so lucky to have this place and each other. But, I'm scared. Can we keep it? Can we keep the farm and everyone here safe?"

I thought about what she'd said. It was all valid reasoning. There were no guarantees. All we could do was try. So I answered her as truthfully as I could.

"I honestly don't know, Marietta. No one does. All we can do is our best. We take care of each other and do what we have to do to keep us all safe. We only get one life—all we can do is live it the best we know how."

Listen to me, being all philosophical and shit. "Let's get something cold ... well, cool to drink. I'll be a mess until Russ gets back, so I need something to take my mind off it. I'm going to try to get that old washing machine started. Nothing like laundry to keep you occupied—especially when it has a wringer to take your frustrations out on."

**\*\*\*\***

The road to the Callen house wasn't clear, but they made their way through with not too much effort. Bill and Sean were riding in the back of the truck, watching for any signs of other people who might pose a threat. There weren't any. The area between the farm and the Callens' was pretty much pastures and farm fields. The fields were plowed, but not much had been planted before the pulse. Most new tractors were computerized—so much so that the farmers had to take them to a dealer for something as simple as an oil and filter change or void their warranty. They passed a field with a big late-model tractor sitting in the middle of it. Monroe shook his head.

"Ya see? Ya see what all that technology is worth? My old tractor is worth ten of those now, ain't it? Maybe a hundred of 'em!"

Russ nodded in agreement. "Yep, you're right. At some point people will have to figure out how to plant crops old style, maybe even using horses or mules pulling plows. It's going to get very interesting, no doubt about it."

"People gotta eat. Ain't no food without farmers. Farmers are gonna get rich in this world, if they can figure out how to farm without them fancy machines."

Russ drove to the Callen place with no issues. As they pulled in the driveway, it was clear something had happened. The gate was lying on the ground; it looked like it had been rammed, as it was twisted from the hinged side. They were driving slowly up the drive when a shot rang out from the house. Russ immediately stopped the truck. Sean jumped out of the back, and Monroe got out as well, hands out to his sides.

Russ called to them. "Careful, guys. You don't know who's shooting. It may not be them."

"That's why my hand is beside my hog leg, instead of in the air." Monroe raised his voice. "Luke! You in there? It's Monroe Warren! I got your friends, Sean Scanlin and his wife, Kate, with me. We're here to see if you folks are alright! Can you come out?"

They waited no more than a minute. A man came out with a rifle in hand, pointed in their direction. It looked like he hadn't slept in days. His clothes were wrinkled, as if, had he been sleeping, he had been sleeping in them. He seemed to be disoriented.

"Mr. Monroe? Is that really you? Who are those other people with you?"

"This here is Russ Mathews, Luke; he's a good friend of my niece. He's like family to me and Millie. This other fella is Bill Lawton; he's staying with us over at my place. Okay if we come on up to the house to talk for a bit?"

Monroe's calm tone seemed to settle Luke down some. He lowered the rifle and waved them toward him. "Yeah, come on up. Casey's inside. She's not feeling well. I'm not sure what's wrong—she can't keep anything on her stomach."

Monroe looked at Kate. She climbed quickly out of the cab. "Sounds like it could be giardiasis. Comes from drinking water that hasn't been purified. We don't have meds for that, so she's going to have to just get through it. I need to get in there."

They all headed for the house. Luke pulled his gun back up. "I don't know those men. I don't want them near my wife."

Sean had stepped to the front of the group. "Luke, they're friends of ours. They saved our lives. Me, Kate, and the girls probably wouldn't be here if it weren't for Russ and his family. They're good men. They won't hurt either of you. You have my word."

Luke lowered the rifle again. "It's hard to trust people these days, you know? We've had some run-ins with strangers. But, if you say they're okay, I'll trust you. It's good to see you, Sean. You too, Kate. Can you take a look at Casey, see if you can help her?"

"Of course I can, Luke. Lead me to her." She walked up to Luke and tried to hug him, but he flinched and backed up a step. She smiled at him and started for the door. He opened it for her, and she walked into the dark living room.

When the others got close to the house, they could see what appeared to be bullet holes in the brick. The windows in front had been broken and boarded up. Something bad had happened here.

As they walked in, they could smell the sickness. Russ covered his nose and mouth with a bandana; Bill turned around and went back outside. "I'll stay out here and keep an eye on the truck; I'll go bring it closer to the house."

Luke looked apologetic. "Sorry about the smell. I've been trying to keep her cleaned up, but with no running water, it's been tough. I've been getting it from the creek down the hill, so I guess that's why she got sick. I'm not sure why it didn't hit me."

Kate laid a hand on his arm. "No one knows why it hits some people harder than others. It could be that her immune system was low, maybe she had a slight cold. Do you guys have vitamins? Have you been taking them?"

"Yes, we had been, but when she got sick, I didn't want to put anything on her stomach that might make it worse. She's been real nauseated, but the diarrhea has been the worst part. She wouldn't eat, so she's too weak to even get up to go to the bathroom. I didn't know what to do."

Monroe sat at the kitchen table. "Why didn't you come to our place, ask for help? You know where we live. We had Kate there for the past couple of days. She could have been taking care of her already."

Luke looked wild-eyed. "I couldn't leave! They might have come back and taken her this time!"

Sean stared at his friend. "Who are you talking about? Did someone try to take Casey from here? Who was it?"

"I don't know who they were. They came up to the house a couple of days ago. They said they needed food, that they were hungry. Casey wasn't quite as sick then. She came out of the house with some canned goods for them and they tried to grab her. I jerked her away, and we ran inside and locked the doors. They shot at the house—shot out the windows in the front. I grabbed my 30-30 and shot back. They took the food and left, yelling that they'd be back for 'the woman.' I haven't slept since. I boarded up the broken windows and we hunkered down, waiting for them to come back. I was afraid you were them when I heard your truck outside."

Monroe was red-faced with indignation. "It wasn't those good-for-nothin' Glass boys, was it? They were at our place yesterday, looking for a handout."

"No, I had never seen these men before. They were older and looked like they had been on the road for a while."

"How many were in their group?" Russ asked.

"I only saw three; two that came up to the house, and one stayed in their truck. I don't know if there were any more anywhere else. Three was enough."

Russ nodded. "I do wish you had come over to Monroe's, Luke. We have a group of survivors there, about two dozen, and we are setting up for a long-term situation, including security. We've been trying to get over here to check in on you two almost since we got there, but honestly, every time we turn around there's something that needs to be handled right away. If you're up for it, we'd like to bring you and Casey back with us. It's obvious you can't secure this place. It will be tight as far as accommodations go, but we'll figure it out. You can't stay here alone."

"If I'd had any idea what was going to happen here, we would have. I thought we'd be safe in our home. It's obvious to me now that we can't be. We'd be grateful to join you all. If you have a place to set it up, we have a small camper we can bring over to stay in. We appreciate the offer, Russ, Monroe. At this point, I think that would be the best thing for us to do."

Monroe grinned at him and replied, "Of course we have a spot for your camper, and that's a damn fine idea, Luke. Maybe we should be keeping an eye out for more campers, Russ. Give those small families an option for alternative living quarters, with a little privacy."

Russ looked thoughtful. "Yes, we've talked about it before and it definitely could help, although they won't be as secure as the house. I'd like to keep them close to the house, just in case. Monroe, why don't you and I go out and have a look at the camper while these guys catch up?"

Monroe gave him a quick nod and they headed for the door.

"It's out behind the storage building. It's still covered from the last time we stored it for winter. It's been at least three years since we used it, so I'm not sure what kind of shape it's in, but hey, it's a roof, a toilet, and a bed. Here, let me give you the key for the door." Luke handed Russ a key ring he pulled from a key holder by the door.

Russ nodded. "You're exactly right. Right now anything you can call home will work. We'll let you know what we find. We'll be back in a few minutes." He opened the back door and held it for Monroe. When they got outside, they saw Bill and motioned him over. They gave him the condensed version of what the Callens had already had to deal with as they walked across the yard toward the camper. He shook his head.

"The world has always been full of assholes. That hasn't changed. With everything gone to hell, the assholes are living large with no repercussions for their assholeness. Any way to find out who they were? Where they came from?"

"Luke said he'd never seen them before, so chances are they aren't from around here. Like everybody else will do sooner or later, when they realized there weren't going to be any more grocery store deliveries, they started figuring out where food actually comes from, and they made their way to the farms. We haven't seen the last refugees either. We just have to be ready to deal with them."

Russ stopped talking as he rounded the corner of the shed and saw the tarp-covered camper. The tarp was still intact, no obvious holes that they could see.

"Well, let's pull this tarp off and see what's underneath, fellas."

Monroe grabbed one corner and released the bungee cord holding it down. Russ and Bill did the same, and the three of them worked their way around until they had all the tie downs released. They then grabbed the tarp by both corners and the center and started backing up. The tarp slid off, revealing a later-model camper, probably twenty-four feet long. Outside of some mildew on the north-facing side, it looked to be in pretty decent shape. There were no holes, no dents, nothing externally wrong that they could see.

"So far, so good. Let's see what she looks like on the inside." Russ stuck the key in the door and opened it.

Inside they found dust, but overall it looked pretty good. No signs of critters using it as a homestead. The bedclothes were still on the bed in back and there was a musty smell to everything, but it was nothing a good airing out wouldn't fix.

Russ grinned at Monroe and Bill. "This is a sweet little camper. What a great idea, for them to bring this over and stay in it. You're right, Monroe—I had all but decided we couldn't grow our group anymore, because we were out of room. Campers could be the answer. The more people we have, the more we can put into the security rotation, and the more crops we can plant, because we have more people to tend them. More mouths to feed, yes, but also more people resources. We could actually look for people with skills we need. What if we could find a doctor, or a butcher, or a blacksmith?"

Monroe laughed at him. "Slow down, son. We ain't even moved this one over there, and you're already looking to hire more folks to live in campers we ain't got yet."

Russ grinned sheepishly. "Sorry. I got excited at the thought of building a little community. We should definitely keep an eye out for more campers, just in case."

"Agreed. Let's go see how they're doing in there. I'd like to get this show on the road, and get us back to the farm. I don't like being gone from there any more than we have to be."

Monroe headed back to the house, Russ and Bill following. When they walked in, Kate had Casey sitting up and drinking water from one of the canteens they had brought with them.

"How's she doing, Kate?" Russ's voice was full of concern.

Kate looked at him. "She's severely dehydrated. We have IVs at the house. If I can get some fluids in her, maybe some Pepto or something, I think we can nip this thing the old-fashioned way—with time. She needs rest, liquids, maybe some broth, and something to stop the bathroom trips. How was the camper?"

"It looks really good. Very livable. Luke, if you guys want to grab some clothes and stuff, we'll hook up to the camper and you can come with us now, if that works." Russ looked at Luke expectantly.

"Really? Leave right now? But what about our place here?"

Russ shook his head. "Luke, you already know you can't defend this place—not by yourself, and honestly, I don't think you could with reinforcements. It's too open. You can see the house from the road. It's just a matter of time before those guys come back, maybe with reinforcements, or someone else finds this place. It's better not to be here when that happens. We can help you gather your clothes, food, guns, and ammo. We can probably be out of here in no more than two hours. Take everything you might need, and anything you can't do without, in case you don't get to come back."

Casey spoke for the first time. It was more of a croak, since she hadn't been doing much talking for a few days. "Pishures."

Luke rushed to her side. "What, honey? What did you say?"

She cleared her throat and said more clearly, "Pictures. Get the photo albums. They're going with us."

He smiled at her and moved her unwashed hair from her eyes. "You've got it, babe. Anything else?"

She shook her head and laid it back down on the sofa arm. He leaned over and kissed her forehead. He stood up, straightened his shoulders, turned to the guys, and said, "What should we grab first? Looks like we're coming with you."

**\*\*\*\***

They crammed everything into any bag they could find, and ended up using quite a few trash bags for clothes. Casey was a serious home canner, so they had a lot of home-canned items and canning supplies. Those jars would be priceless in the future. The guys grabbed all they could, along with the jars and lids. She had a few dozen of each size lid in a reusable form, which were now worth more than their weight in gold. They gathered all her canning equipment and loaded that in the truck. There was already similar equipment at the farm, but can you ever have too many canning supplies? Especially when you couldn't go to the store to buy more. Since they were bringing the camper, it was easy to just throw everything inside it and still leave room for the people in the truck.

Kate had them leave the area around the sofa in the camper clear, so they could put Casey there for the short ride to the farm. Kate wanted to ride with her, so the guys piled in the pickup. Within two hours, they had loaded up what Luke and Casey needed to relocate. As Luke was locking the door, he turned to Russ.

"Any idea if there's a chance we get to come back here someday? If we do, will it even be here?"

Russ laid his hand on Luke's shoulder. "I wish I knew. I have a feeling life as we knew it will never be the same, buddy. All we can do is move forward and deal with whatever life throws at us."

"Any chance life will stop hurling turds at us any time soon?"

Russ snorted at the unexpected humor from a new friend. "That sure would be a welcome event, Luke. Let's hope so."

They were still laughing as they climbed into the truck. Russ turned the key, and she fired up. Just as he was putting it in gear, another pickup pulled into the driveway, blocking their path. Why hadn't they heard it coming?

Luke yelled, "It's them! That's the guys who tried to take my wife!"

# Chapter 15

Russ slammed on the brakes, turned the truck off, and grabbed his pistol. Sean and Bill, who were in the truck bed, followed suit, as did Monroe in the cab. Luke stood up in the bed with his rifle laid across the roof, aimed their way. Russ leaned out the window so the guys in the back could hear him, along with the ones in the cab.

"Don't do anything yet. Let them make the first move. There's still just the three of them, so we definitely have them outnumbered. They don't know what we have for weapons, or what our level of expertise is with them, so, if they're smart, they'll find that out first. Monroe, do you know them?"

Monroe was squinting in their direction. "I don't recognize the truck. I can't really make them out, but I don't think I know them, no."

"Then they're not locals. Hold tight for now, guys. Let's see what they do."

The strangers were talking among themselves. The one by the passenger side door finally got out. He was armed, but not holding his weapon. He addressed Russ's truck.

"Hey, fellas! We was just wonderin' if y'all had any more food you could spare. We was real grateful for what you gave us the other day, but we ain't been able to find any more anywhere, so we was hopin' y'all could help us out again."

Luke jumped out before anyone could stop him. "*Help* you? You tried to take my wife, you dick! I ought to shoot you where you stand—all of you!"

Luke started to raise his rifle, and a shot rang out from the cab of the other truck. It missed him, fortunately, but it didn't stop the guys from all jumping out and training their firearms on the three men. The shooter, who was the driver, put his gun on the dash and held up his hands. The other two men did the same.

Monroe took the lead. "You boys step on out of that truck, nice and easy now. No sudden moves, and no one will get hurt. Hands where we can see them."

The other two men got out, hands to their sides. The spokesman calmly replied, "None of us want to get hurt. We're just looking for some food. And we didn't try to take his wife. I was just tryin' to take her hand, to thank her for the help, and she misunderstood; started screamin' and shit."

Monroe looked him in the eye. "Well, I'm afraid you're out of luck, boys. No food left here. Y'all best get on down the road, see what else you can find."

"Well, what about where you're stayin', old man? Got something there you could give a neighbor, just to get us by?"

Monroe was getting mad. "First off, you should respect your elders, boy. Calling me 'old man' ain't curryin' no favor with me. Second, you ain't my neighbor. I've never seen you before, and I've lived in these parts most of my life. I don't know where you're from, but it ain't here. Last, I got nothing for you or your kind. I see you again, I'll be the last thing you ever see. Now get in your truck and get the hell off this property!"

With the last word, Monroe cocked his revolver and aimed it at the man's head. The scavenger smirked at him, but backed up to the truck door he had left open. The three of them climbed into their truck and it started up. The man leaned out as they were pulling away and said, "I'm sure we'll see each other again, *sir*. I'm lookin' forward to it."

Monroe yelled after them, "Not nearly as much as I am, asshole!" He turned back to the group. "Listen for that truck to go away before we head out. Make sure they don't follow us to the farm. Damn, I need a snort."

"Sounds good to me. As soon as we get back, let's make that happen." Russ climbed in and started the truck again. He sent Sean back to check on the girls. When he returned with a thumbs up they pulled out onto the road. They stopped to listen for the truck but didn't hear anything except the one they were in. They took the chance the scavengers weren't around and headed back to the farm. It was a chance that would cost them later.

****

When they came through the gate pulling a camper, we all knew we had some new folks joining. We waited in the yard for them to come to a stop. A man jumped out—it must have been Luke Callen—and rushed to the camper door without acknowledging anyone. He opened the door and stepped inside. I walked over to the camper to see if I could be of any assistance. Luke was kneeling beside the sofa. He touched the forehead of a pale woman, and looked at Kate.

"She seems to have cooled off a bit, doesn't she? Is she going to be alright?"

Kate smiled at him reassuringly. "I think Casey will be fine. We have a mini clinic set up in the basement, and I'd like to get her down there as soon as possible, so I can get an IV in her. Just a saline drip, to get her rehydrated. I'll get one of the guys to carry her down."

"No! I'll do it! I can do it!" Luke seemed to have a problem with any other men getting close to her. He leaned down. "Honey, are you okay? Was the ride very hard on you? I'm going to pick you up now, and carry you inside. Kate's going to take care of you."

He struggled to pick her up; he looked thin and tired, as if he'd been too busy taking care of his wife to look after himself. But he still refused help when Sean tried to step in, and he carried her up the front steps.

Millie was waiting at the door. "Luke, I'm so glad you're both here. Bless her heart, has she been sick long? Follow me, I'll show you where the clinic is."

He followed Millie inside with Kate right behind them. The rest of us went out to the truck and got the rest of the story. No wonder Luke was so protective.

"I'd be acting exactly like him if that had happened to Janet. Or Anne. Hell, any of our women. There's a bunch of low-life scumbags out there, ya know?" Bob was getting himself worked up. I didn't blame him. I was furious at the thought of those men trying to grab Casey, and I barely knew her. If it had happened to one of our people? No effing way they'd have walked away from that.

Mike was nodding slowly. "Yes, there are, and sooner or later we'll run into some more of them, or possibly these guys again. Luke and Casey's place was only about five miles away. They could easily find their way here. We have to finish the security measures. We need to fortify the gate. We are about to hunker down for the long haul—I can't think of any reason we need to leave again any time soon, so it's time to go into lockdown mode. We need to stay hidden while the outside world tears itself apart—at least as long as we can."

# Chapter 16

Alan Byers had never really held a steady job. The last one he'd had was as a day laborer on a demolition crew. He had been on that job site when the power went off. If not for all the equipment suddenly stopping, they might not have known right away that anything had happened. A job site is a pretty noisy place until all the power tools and forklifts shut down. The foreman had instructed them to continue working, as they could still be manually moving materials and cleaning the site up. It didn't dawn on him that a normal power outage would not have taken out the equipment, but as soon as one of the gofers tried to start his car to go on a coffee run, that brought things to a screeching halt. Everyone ran to their own vehicles to see if theirs would run. Most of them didn't; Alan's 1960 GMC pickup did. He laughed, flipped off the rest of the crew, and peeled out of the lot in a plume of dust, with his former co-workers running behind, trying to get him to stop. He didn't know what was going on, but it sure looked like it might be his lucky day. He headed home to see what Rich and Steve thought about the situation.

Alan had been friends with Rich Hawkins and Steve Carpenter most of his life. They met in middle school, stayed friends through high school—from which none of them graduated—and now lived together at Rich's house. They had gotten into trouble with the law on occasion, but never anything major. The sheriff's deputy, Tim Miller, was another buddy from high school; only difference was he managed to graduate and landed a job at the department. He mostly left them alone if he found them on the wrong side of the law, unless someone else was around, like the sheriff; then he'd come down a bit harder on them. They'd never stood before a judge though—even if he locked them up, he'd let them go the next day, the charges mysteriously dropped.

Alan had to go around quite a few dead cars on the way home. Folks were waving and hollering for him to stop, but he just kept going, laughing and throwing empty beer cans from his floorboard at them. *Stupid snooty assholes. Your high-dollar rides ain't worth shit now, are they?* He was feeling pretty smug when he finally pulled up to Rich's place about an hour later. Rich lived in his dad's old house, which was pretty much the only thing he got when his old man died. It was out in the boonies, so they could drink, shoot, and raise hell all they wanted without anyone calling the cops—not that it was really an issue if they did. Steve was already there, since his pizza delivery job was on the night shift. They were sitting on the front porch drinking beer and laughing when he pulled up. He jumped out of his truck and started up the walk.

"Man, toss me one of those. There's some crazy shit going on today."

Rich tossed him a beer. "Don't I know it. Nobody's got power, nobody's cars run—'cept yours, it looks like—no cells or regular phones; this ain't your usual 'somebody hit a pole and took out a transformer' power outage."

"No, it ain't. The radio in my truck was nothing but static. What the hell could cause something like this?"

"I don't know, but since you're here and your truck works, how 'bout we head to town, see if we can find out what's going on?"

"Hell yeah. If I've got one of the few trucks running, I might start me a taxi service. Fifty bucks a mile." Alan laughed long and hard at his own joke—but maybe it wasn't a joke. Maybe he could figure out a way to make some serious money off this mess, especially if it lasted a while. Maybe they could have some fun, too.

****

Now, weeks later, the three men had been to most of the homes in the vicinity. One of the first ones they "visited" in the beginning had a stash of crystal meth. The chick was high on something when they got there, probably heroin since she was pretty much out of it, so they grabbed her meth and took off. She was a skank, as Steve referred to her, named Chris. He knew her, knew she was a cooker of the stuff, and figured they'd be able to score some from her. He had no idea she'd have as much as she did. Apparently she had gotten her hands on a big pile of the pseudoephedrine used to make it from somewhere; probably robbed a drug store when the lights went out. They started smoking it immediately, and things escalated soon after.

They left behind the bodies of the husbands of the wives they had held hostage and used for days, before they got tired of them and decided to go find "fresh meat," as they referred to the women they were repeatedly raping and sodomizing. The women were left for dead, their bodies broken, no food to eat, no one to help them. At first, in their meth-induced frenzy to grab as much fun as they could before the power came back on, they had killed two families, somewhat accidentally. One of them had two young children, a girl and a boy, both not quite teenagers. Neither of them had escaped the sexual abuse, or the welcome death that followed. The other family had a toddler that screamed until they held a pillow over his face. No more screaming. In a matter of a few days, the three men had gone from lazy good-for-nothings to murdering wild animals. And they were enjoying their new lifestyle, Alan especially.

As the days went on with no sign of anything changing, they had gotten bolder and more strategic. They chose homes they thought had either food or women. If they had both that was a bonus, but the meth took away their appetite for food, while it increased their appetite for sex, so the females were their main objective. They had grown so brazen they didn't even try to hide their intentions once they had gained access to a property. It had served them well—country folks were just naturally more trusting and more giving. They'd play the poor, hungry travelers act to get close to the house. If there was a man, they'd wait to see if he was armed. If there was a woman they could get to, they'd grab her and put a gun to her head, to get her old man to comply. Once he gave up his gun, they would either kill him outright or play their new sick game, which was to make him watch while they took turns raping his wife, or daughter, or both. They'd do this for only a day or so, because the yelling and wailing got on their nerves pretty fast in their constantly strung-out state. They'd end up smothering, strangling, or just shooting them when they were done with them. They'd take whatever weapons and ammo they had, and some of the food, just in case they got hungry before they got to the next house. If they had booze, though, they always took that, and any good prescription drugs.

In the first few days, they took the people's wallets, for their credit cards and cash. When nothing came back on, they figured out the credit cards were a waste of time and tossed them; they kept the cash. They also took jewelry, including wedding rings off the dead—it wasn't like they were going to miss them, right? They were building up quite a pile of assets, which they kept in a couple of plastic trunks in the back of the truck. They were more like gypsies than anything else these days. They'd find a house and hole up there while they hit the houses around it. When they got ready

167

to move on, they would go to the furthest house they had already cleared out of people and resources, and make that their new base camp. They were about done with the area they had been working when they found the Callen homestead. They had already decided that once it was clear, that would be the next squat site for them.

They were parked about a mile down the road, trying to figure out their next move. Rich was pissed off at that old man for pointing a gun at him.

"I bet that couple ain't even there anymore. They were hooked up to a camper. Looked like they were leaving. I bet that place is abandoned. We should go check. If it is, we can stay there to work the next area. Maybe we'll run into those dicks that was there today, teach 'em some respect."

Alan gave him a gray-toothed smile. "I think that's a great idea. That was a sweet-looking piece of ass that lived there. Maybe they'll come back for some more of their stuff. I'd love to be there to welcome them home."

Alan was turning the truck around when he heard another vehicle, heading away from them on the road. *It must be those assholes. I bet they're headed home, and I want to know where that is.*

The Callen house would become their new base, but first he wanted to know where the former tenants and their saviors were headed. *I bet that will be a sweet score.*

# Chapter 17

The day after the guys brought Luke and Casey in saw the front gate secured per Mike's instructions. Extra posts at each end of the gate, with a big post the size of a small tree sunk in the ground on the inside of it, just as he had suggested. It's not like we were planning to go out again anytime soon. He also had some razor wire wrapped around the top edge, then hidden with the fake foliage. Yes, someone could still climb the gate, but it would not be easy—or without pain and bloodshed. The Gopher Holes had been dug out deep enough for a man to stand in, with pallets over the top to act as roofs. The pallets were covered with black tarps to keep the rain out, then more of the ghillie material and some brush to complete the illusion that there wasn't a hole there, with a guy in it holding a rifle watching for someone to try to breach the front. Just some random bushes on the sides of the drive. With the Bird's Nest completed as well, we had done what we could to secure what we felt was the only potentially viable and vulnerable entry point to the property.

The plan for three-man security teams had been modified to four. We needed one in each hole and at least one in the tree hide, and they decided to add one on the ground, walking the area between the two. There was a radio on one of the guys in the holes. Whoever was in the treehouse had one. The roamer had one. The last one was in the kitchen in the house, and there was always someone monitoring it. Even the dogs did their part, spreading themselves out between the front and the house area. It was like they knew there was a job for them to do as well.

Mike kept the security watch schedule and had added Luke and Casey at their request, but Casey wasn't ready just yet. She was getting stronger every day under Kate's care. She still spent a good bit of time in the bathroom, but her color was better and she had been eating some—if you call chicken broth eating. Yeah, actually more like drinking her food. With Millie's input, Casey was on a homemade sports drink type of mix to boost her electrolytes. She had strict orders to drink at least one liter of it daily. The liter consisted of water, a half-teaspoon of salt, and four teaspoons of sugar, with a little lemon juice and salt substitute for the potassium and flavor. It is a natural remedy for diarrhea and it was definitely working for her. Kate agreed to Casey taking a security watch, but only after she could get through a day without going to the bathroom more than once. She hadn't accomplished that yet, but she had at least graduated to applesauce and plain toast. Applesauce contains pectin naturally, which is a soluble fiber that soaks up fluid in your intestines. Toast is bland, but when you've been on a liquid diet for a couple of days, anything that you actually had to chew was wonderful. She was smiling and laughing more; both good signs she was on the road to recovery.

The guys had set the Callens' camper up beside the bunk-house, which still wasn't finished. Hopefully, with the security projects completed, they could focus on that one now and, with all the manpower available, finish it pretty quickly. They leveled the camper and filled the holding tank with water. Monroe watched the process thoughtfully.

"Ya know, Russ, you're right. We could build a nice little trailer park here. Well, not right here, but maybe between that shed and the barn. We could probably get a half dozen or so campers in there. If we can get a couple of days of peace and quiet, maybe we should go out scouting for some. I know a few places around here that had them sitting outside last time I was by. If the owners are there, maybe they'd trade us for them, or, better yet, we could get them to join us—you know, if they aren't assholes. If they aren't there, they probably won't be again, and we could 'borrow' them. Figure it's better for someone to get some use out of them than to just sit there and rot."

"Yep, I agree with that idea, Monroe, especially the part where we get a couple of days of peace and quiet. I really didn't expect things to be as bad out here as they were closer to town, at least not right away. I thought folks in the country were used to harder times and would become more of a community in a situation like we're in right now. Was I wrong in my thinking?"

Monroe shook his head. "No, son, you weren't. Country folk *are* more self-sustaining. Problem is the good-for-nothing, living-off-the-government, lazy asses that are out there too. Rent is cheaper in the country. Most of them have never had to fend for themselves, never even tried to grow food, or hunt or fish. They've been so busy playing video games, and sending pictures of their lunch to their friends—what's the point of that, by that way?"

Russ shrugged his shoulders, so Monroe went on. "Add in the criminals and the law breakers, who have nothing to lose now with no police or sheriff around, and you've got a whole mess of trouble. And even though none of them have ever had to work for food, they know where it comes from. They know their grandparents lived in the country and had gardens, and farm animals; they remember Granny making biscuits to eat with vegetables she poured out of a jar she had filled with something at some point. They don't know *how* it comes to be, but they know *where* it started: on a farm. It's gonna get worse. I think we're gonna need more folks."

"You're right. We need more people on security watch, especially at night. We should have at least a half dozen on watch at all times, which means we need at least a dozen more folks. Can we swing that? Do we have the resources?"

"We've cleared about five acres for everything we're using right now. That's only a quarter of what we have. We can plant more food. We can breed more livestock. We can hunt on this land, and probably another forty or fifty acres behind us. It's all wooded, no one lives there. Yes, we can handle that number of people. Question is: who do we get? We ain't bringing in those worthless Glass boys, or those assholes we had the run-in with at Luke's place."

"Didn't you say there were others out here you wanted to check up on? If you felt that way about them, surely they're good people. I think we should give it a few days, finish the bunkhouse—which will give us more sleeping quarters for folks—and maybe take a little trip out. What do you think?"

"I think that's a damn fine plan. Let's talk about it some more over lunch. I'm starving. All this supervising is hard work!"

****

"Kids! Lunch time!" I yelled across the yard to where Sara and Marietta were helping the kids pull weeds in the garden. They both had their positive qualities working with the kids. Sara was a teacher and had a natural gift with them. Marietta had grown up the oldest of six kids in a very poor home, so she was comfortable leading them in their chores. These two women had come a long way in the past few days, both in dealing with the world as it was now and in increasing their knowledge of things here on the farm, like what was and wasn't a weed, and determining when vegetables were ready to harvest.

Sara was like a sponge, trying to soak up every bit of information she could get her hands on. She took one of the e-readers to bed with her every night, to learn for herself, but also to be able to teach the kids. With no textbooks, school was completely different now. We were still trying to figure out what to do about paper and pens or pencils. We had some, but they would go fast once the kids started using them to figure out math problems and take spelling tests. What we really needed was some chalkboard paint and chalk. We could make slates, like kids used to use for school. Maybe we could find some at an abandoned craft store. Pretty sure that wasn't a highly valued item in the apocalypse; if we could find the store, we could probably find the materials. I knew there was no way that was going to happen any time soon, though. Not with the trouble we had already run into leaving the farm. Oh well, I'd file that away in my mental wish list for the future.

Marietta just wanted to contribute wherever she could, but she loved working with the kids the best, so whenever the laundry was caught up—which wasn't very often, but seriously, how many people can wash clothes at the same time anyway?—she was with Sara and the kids. They were both great with them, and Marietta kept a sidearm on at all times, just in case. Sara was still not carrying one, but she had attended firearms training classes ever since they had come back from the run to their neighborhood and the subsequent run-in with the road gang. I guess finding out just how bad it was getting out there had been enough to open her eyes to the world that was forming around us. The sucky one on the outside of the fence, anyway.

The kids came running and headed for the wash station we had set up outside. They didn't even have to be told anymore that washing came before eating, brushing came after. Their knees were dirty, but their hands and faces were clean. When they finished washing up, they headed for the picnic table Lee had built for them. The four older boys sat at the big table. If the sky was clear, we ate outside. We were up to twenty-seven people now, and while we could squeeze everyone into the house when we needed to, we liked to spread out whenever possible. It was starting to warm up now we were at the end of April, but there was still a wonderful breeze under the tree.

While breakfast could be anything from eggs and country ham with biscuits and gravy to oatmeal or pancakes, lunch was almost always cold sandwiches. The kids never got tired of peanut butter and jelly, and we had lots of peanut butter, as well as homemade jams, jellies, and preserves, courtesy of Millie. She was also making at least four loaves of bread every day. If it was nasty raining, which we got at least one day a week in Tennessee in the spring, we might throw in some soup to warm everybody up. We added fresh veggies from the garden to the sandwiches: carrots, broccoli, cauliflower, celery, and my beloved radishes. We tried to use the fresh food when we had it, to keep from having to break into our food stores for as long as we could.

Supper was our big meal. We were getting pretty good at cooking for a group. We did big batch foods that would feed a bunch of folks with a minimum of ingredients: soups, stews, chili, spaghetti, chicken and rice, goulash, just to name a few, and always with some of Millie's homemade bread, cornbread, biscuits, or yeast rolls. She kept a sourdough starter going all the time on the counter, so even if the yeast was gone someday, we'd still have bread, and who doesn't love sourdough bread?

Sara and Marietta came over to grab a sandwich and watch the kids wolfing theirs down. Marietta didn't talk much, but she had a big grin on her face as she kept her eye on Moira and Aiden in particular.

"They really do work up an appetite doing their chores every day. I think it does them good to keep busy—they don't seem to be as sad about losing their mom when they're working."

I was watching them as well, and nodded at her. "It will take some time for them to heal, Lee included. It's good they have things to keep them busy, at least during the day. How are they all doing with the gardens? Do they seem to be grasping what gets eaten and what doesn't? We'd prefer it if we didn't have Bermuda grass in with the collard greens."

Sara laughed. "Yes, Anne, they are doing great. The girls are awesome at getting in and getting all the little tufts of grass. They're much more thorough than the boys. I think we should get the older boys to step up their wood chopping, to give the younger kids more to do. They can get through the garden in about thirty minutes now."

"We can do that for a bit, but I think we're going to be tilling up another piece of ground to start a new garden. We have a lot more people than we have ever planted for in the past, and we still have plenty of time to plant more crops. It's better if we can turn it early so the bugs get out of the ground, but we'll just deal with it for now. We're going to need more food—not just for our daily meals now, but to put up for the winter. Now's the time to do it. Pete should be starting that either today or first thing in the morning. They're almost done with the bunkhouse."

At the mention of it, we all looked over to the newest structural addition to the place. It wasn't fancy, but it had turned out great, much better than I had imagined. There were doors at both ends, and three windows on each side to let in natural light. The whole building had been wrapped in tar paper around the outside to seal the walls, as well as the roof. With most of the men able to work on it full time, they had knocked it out quickly. True to his word, Lee had built six bunks into each wall, for a total of twelve. The old wood stove Monroe had donated had been set up in the back. The floor had been laid like a deck with five-quarter boards but without the spacing normally used for a deck, to keep the drafts and critters out. An old card table and four folding chairs completed the décor.

We didn't have mattresses, but when the group had gone for the clothes they had grabbed all the blankets and sheets they could rustle up, as well as any sleeping bags. The Lawton brothers had been hauling freshly line-dried sheets and blankets in for the past hour. Ryan saw us looking that way and waved us over.

"Ladies, come check out the new digs!"

He was so excited; you would have thought it was a million-dollar mansion he was moving into. Funny how your priorities change with the circumstances, isn't it?

We grinned at him, checked the kids one more time, and headed that way. As we were walking up the steps, Lee came out to dust the sawdust from his clothes. He saw us and gave us a small smile.

"Hey, ladies. Are my kids behaving and doing their fair share?"

Marietta smiled back. "They are doing great, Lee. They mind well and don't fight much, considering they're brother and sister. I fought with mine like a wildcat. They are very well behaved. You should be proud."

"Well, to tell you the truth, the not fighting thing is new. They used to be at each other all the time. I think losing Jackie got them to thinking about how they'd feel if they lost one another, too. If I am able to find anything good in this mess, that'd be one thing I'd pick. And thank you for the kind words."

The sadness in Lee's eyes whenever he mentioned his wife always made me feel like I was going to cry. I wished there was some way to find her and bring her here to her family, but I knew that couldn't happen. We had to leave our own home because of the lawlessness that had manifested so soon. What would the city be like, with all those people trying to find food and water? And how would we find her in the vast sea of humanity that would have been there?

I cleared my throat to clear the tears and put on a smile. "Well, let's see this new building of yours, Lee. Care to give us the grand tour?"

He laughed, surprising all of us. He didn't do that very often. "I hope you didn't carve out a lot of time for the tour. It'll be over in about thirty seconds."

We followed him in and again I was awestruck at his skill. The bunks were built similar to berths on a train. They were attached to the wall, with the ends closed off with plywood. That would give the inhabitants a little bit of privacy. The bottom ones were about eighteen inches off the floor, and I saw the guys were using that space for storage; they had totes and duffel bags under the bunks. There was a short ladder attached between the top and bottom bunks for the top sleeper access. The beds were made up of a combination of sleeping bags, blankets, and sheets. While it wasn't a mattress, it was clean and dry, and I would think much preferred to sleeping on the ground in a tent.

Ryan was laid out on the right-side bunk closest to the front door. With a big toothy grin, he said, "Well, what do you gals think of the new frat house? Isn't it awesome? Lee is a building son of a bitch. No offense, Lee."

"None taken. Is it comfortable at all? There's nothing I can do about the wood base."

"Dude, are you kidding? I've been sleeping with a big honkin' rock in my back for the past two days. This is heaven!"

He wiggled like he was getting comfortable, then closed his eyes and started fake snoring. We all laughed at our resident joker. Ryan seemed to always be able to find humor in any situation, including getting a face full of glass. His face was healing, thanks to the "farmacy," as we called our healing herb plants. Seeing how much better his cuts were reminded me of the conversation I'd had with Kate the day after they got back from their neighborhood. She was learning stuff they didn't teach them in nursing school. She was learning old school healing. With the state of things, this was a skill that would be priceless.

****

Kate wasn't as well versed in the natural options, but she was working with Millie every day on learning them. Millie knew them all. Ryan's specific issue called for twice-daily applications of aloe vera. Aloe is a natural scar-removal remedy due to its anti-inflammatory and antibacterial properties. It works as a natural emollient to help repair damaged skin and promote the growth of healthy skin. Kate knew about its use for soothing burns, but she was amazed at how well Ryan's cuts were healing. She was also eager to learn other alternatives to traditional medicine. I had given her the e-reader with the medicinal plant listings on it the day before.

"We have most of the important ones that will grow here in a portable tiered planter in the screen porch. They can get the sun they need, but we can bring them in if it gets cold. We try to keep some already dried, too. Those are in the root cellar."

She was really excited at the prospect of learning about the healing plants. "What all do you have? What are they used for? I know it's in the e-book, but can you show me? I learn better by seeing and feeling than reading."

"Sure. Let's go to the drug store." I grinned at her and headed out to the porch. When we got out there she looked hard at the far corner of the room.

"Oh my gosh, Anne. I saw the plant stand, but I just figured they were house plants. You can use all of these for medicinal purposes?"

"Yes, ma'am. The aloe you know about and recognize is on top. They can get pretty big, so we give it room to spread out. They have what I call 'babies'—they're really called pups. They're offsets that pop up in the pot. You can replant them. You already know about aloe's use on the skin, but you can also use it internally,

181

specifically for digestive issues. You can put it in water and drink it. I have not taste tested that yet."

I shuddered a little, and Kate giggled. I went on, pointing to each plant as I moved down the plant stand.

"Burdock: great for skin diseases. Pot marigold: insect bites and sprains externally; fever and infections internally. Chamomile you have probably heard of for a calming sleep aid. It can also be used for tooth and earaches in a poultice. Echinacea ..."

"That one I know! I kept it at the house in capsules all the time. If anybody started sniffling or coughing, everybody got it."

"Excellent. We can skip that one then, but you'll find more uses for it in the book. Lemon Balm: smells great, and makes a decent bug repellent. Infused, it can help treat colds, fever, headaches, and more. Peppermint you may already know helps with digestion; that's one of the reasons you get them free at a lot of restaurants. It can also help with fever. Sage: internally, stomach and nerve issues; externally, skin infections, mouth infections, bug bites. Dried and smudged, it wards off evil spirits."

We both snickered, and I went on. "Comfrey: it has a lot of uses, which I can't remember all of, but I know we planted it specifically for compresses for bruises and sprains. This last one is called Feverfew. As the name denotes, it is used in the treatment of fevers, as well as colds, and can ease the pain of arthritis.

"There's more information and uses on all of these in the books. There's more than one book on medicinal plants, by the way. There's a whole section on the e-reader for them. Without doctors and hospitals, we have to go back to the old ways of the medicine men and women and use what nature has to offer. We have supplies to last a while, but we should probably start working some of these in from time to time, to extend the preps we do have. You can start with the easy stuff, like cuts and scrapes and bug bites. If you're comfortable with their effectiveness, you can move on to using them on the bigger booboos."

She grinned. "This is so awesome. I'm ashamed that I am in the healing industry and never thought to learn alternative methods. They brainwash you in school that modern medicine is the only real option, and the 'old ways' are ineffective. I can't wait to find out what all we can use these for to keep our people healthy."

"Oh, there's one more plant I need to show you. Come outside with me."

We walked out into the yard a bit to a patch of fuzzy-leaved plants. I plucked a leaf and handed it to her. "This is called lamb's ear. It grows *really* well. I don't think you can truly kill it off. It is very prolific, like spearmint. They're actually in the same family, I think. It has great medicinal properties. It can be used as a bandage. It's absorbent, and it has antiseptic, anti-inflammatory, analgesic, and antibacterial properties. It's been called 'nature's bandage.' They can also be used for 'that time of the month' in place of pads. This one plant will cover a *lot* of areas for us."

Kate stood there staring at the leaf, running her fingers over the velvety softness, with a look of sheer amazement. "All that from this one plant? How come I've never even heard of it, much less what all it can be used for?"

"Because you grew up in a time when Band-Aids were in every home, when if you needed anything for feminine hygiene or a stomach bug you ran to the store and bought it. You didn't need to know about things like this then. We all need to know it now. Knowing alternative ways to do things is the only way we survive in this world. Speaking of alternative ways, we should probably get Sean to get the still set up soon. Depending on how things go, we may need that alcohol sooner than we had planned, if the last few days are any indication."

"We've partaken of plenty of his moonshine, and frankly it was awesome. I never once considered it might be used for something besides a good buzz."

I smiled at her. "I'm sure we'll use it for that, too. I just hope we can come up with whatever he needs to make it. I've read about it, but since we didn't have a still, I don't know a whole lot about it—although I think there's a book on making moonshine on one of the e-readers."

Kate laughed. "Imagine that. You having an e-book on it. I'm pretty sure all he needs is corn, sugar, and water. He can use livestock feed, like sweet feed you get for horses, or the cracked corn you feed chickens. He's bought more from the feed store than the one that specialized in home distilling. Much cheaper. It takes a few days for the fermentation to start, so yeah, we should probably start gathering supplies to get him set up. Thank you so much for all the info, Anne. It looks like I'll be going to school in the mornings too."

I had an idea. "You know, we could add learning the uses of the medicinal plants to our Laundry and Learning sessions. That will be just as important as learning what plants we can eat. Yep, I think that's a great idea. You learn it, then you can teach it."

"Are you sure I'm the right person to do that? I mean, I'm learning as much as everyone else."

"Yes, I'm sure. Once you look them up, and find out what all they can do, you'll be able to dumb it down, so to speak, for those of us who aren't as well versed in the healing arts as you are. You know, something like, 'if you get a cut, grab one of these leaves and stick it on it'—and show them the lamb's ear. Heck, we could tell that one to everyone. 'Grab a fuzzy leaf, slap it on the cut, and go see Kate.' Might make your job easier. Anyway, you'll do great. Just don't teach one until you are confident you know what all it can do. Then, just share."

She looked apprehensive, but she nodded. "Okay, I'll give it a shot. If I suck at it, we'll call in reinforcements—namely, Millie."

I grinned at her. "Sounds like a plan. Now, how about a nice glass of lukewarm tea? Man, I miss ice."

# Chapter 18

The next few days were quiet, so we should have known something was coming. In this kind of world, peace doesn't last long.

The bunkhouse was done. Luke and Casey were set up in their camper, with Casey well enough to stand security watch. Sean had some of the cracked corn we used to feed the chickens soaking in a big cooler to start the fermentation process. Pete had gotten us another acre tilled up with the tractor, after much berating from Monroe.

"Ain't you ever plowed a field before? Them rows are as crooked as a politician on votin' day!"

A group of us were standing off to the side, watching. Snickering.

"Well, to tell you the truth, no sir, I haven't ever plowed a field before. I said I could drive it. I didn't say I was experienced with the accessories for it."

"You ain't gotta say it! I can see it! Get off my tractor and let me see if I can fix this mess you made!"

Pete looked crestfallen, but we were all laughing so hard we could barely stand up straight. He climbed off the tractor as Monroe was climbing on the other side, mumbling, "City slickers don't know a damn thing about farming. Without farmers, they'd starve for sure!"

Bob walked over to Pete and laid an arm across his shoulders. "Don't take it personal, bubba. He ripped me a new one the first time I tried to drive it, too. Except I took out a whole section of fence over by the barn. Took me the rest of the day to fix it, and he made me fix every inch of it. He still gives me hell about running over his horse pen."

Pete was listening to Bob, but he was paying more attention to what Monroe was doing. He seemed to be trying to absorb the actions needed to keep the tractor, and thus the discs behind it, moving in a straight line. Monroe made it look easy. Of course, he'd been doing it for most of his life. He got to the end of the row Pete had made and turned around and looked back at his work. The rows were now straight as an arrow. Monroe had a smug look on his face.

"There, you see how easy that was? You think you can follow that last one to make the next set, or is the oldest guy out here gonna have to do all the work while all you young'uns stand around in the shade laughing?"

Pete now had a determined look on his face, and he started for the tractor. The rest of us were doing our best to stop laughing—at least so far as Monroe knew. Coughing and throat clearing were rampant at that moment.

"Yes, sir, I think I can handle it now. Would you ride along for the first few passes, just to make sure I get it right this time?"

Monroe grinned at him. "I love watching other people do my work. Hell yeah, I'll ride with ya."

Under Monroe's tutelage, Pete managed to plow the new field in a few hours. We'd give the dirt the rest of the day to dry out some and be back out there first thing in the morning, pulling grass out of it and getting some more food in the ground. We couldn't wait if we wanted to get things like potatoes and corn started. We were coming up on the first of May, and while we have a pretty long growing season in Tennessee, a drought or an early frost could take out everything in the ground. The more we had planted, the better our odds of having something to harvest. The more we could harvest and put back in storage, the better our chances of making it through the coming winter with the mouths we had to feed.

At supper that evening, we got into a discussion about what might have caused the pulse and what, if anything, our government was doing to get things back online. We had been so busy planning and preparing we had completely forgotten about the radio broadcast we had heard while we were still at our house. I asked Russ if he wanted me to pull out the little handheld ham radio we had up in our room, but Monroe interrupted with a derisive snort.

"You don't need that baby radio. I'm surprised you even picked up anybody with that puny thing. My big rig is set up upstairs in our room. I heard that broadcast early on too, but to be honest there's been so much going on since y'all got here, I ain't even thought to turn it back on again. It didn't matter anyway—wasn't nothin' on there anybody could say to change what we had to do. I reckon now that it's gotten a little quieter and we're pretty much settled in, we should probably find out what's going on out there. We'll fire it up tonight, after the sun goes down."

Monroe was a licensed ham radio operator. He had gotten his license after returning home from Vietnam, so that he could stay in touch with his army buddies who were lucky enough to have made it home as well; it meant they could talk to each other without having to pay long-distance phone charges. There was no such thing as "free long-distance" back then, and it was very expensive.

As many ham operators do, Monroe built his set himself, to defray the cost of a brand new unit. He could build it in pieces cheaper than he could buy one complete. He bought a kit that allowed him to build the receiver first, then the transmitter. The final piece was the antenna, which was basically an antenna wire thrown up in a tree. He could run it from a wall plug, but he also had an inverter set up so he could use a twelve-volt deep-cycle marine battery as well.

On clear nights, he could reach people hundreds of miles away, and had. His army buddies were all gone now, but he had "met" other hams—as they called themselves—through the years and, until everything went down, talked on his radio at least one or two nights a week. With his set, we should have no problem getting the broadcast—if it was still out there.

**\*\*\*\***

It was decided they would bring the radio equipment downstairs, so we could all hear what was said without cramming twenty adults into Monroe and Millie's bedroom. With the kids settled in the screen porch playing, Monroe connected the radio to the generator the guys had brought onto the porch. He had kept the radio turned off and unplugged when he wasn't actively using it, which is probably why it still worked. The components of his forty-plus-year-old radio were not as susceptible to the pulse, and being unplugged had pretty much guaranteed it making it through, just like the older cars and trucks. He'd tossed the antenna out the upstairs window, so Bob picked it up and handed it to him through the living room window they had run the power cord out of for the generator. As he flipped the power on, we heard talking immediately. He had obviously left it on the same channel we had found.

*"Look, I don't know who's behind this either. All I can tell you is what I saw—not heard from someone who heard from someone else— SAW with my own eyes. It was a line of armored vehicles with the UN symbol on the sides. They were headed to DC from up north—possibly*

*New York City. I don't know if they had supplies or food, but I didn't see any Red Cross or anything like that. It was all armored vehicles, with machine guns on top. It looked like an invasion to me."*

*"An invasion by the UN? Sounds all tin foil hatty if you ask me."*

*"Then take yours off so you can hear what I'm saying. We were set up for this by that illegal small arms treaty that was signed, along with allowing the UN ANY say in what we do as a nation. The administration and the UN have been chomping at the bit to get in here and start taking away our liberties and freedom. Some radical whack job country sets a nuke off in our atmosphere, sends us back about two hundred years technologically, and guess what: we're now a third-world country. We have no utilities, no food or clean water, people dying in the streets due to illness or lawlessness, and no one is doing a damn thing about it. Did you hear that ridiculous address from DC today? I recorded it."*

We heard the sound of a recording start playing. Man, that guy must have had some really good Faraday cages—or some *really* old equipment.

*"We know you're struggling, but there just isn't anything we can do right now on a large scale. We are doing everything we can to hold the government structure together. We have FEMA camps set up outside almost all major cities now. While our resources are severely limited, you can get some food, water, and medical attention there if needed. Just don't expect it to be a long-term solution for you. Everyone needs to buckle up and hunker down, because this is going to be a rough ride. Martial Law has been in effect for weeks, but it doesn't seem to be*

helping with the illegal activities being perpetrated on the American people by their own countrymen. We just don't have enough men and women to police the entire country. We encourage you to protect your families and to assist your fellow man when you can. While this is not an open invitation to take the law into your own hands, you should defend yourselves. If your neighbor comes to you asking for help, share whatever you have with them. Only together can we come through this tragedy stronger than ever.

"We also need food and ammunition, as well as working vehicles, for our troops and law enforcement who are gearing up to protect this country from an invading force, so I am enacting the Executive Order for the National Defense Resource Preparedness. If you are contacted by any representative of our government or the United Nations, do not resist them. Provide them the supplies they are there to collect. Without our military, we are open to invasion by other nations who would see us annihilated. We must maintain order in our government and control of our country. With that said, the upcoming elections have been suspended until we get back to some semblance of what we were and what we had. To be perfectly honest, it could take years. The Posse Comitatus Act has been repealed as well, so that our military can protect us here at home. We may have to sacrifice some freedoms to get through this situation. I know you will all agree that these are the best options we have at being successful in returning our country to what it was just a few short weeks ago."

The recording stopped and the speaker came back on.

"Seriously? That's the solution? Take away our freedom, stick us with your sorry ass for the unforeseeable future, oh, and by the way, give us most of your supplies. There was a guy on here yesterday who lives in Maryland. He said the UN forces came to his house, kicked in the door, and demanded all but three days' worth of his food. They took every gun except one pistol and one rifle, and all but a box of ammo for each, AND they took his truck. He said before that he had enough food to feed his family for a couple of years, and thousands of rounds of ammo. So, tell me how we are supposed to fend for ourselves with no food and no ability to get more by hunting? If you use the ammo for hunting, what do you have to defend yourself and your family with?"

"Was he the only one in that area they took supplies from? Do you know?"

"I do know. He has a prepper group he's part of in that area. All of them were hit. But none of the other residents, the ones who didn't have a bunch of supplies stored up. They knew who would have the stuff they wanted."

"How'd they know?"

"Do you buy things online or at warehouse stores with credit cards? They know and track everything you purchase. Specific items like ammo, guns, and mass quantities of food stuffs trigger their tracking code. They may not have a gun registration, but they know who buys guns. They've kept all that info on all of us, just waiting for something like this to happen, so they'd know where to go to get the things they need. Oh, and they're probably listening to this conversation."

Monroe turned the volume down. We all stood there staring at the radio, then at each other. The UN was in our country, taking people's food and supplies?

"I knew about the EO, but I never thought they'd use it." Mike was looking around the room. "This changes things—this changes everything. Marauders, beggars, and scavengers are one thing. An invading army is a whole other ballgame."

Bob looked bewildered. "Would our military do that? Would they take from people who are just trying to get by, taking care of themselves, not asking for help from the government, or anyone else for that matter, for the 'greater good'?"

"I don't think our troops would do that, even if they were ordered to. We all took an oath, and it said specifically 'all enemies foreign and domestic.' As a former member of that group, I personally would tell them to take a flying fuck if they ordered me to take anything from folks like us, and I hope those currently serving feel the same way. That said, the UN 'peacekeepers' is a whole other scenario. They want a new world order where there is no local, or even national, law enforcement, but a global police force. They care nothing about our Constitution, they despise us for our Second Amendment rights, and the majority of the countries in the UN want to see us knocked off our high horse. Looks like this is their chance. We need to talk about some things when we get done listening here, but I'd like to hear more, if we can, first."

We were all in shock, but definitely wanted to know what else was happening out there. Monroe turned the volume back up.

*"We can't fight UN forces alone. I strongly urge everyone listening to find like-minded individuals to team up with if you haven't already. I'm betting if they come up against a force of more than just a couple of folks, they won't be so eager to exert force and take your things. The guy from Maryland said it was six guys who showed up at his place. I don't know how we can hook people up with each other without them knowing where we are, but we need to figure that out. I'm completely open to suggestions, people."*

There were a bunch of people trying to talk at once, so Monroe turned it back down again. Russ and Monroe shared a look, and Monroe nodded at him.

"We've been talking, and we think we can take at least a half dozen more people, maybe up to a dozen here. With the bunkhouse, and more campers if we can find them, we can beef up our numbers. We can plow more ground for more crops, and put the breeders together in the livestock pens. We need more people. We need to find more folks like you guys"—he gestured to the group—"to maintain this place. If we have three dozen people, I'm betting most outsiders will leave us alone, if they find us. Monroe knows other folks in the area he thinks will be good additions to the group. In the next few days we are going out to see if they want to join us. We will protect this place, and our supplies, against all enemies foreign and domestic. Count on it."

We all nodded in agreement with Russ's comments. We listened to the irate survivors on the radio for a couple of hours. No one knew who had set off the EMP. From what we could tell, we hadn't been invaded by any forces, outside of the UN. Did it really matter who had done it? I mean, we were where we were, regardless of who was responsible. All we could do now was live the life we'd been dealt, take care of each other to the best of our abilities, and get ready for whatever was coming. We knew something was coming, we just didn't know what it was—or who was bringing it.

# Chapter 19

"The first thing I want to say to all of you is if you have a rifle, you should be carrying it with you at all times. Pistols are for up close, when you can see your target well. Rifles will hopefully keep the target from getting up close."

Mike had brought this up over supper the next night. We had spent the day with the standard chores, as well as getting some more food planted in the new garden. Mike had been walking around all day, observing our actions as we went about the daily routine of life on a farm.

"As I walked the area today, I saw everyone who has them wearing sidearms, which is good, but you need to get in the habit of slinging your rifle over your back as well. If something goes down, you don't want to have to be scrambling around trying to find it. If you're working the garden, prop it up against a tree. We can put up hooks and nails in them and on fence posts so you can hang them for easy access."

"But what about the kids? Isn't that dangerous, having guns lying around they can just pick up?" Ah, Sara—she was trying to get it, but sometimes she still had a hard time grasping it all.

Sean answered her question. "You tell them not to touch any gun until they are taught how to use one, and if they do, they get their butt whipped. I've already had that conversation with my kids a long time ago. They know better. Tony should probably be learning how to use one now, but that's yours and Pete's decision, not ours. Either way, if I see any of them trying to get their hands on one without an adult involved, I'll whip their butt. Okay with you, Lee?"

Lee gave a short nod. "More than okay with me. Every adult here has permission to instruct and discipline my children if they see a need for it."

Sean nodded back. "Same goes for ours. Kids need to learn respect for all grown-ups, and that misbehavior will not be tolerated from any of them by any of us. The most important thing to remember is guns protect us from those who would try to harm any of us, or particularly our children. They are an important and necessary tool in this reality."

Mike went on. "Make sure you have a bag with at least two full magazines for any weapons you're carrying. We have a bunch of backpacks we brought back from the neighborhood, so we should have extras if anyone needs one. I don't want us to get caught unprepared like we were when those Glass brothers showed up. If that had been actual marauders, we would have been in real trouble, possibly even losing some people. Bad guys will come in guns blazing. We need to have some firepower to meet that with on our side."

Brian looked at Mike solemnly. "What if it's soldiers? Are they bad guys now?"

Mike was silent for a moment, then stood very tall. "If they come in guns blazing, yes they are, and we will return in kind. If they come in guns drawn, we will match their stance. If they try to take anything, we will resist. This is America. We have rights, we have freedom, and we have a Constitution that lays all that out. *No* edicts from a wannabe dictator change any of those things. *No* illegal laws can take away our God-given rights. I don't know about all of you, but I for one will go down fighting for every one of those things."

To a chorus of "Hell yeah!" and "Amen!" it was decided that we would not be able to comply with the requests of the current administration. While Pete and Sara seemed less than confident, the rest of us knew we would do anything to defend the people here from any enemies that came. It was time to find more people we could trust and make them a part of our family too.

****

With the prospect of more folks coming, we started trying to think of what other accommodations we needed to get set up to handle more people. We were pretty much done washing and drying all the clothes that had been brought back. While the owners took a fair share, they also donated quite a bit to whoever might need them. We ended up with a nice pile of extra clothes, including some from our family and the Hoppers, sorted into totes by size. These were stacked up in the trailers we had brought our stuff out to the farm in, currently parked in the big garage. No sense wasting good storage space, and they were perfect for this, since we wouldn't need to be in them on a regular basis.

Adding another dozen people was going to be challenging in the food prep department. While we were concentrating on a lot of one-pot meals for supper now, even that would be harder with three dozen people. Too bad none of us had ever worked in a school cafeteria.

We were sitting at the kitchen table the next evening, discussing our options while the kids washed the supper dishes. Yep, any of them who were not old enough to stand security watch were now on a dish-washing work rotation. Plenty of work to go around on the farm.

Millie was mulling the possibilities over. "We're using the biggest stock pots we have now. We can use Casey's water bath canner, as well as mine, if we need them. The challenge is going to be where we do the cooking. With pots that big, my old stove will probably only be able to handle two at a time. I suppose we can fire up the wood cook stove if we need to—no time like the present to learn new skills. I can cook on it, I'm just not as confident of its use as I am my old reliable.

"I think we should keep on the way we've been doing it so far: soups, stews, and big pasta dishes with bread. If we happen to get a nice batch of something from the gardens, we throw it in. We just cook half again as much as we're cooking now. We may have to split it into two pots, but we can do it. I do think we'll need to use the wood stove to make more bread each day."

"Okay, Aunt Millie, but you have to take on at least one helper, full time. I'll volunteer." Janet was watching her aunt for any signs of resistance.

Marietta raised her hand. "I volunteer too. I used to cook for my family, what little we had, so I know how to stretch food. I've also been dying to get the secret to Millie's fluffy bread."

She grinned at Millie as we all laughed. Millie smiled back at her. "No secret, dear. Just don't overwork the dough. Let the yeast do the work. And I would be very thankful for the help, especially with the kneading. My old hands just don't always do what I tell them to these days."

As she said it, she held her hands up. I was shocked to see they looked enflamed and swollen.

"Millie, why didn't you say something? Kate, have you seen this?"

Kate got up and hurried around the table to her. "No, I have not. Millie, why didn't you tell me your hands were bothering you? We can give you something to help with the arthritis." Kate was standing there with her hands on her hips, looking every bit the charge nurse.

"It usually isn't this bad. I think it's from the extra bread making, to be honest." Millie held up a dark glass bottle with a dropper top. "I've been treating it with an essential oil mixture one of the ladies from church gave me a year or so ago, but I just ran out yesterday."

Kate took the bottle, took the top off, and smelled it. "Hmmm. I smell peppermint, eucalyptus, I think, and a slight hint of olive oil. Do you know the recipe, Millie? Does anyone have more of the oils?"

Janet stood up and headed toward the door. "Yes, we have most of the popular ones in the root cellar. I'll be right back."

Our prepping had included a variety of essential oils, particularly the ones with medicinal or healing uses, but we also had some that would help with dry skin and soothing balms. We had beeswax, shea butter, and coconut oil to use as carriers or to make blends, as well as vitamin E capsules. Janet and I had no doubt the ability to make hand and body lotions would be a valuable asset when the stores were gone. We could also make salves and antibiotic ointment if needed. Supplies were the new currency, and the people who knew how to make things you couldn't buy anymore, including those considered luxury items, would have more bargaining power. And yes, I had quite a few books on the e-reader with information and recipes for those things. Did I say how awesome it is to have a device that holds thousands of books?

"I don't know the exact amounts, but you're right about the ingredients. I do know it opens my sinuses up when I use it, so I get a bonus benefit." Millie laughed at her own joke, and we joined her. Janet came back with the essential oils and handed them to Kate.

"Great. Anybody have any idea how to do this?"

I took the bottle. "I think I can wing it. Millie, where are those small funnels we brought you?"

"Look in the gadget drawer by the stove, Anne."

I went to the drawer that every woman has in her kitchen: the gadget drawer. The drawer that holds all the things you use only sporadically. The place cookie cutters and corn holders go to hide. The spot for the nut cracker and picker you bring out only at Christmas. The location of all those things you bought that were cute or cool, or that you really thought you needed, but used only once. I rummaged around until I found the small set of funnels we had given Millie. Janet and I each had a set, so we thought Millie should have one too. Now I was really glad we had.

The rest of the group gathered around as I set the opaque bottle on the counter. I put in five drops each of the peppermint and eucalyptus oil, then a couple of tablespoons of the olive oil sitting by the stove. I put the lid on and gave it a good shake. When I took the lid off, I let Kate and Millie sniff test it.

Kate smelled it first. "Close, but I didn't get that distinct of a smell of the olive oil in the original. What do you think, Millie?"

She handed the bottle to Millie, who gave it a sniff. "Yes, Kate's right. I'd go heavier on the essentials."

I added another five drops of each, gave it another swish, and passed it back. Kate smiled when she smelled it. "I think that's it. Millie?"

Millie took it, inhaled, and smiled as well. "I do believe you did it, Anne. Do you remember the recipe?"

"Yep. Ten drops of each, plus two tablespoons or so of the olive oil. Get that on your hands right away, Millie. New meal prep rules, starting now: you supervise. You may participate, but you are not the primary cook anymore. Marietta, Janet, and myself—"

Kate chimed in. "Me too! If I don't have any patients, I can help. If I do have patients, I can still help, because this will keep me close."

I nodded and went on. "We will take on the cooking duties. There may be some of the guys who want to help, but I know from experience Russ and Bob can barely grill out. We do not want to subject all these people to their culinary deficiencies."

Everyone giggled. I went on. "Kate, there are some books on the e-reader on essential oils you can use for medicinal purposes. I completely forgot about having those in the root cellar because we haven't used them up to now. Janet and I have experimented on a couple of things, but it's been a while and nothing really serious. She can show you where they are, as well as the dried herbs I told you about. There's a few big bags of Epsom salt in there as well."

"Perfect. We can do a soak in a bit. Millie, I'm going to get you some acetaminophen and ibuprofen to take for now. I'll be right back." Kate headed for the basement.

Millie looked at us. "Both?"

I shrugged. "She's the doctor, so to speak. Ask her when she gets back."

Kate came back with one of each in her hand, and both bottles in the crook of her arm. Millie was hesitant. "Shouldn't I take one or the other? I've never heard of taking one of each."

Kate handed her the pills. "These two work together at fighting pain and inflammation. Each one has its own unique properties and abilities, so they complement each other. If it doesn't feel better in an hour or so, we can give you two more ibuprofens. It's the best we can do without something stronger, but this method works very well with pain management. I use it a lot for my back and legs when I've worked a double shift."

"Well, if it's good enough for you, it's good enough for me." With that, Millie took the meds, then looked at us. "Now, let's get to working on the meals for tomorrow. If you're not going to let me do the cooking, I can at least help with the planning."

We settled back around the table, and we were just starting to discuss ideas for meals for the next day when we heard gunshots. Again? Dammit!

****

Lee and the Lawton brothers had been in the bunkhouse getting it ready for more inhabitants. They made up beds on all the bunks to make sure there were plenty of bedclothes. They condensed some of the totes and duffels under the bunks so that any newcomers had room for their things as well. They had added hooks for coats and hats, and some simple gun racks for rifles and shotguns. Bill was sweeping the floor while Lee and Ryan finished up the last bunk.

"You're going to make someone a fine wife someday, big brother."

Bill took a swipe at Ryan with the broom. Ryan dodged and laughed. Bill gave his little brother an evil look.

"I doubt I'll ever get married, because they probably won't want to taint their bloodline with someone who has a moron for a brother."

"Man, you shouldn't talk about yourself like that. You're not a moron."

Ryan laughed at his own joke, then took off running out the door as Bill came after him with the broom. Lee was watching them with a grin on his face, until he heard the shots. He took off out the door to find his kids, while Bill dropped the broom in the yard, and he and Ryan headed toward the front, pistols drawn. Remembering Mike's admonishments regarding rifles over handguns, they turned around and raced back to the bunkhouse to grab them. They didn't know who was shooting, but it sounded too far off to be the people living at the farm. It wasn't. At least, not yet.

****

Russ, Monroe, and Bob were scoping out an area for more campers. They had pretty much decided on the space between the car shed and the old outhouse. It would not be as close to the main house as the bunkhouse, but it would still be shouting distance if something happened.

"I think we ought to hook the blade up to the tractor and do a little grading. There's a slight incline that might make it harder to level a camper. I know it doesn't have to be perfect, but the more level the better. Have you ever been in a camper that wasn't level, or wasn't set up properly with jacks? Every time someone breathes you can feel it move."

Bob seemed to be remembering the situation he was describing. Monroe looked at him. "I didn't know you'd ever been in a camper. I thought y'all were tent campers."

"We are—well, were—but we went with some friends once who were on their maiden voyage with their camper. To say they were green would be an understatement. I got seasick just stepping up in the thing. I had to show them how to use the jacks to steady it, but the spot was gravel, so they still didn't get a good solid base. I think they got rid of it right after that. The wife said that was the worst night's sleep she had ever had, and she would not go again."

"Sounds like someone got a good deal on a slightly used camper right after that. I can see the ad: Camper for sale. Used once. Wife said either it goes or I do. Make me an offer." Russ was grinning as he said it.

"Dude, that was it almost word for word! He practically gave it away. I'm kind of wishing now I'd bought it, but Janet was pregnant with Benny then and we couldn't swing it."

"It'd be at least sixteen years old now. They're making campers like mobile homes these days, using very sturdy materials. We'll find some late models we can bring in. Unfortunately, I'm pretty sure there are more people out there who never made it home. We'll find some we can use, I know it."

Russ's confidence was infectious. Bob and Monroe were discussing how much grading they needed to do when they heard the shots. They immediately took off at a run toward the front gate, where it sounded like they had come from. The two younger men were unslinging their rifles as they ran, but noticed Monroe was no longer with them. They turned to look and saw he had changed course and was headed for the house.

"Go on ahead!" Monroe yelled back at them. "I'm gonna make sure everyone is secure inside, and the kids are all accounted for. I'll be up there as soon as I can! Call on the radio if you need anything from the house."

They nodded and continued to the front at a dead run. Who was shooting? What were they shooting at? How did someone get close enough to shoot without the sentries seeing them? Too many questions that needed answers, and fast.

****

Mike was on security detail and had been walking back toward the house from one of the foxholes, where Brian had been keeping watch, when the shots rang out. Matt Thompson was in the treehouse and immediately brought his .308 up so he could use the scope to try to determine where the shots had come from. Luke was in the other hole. Mike hit the dirt and worked his way to the tree line in front of the treehouse.

"Matt! What do you see? Who's shooting?"

Matt was scanning the area through his scope. "I don't see anybody, Mike. I don't think whoever is shooting was aiming our way. Maybe someone out hunting?"

"Could be. Let me know if you see anything. Use the binoculars hanging inside if you need them."

Monroe was calling them on the radio. "Who is it? Who's shootin' at us? If it's them Glass boys again, I'm gonna tear them a new ass when I get out there!"

Mike answered him. "We don't know yet. Matt doesn't see anybody out there. Maybe somebody hunting close by. The shots don't seem to have been aimed toward us."

"Alright, give me a minute or two and I'll be up. Out."

Mike climbed up to Matt to take a look for himself. When he got up Matt tried to hand him the binoculars, but Mike waved him off.

"Thanks. I've got my own." He pulled his minis out and scanned the area. He couldn't find the source of the shots at first either. Just as he was about to give up, he saw a muzzle flash and heard another shot. Definitely not toward the farm; it looked like the shooter was in the field across the road, possibly rabbit or turkey hunting. As there didn't appear to be an immediate threat, Mike climbed down and headed off everybody coming down the road.

"Looks like it's just somebody out hunting. I don't think they're looking for trouble. We should probably just hang tight."

By now Monroe had gotten to them and was looking toward the gate. "Did you get a good look at him? Could you tell anything about him?"

"Medium build, maybe late fifties, early sixties. Had a braid of gray hair about halfway down his back. Do you know him?"

"Yes, and he's one of the ones I wanted to talk to about joining up with us. I believe it's Jim Dotson. He lives about two miles as the crow flies, straight in front of us. He's got a wife, Charlotte, and two girls, Ashley and Carrie, I believe are their names. I think Ashley just got divorced and moved back in with them with her teenage daughter … I can't remember her name. Carrie has been there all along; Charlotte is disabled, so Carrie helps take care of her."

"What happened to Charlotte, Monroe?"

"She got hit by a drunk driver about ten years ago. Messed her leg up bad. The driver was a judge. They sued and got enough to take care of her medical bills, ongoing therapy, and they both got to retire. She can get around, but she needs help in the bathroom sometimes and with getting dressed, that sort of thing."

He paused, looking thoughtful. "I'm not positive, but I think they still have an older-model RV at their place. Jim got a deal on it right after they got the settlement money. They're good people, and I think they'd be a good addition. Jim's a hell of a hunter. He's like a quarter Cherokee. He can track like you wouldn't believe and never comes back from hunting empty handed. And Carrie is a nurse—she got her degree right before Charlotte got messed up. I think we should go out and talk to him. He knows where we live, so we won't be revealing our location to anyone who didn't already know we were here."

With that settled, most of the group went to the gate. There hadn't been much going on outside of the day-to-day grind, so meeting new people was a little bit of an adventure. It took three of them to wrestle the middle post out of its hole. Mike wiped sweat from his brow.

"I think we need to figure out a better way to move that thing when we need to. It's a great defense mechanism, but damn it's heavy!"

Bob laughed at him. "It was your idea. Figure it out, Sergeant."

"So, you're saying I have to do all the heavy lifting *and* thinking, Pinky?"

Bob started to say something, closed his mouth, shook his head, and turned to walk away. Everyone else was laughing hysterically, since by now they were all in on the Pinky nickname.

Monroe was trying to compose himself as he unhitched the gate. "You're killing me with that Pinky business, Jarhead. Now let's go talk to Jim."

No one from the group was aware that Jim wasn't the only one out there.

# Chapter 20

Alan had followed Russ's truck from as far back as he could while still trying to keep it in sight. The thing about older vehicles is they tend to be pretty loud. There hadn't been inspection stations that tested your emissions back when this truck was built. When they started hitting houses for supplies, Alan had stuffed the muffler with steel wool to quiet it down so people wouldn't hear them coming too soon. It helped a lot. They were able to be in the driveway before anyone knew they were there. Still, he didn't want to take a chance, so he had stayed well back from the camper. When he thought he heard the truck's engine sound change, he guessed it had been placed in park. He wanted to get a look at where they were, but he didn't want to take a chance they were outside of the truck and could hear his, so they parked and took off on foot.

They were approaching a bend in the road when they heard the truck's engine sound change again. They took off at a trot to get past the corner, but by the time they had a good view of the road again, the truck and camper were nowhere in sight.

Rich hissed at Alan. "What the hell? Where'd they go? They got a bat cave or something?"

Alan smirked at his buddy. "Not likely. Their place is here somewhere, in this stretch of road. Let's find it. Stay to the edge, close to the trees. If we can't see them, then by God they ain't seein' us."

To their left were open fields that looked like hay or wheat, so it couldn't be that side. That left only the right side of the road. It was solid trees and brush, or so it seemed. They walked the road slowly, peering into the foliage and trying to see past it. It was just too thick.

Steve looked at the tree line, then at Alan. "You think we should try to go in there, see if we can find 'em?"

"Do you see any place that looks like someone has been drivin' through here, dumbass? You think they drove that truck through that thick shit right there? If we can't get through it, they can't either. Keep walking and keep looking. There has to be a driveway or a gate or something."

They walked the road for over a mile and could find no sign of a track or driveway. Alan stopped and looked back the way they had come. In the dusky dark, there was no indication of an entrance to anything. He picked up a rock and hurled it across the road.

"It has to be here somewhere! They didn't just disappear! If they're hid that well, you know they're sittin' on a pile of goodies stashed in there, and I want 'em! We've got to find this place, but it's gettin' dark, and with no moon out, we won't be able to see shit, so let's get back to the truck. Be quiet, in case they're close and we just can't see 'em."

They headed back the way they had come, still peering into the tree line, trying to see anything out of the ordinary. They saw no more on the way back than they had on the way out; even less, since the sun was dropping rapidly in the sky. When they got back to the truck, Alan turned to his buddies.

"We're coming back here every day until someone shows their face. Then we'll know where they are. That's when we'll make our plan to take everything they have, including their place."

Steve looked confused. "How are just the three of us going to take them out and take their place, Al? They had us outnumbered already. They could have a bunch more folks back in there, wherever they are."

"Don't you worry about that, Stevie. When the time is right, we'll have what we need to take them down."

Even in their meth fog, Alan saw Steve and Rich look at each other in confusion. He laughed to himself. *I bet they're thinking, "What the hell is he getting us into now?" Well, they're about to find out.*

****

"Did you hear something?" Nick said softly to his brother, Matt, who was in one of the holes. Nick had been on patrol, and had stopped to check on him before he made his way back toward the house.

Matt held still and listened. He replied in a hushed voice, "I don't hear anything. What did it sound like?"

"Kind of like people talking, but it could have been the leaves rustling in the wind, I guess. It's still kind of creepy with no background noise, like the hum of the yard light. When it starts getting dark, it's like all the sounds are magnified."

"Awww, is da wittle baby afwaid of da dark? Does him need his bwankie?"

Nick kicked dirt in his older brother's face. "Jerk."

Matt shook his head, wiped his face, and spit a few times to clear the dirt from his mouth. "Buttwipe!"

Pete hissed at them from the other hole. "Knock it off, boys! If there is someone out there, they'll be hearing you instead of you hearing them!"

The boys stopped talking, but Nick flipped his brother off. Matt snickered at him as he poured water from his canteen onto a bandana and wiped his face with it. Pete radioed the nest. "Brian, you see anything up there? Nick thought he heard someone talking."

Brian scanned the area, trying to see past the tree line, but with the sun past the horizon, it was almost completely dark.

"No, I don't see anything. Stay sharp just in case."

Their watch was almost over and the next shift was starting to arrive. Pete had Nick tell them what he thought he had heard. As the next one up was Russ's shift that night, he listened, asked a few questions, then sent them to the house for their late supper. The four to eight shift in the evening ate when they got done.

"Make sure you tell Mike about it, so he can put it in the log."

Nick looked hesitant. "Are you sure, Russ? Maybe it was just the leaves."

"Yes, I'm sure, because maybe it wasn't just the leaves."

\*\*\*\*

Monroe walked out the gate and hollered across the field. "Jim! What ya huntin' out there?"

Jim Dotson turned to the sound of his name. He smiled at his old friend and waved. He started walking that way. "Hey, Monroe! Just gettin' a few rabbits for dinner. Charlotte likes the tame ones, but I kind of like that wild taste sometimes, ya know? How you doing, fella? I was gonna come see ya, see how you and Millie were farin', but the way you had the gate hidden, wasn't sure you were taking visitors, and these days it don't pay to show up uninvited, if you get my drift. Y'all makin' it okay with all the craziness going on?"

"Well, if you're just talking about the power being gone, yeah, we're doing alright. Got some kin, some old friends and some new ones staying at our place now. C'mon over, gang."

Monroe made introductions all around. Jim smiled and nodded and shook everyone's hand, and patted the heads of the dogs that had followed. "You do have quite a crew. Can't say I blame ya. Them Glass boys been by your place?"

Monroe snorted and spat on the ground. "Yeah, they came around begging a week or so ago. We sent 'em packing. They'd be like a stray dog. Feed 'em once, and they'd keep coming back for more. Everybody needs to learn to take care of themselves now. They come to you, too?"

Jim nodded sheepishly. "Yes, and unfortunately we gave them some supplies. Peanut butter, crackers, tuna, and some cans of soup. And you're exactly right. Three days later they were back for more. Said they ate all that and needed some more 'help.' Charlotte wanted me to give them more, but I said no. I told those boys if they wanted any more help, the only thing I could do for them in that department was to teach them how to hunt and fish. One of 'em seemed to want to do that, but the other one didn't want any part of actually having to *do* something to get to eat, and they stormed off.

"That night, I heard glass breaking. I jumped out of bed, grabbed my shotgun, ran into the kitchen, and caught the lazy one trying to climb in the window. I pointed my shotgun at him and said, 'This is the only warning you're gonna get. Get off my property and don't come back. I see you here again, and you won't be leaving.' He hustled back out the window, and I ain't seen hide nor hair of 'em since. Doesn't mean he won't be back. Just means he ain't figured out how to do it without gettin' shot."

Monroe was shaking his head. "Clay Glass. Ya know, if he spent half as much energy learning to gather food as he does trying to get someone to give it to him, or trying to steal it, he'd be able to feed himself and his family. I don't get it."

"I know what you mean. They've been taken care of by the government for so long, they don't know how to take care of themselves, but more importantly, they don't want to. But those boys aren't the only ones we've seen. There's been a few bunches come through. Our place isn't right on the road, but we don't have as much tree line as you do, and the gate is easy to see. We've had people come up, open the gate, and walk right up to the house. Mostly younger men, but a few women and kids.

"At first, Charlotte was giving everybody something. She loves canning veggies from the garden, and meat from my hunting trips, so we have a lot put back. But again, we were getting repeat customers, and when I said no more, they started gettin' hostile. I put a stop to all of it. I put a chain and a lock on the gate and a sign that says 'ALL TRESPASSERS WILL BE SHOT ON SIGHT.' That slowed the flow real quick. We still get a brave or stupid one every now and then, but I got the girls sitting watch with a rifle day and night. A shot over their heads usually sends them runnin', sometimes with piss runnin' down their legs."

Monroe chuckled. "Well, it sounds like you got a pretty good handle on things, Jim, but we were gonna come over and see if you and yours wanted to move over here with us. We have lots of room for campers, and we have over two dozen folks here now. Some younger kids, but plenty of adults to share security watch. As you said, our place is a lot more secure. We really only have to keep an eye on the front gate area, and as you can see, if you don't know where it is, you don't know where it is. I know it would be tough to leave your home, but things are going to get a lot worse, and you and your girls can't protect yourselves and your place alone. Not only that, but there's people out there grabbing women and kidnapping them. I don't think I have to tell you what for. I think you would all be safer with us."

Monroe told him what had happened to Casey, and that they had actually confronted the men as they were leaving to bring the Callens to the farm. He could see when Jim realized what he was talking about when he mentioned kidnapping women. Jim's eyes looked almost red as his anger seethed at the thought of what could happen to one of his daughters or his granddaughter.

He shook his head as he spoke quietly, dangerously. "No one is touching my girls. Ever. I will die protecting them if I have to."

Mike stepped forward. "That's what we don't want to happen, Mr. Dotson. That's why we'd like you all to join us. There is safety in numbers. Where a group of five or six guys might try to storm your place, they wouldn't have a chance at ours. Monroe said you had an RV at one time. If you still have it, we can load up all the things you need to bring, and get you and your family moved in with us in a day or so. I'm sure you'll want to talk to them first. We just want you to know that if you decide to take us up on our offer, we'll have a crew over there to get you loaded up and over here in a matter of hours."

"I don't think the RV will run. How will we get it over here?"

Monroe waved him off. "My tractor will get it here. Don't worry about that. You just go talk to your family. If they're in agreement, come back here. Go to the gate, and shoot one shotgun blast in the air. You'll get a shot back in return. Fire two shots after that. We'll meet you at the gate."

Jim reached for Monroe's hand. "Thank you for the offer, Monroe. Thank you for considering bringing my family into yours. I'm going home to talk to my girls right now. You'll hear back from me in the next day or so."

Monroe shook his hand and smiled at his friend. "No thanks needed. There's plenty for everyone to do. You'll earn your keep."

"You bet your ass we will. Talk to you soon." With that, Jim headed back across the field.

The gang watched him as he walked away for a moment, then turned back to the gate. They went through, closed it, and locked it. They didn't put the center post back, because they were expecting to bring Jim and his family over the next day, two at the most. They were talking among themselves, discussing the things Jim had shared with them, so they didn't see Alan and his boys down the road, peering at them from the ditch where they had taken cover when they rounded the corner and saw them talking to Jim. They weren't aware they were being watched. They had no idea that they had inadvertently led the wolves to the door.

****

"I told you if we watched and waited long enough they'd show themselves. We've got those assholes now!" Alan was full of himself right about then. They could hear it in his voice as he spoke. "Give it about ten minutes, enough time for them to get on up the drive, then we're going to see where that gate is."

Steve glanced at Rich; Rich was shaking his head. "Al, did you see how many people were out there? There had to be eight or ten of them, and I'm betting that wasn't everybody. And they all had guns. And some pretty big dogs. There's only three of us. Do you want us to get killed? What's the plan, man, cuz this sounds bad to me."

Steve added, "Me, too. Dude, we can't take that place. We should just keep on like we have been. It's working good for us. We got food, booze, drugs, and chicks. What else do we need?"

Alan looked back at his two so-called friends disgustedly. "So, you're okay with those dicks threatening us the other day, huh? You're fine with them pointing guns at us, right? You've got no problem with being a little bitch and tucking your tail and running to hide, is that it? Well, I ain't nobody's bitch. That old man was disrespectful to me and I ain't forgot it. They got us outnumbered? Then let's go find some more bodies. There's got to be other guys around here that we could get to join up with us. We're getting in there somehow. They're gonna pay for how they treated us—with everything they have."

Whether it was the meth making him delusional, or some kind of character flaw that had him believing he was more powerful than he truly was, Alan thought they could breach the defenses of the farm and take the place. Steve and Rich knew it was insane, and not possible, but that wouldn't stop him from trying. That path would have consequences on both sides.

\*\*\*\*

News of the Dotsons possibly joining us very soon was the discussion over supper. With the addition of another nurse, Kate was confident we could handle most any minor to medium medical treatment needed.

"As long as no one needs anything along the lines of open heart surgery, we should be good. If you've ever been in a hospital, you know the nurses know damn near as much as the doctors. I can remove an appendix, do a C-section, set a broken bone, stitch up a cut, and I'm a pretty good diagnostician. It will be great to have another set of eyes, ears, and hands though. I'm worried we haven't seen the worst of the bad yet."

"I'm sure we haven't," Mike replied. "I expect the Glass brothers back any day, and those guys from Luke's place will probably find us sooner or later. I hate to sound like a stuck record, but we need to stay on our toes, gang. It's definitely gonna get worse before it gets better—if it ever does get better."

"Well, I've been thinking about it, and I feel like it's best if my family trades space with Pete and Sara. They can take the upstairs room, and we'll take the basement. That way I can be right there if we have someone who needs to stay in our clinic. The double bed is fine and we'll put the girls on a pallet on the floor."

"No, you won't," Lee said. "You'll let me build them a set of bunk beds."

Kate smiled at him. "Even better. Takes up less floor space. We can make the move as soon as you have those ready then, or if we end up with anyone needing to stay down there, whichever comes first. Thank you, Lee."

Lee returned her smile and gave her a nod. "Anything else anyone needs built that will make things easier, just let me know. I'll build until we run out of supplies, then we'll go find some more."

"Since you mentioned it, Lee," Millie replied, "I think we should move the dining room chairs to the attic or the shed and put some benches at the dining table instead, long ones for the sides and short ones on the ends. We could seat a lot more people at the table that way. With all the leaves in place, that table is huge; we could possibly seat close to two dozen people in there. I'm sure we'll be getting into the summer storm season soon, and we need to think about some alternative eating arrangements. We should probably go ahead and do that for the kitchen table as well. No rush, dear. Whenever you don't have anything else you're working on."

"I'll start on them right after I finish the new bunk beds, Miss Millie."

Millie smiled at Lee, and Kate continued. "Oh, Anne, I forgot to tell you earlier. The e-reader battery needs to be charged. How do we do that with no electricity? I didn't know—"

Bob interrupted her. "Is that a dig at us for not having the solar panels set up yet? I was shot in the leg, you know. Mike was shot in the arm. Can we get a little sympathy around here?"

While those who didn't know Bob as well as we did sat there in stunned silence, Janet punched her husband in the arm. "Ow! And now I have a bruised arm!"

"Stop whining. You're gonna live. It was in the upper eighties today. Fans will make for less cranky people, me being one of them. Ignore him, Kate. He's just acting like a baby."

I was laughing as I got up. "In the meantime, I have something we can charge it with, Kate. Be right back."

I went into the house, ran up to our room, and got out one of the ammo can Faraday cages that held a solar power pack. It was a fifteen thousand mAh power pack that would charge the e-reader to a full battery at least three times from its full capacity. While solar charging on the unit was a slow process, the e-reader would go for weeks on a single charge, so we had plenty of time to build it back to full capacity on the solar side, unless we got power before then. The power plan had kind of gotten pushed down the priority list, so maybe with no other projects going on we could get that started now. I for one would love a real shower, even lukewarm.

While I was gone, Kate had retrieved the e-reader from the basement. She handed it to me, so I took the opportunity to show everyone how the power pack worked. Not much to it, but it did have a power switch to keep it from draining its own battery when not in use. Ryan was watching intently.

"Hey, Anne, would that thing have charged my tablet—you know, if it wasn't a door stop right now?"

Everyone laughed and I nodded at him. "Yep, it would have, hun. I charged my cell, e-reader, and tablet all off one full pack. It's a beast."

"Well, if the world ever turns right side up again, I'm getting one of those. Right after I get a new tablet." He grinned and went back to trying to get every drop of gravy off his plate with a biscuit.

"Alright, what's the plan for the Dotsons coming in? Are you guys going to go get them tomorrow?" I was anxious to meet them.

"I told Jim to let us know what their decision was after he talked to his family. From all the problems they've had, I'm pretty sure they're gonna come in. We'll probably have to tow their RV in here. It's too new to still be running." Monroe looked over at Pete. "You think you can haul a motorhome with the big tractor, Pete?"

Pete considered it, and nodded. "If we go slow, yeah, it should handle it. Are there any big hills between here and there?"

"Nah, this is farmland. It's all pretty flat. It's only about four miles of driving over to his place."

"Then we should be good to go. Just say when. Do you have a spot scoped out already that you want to park it in?"

"Yeah, I think we're gonna set it up on the other side of the car shed. It'll give them a little privacy. Charlotte is a little shy about her leg." Monroe pointed to the spot he was referring to. Pete leaned over to get a good look at it.

"Hmm. Might be tough to get it in there with no engine to drive it. We may have to push it in, and it could damage the front end if we do."

"Son, at this point, a dented bumper is going to be the least of their worries."

"True. So, yeah, no problem. Just let me know when we're a go."

Mike stood up. "Well, I guess since we don't have anything else going on, we should see what we can do about getting some electricity going. We've got a couple of hours of daylight left. Who's in?"

"I definitely am. I don't want anyone accusing me of not doing my part, even if I was shot in the leg." Bob sounded indignant, but then broke out in a huge grin. Janet was shaking her head as she picked up their plates.

"How long are you going to milk that leg wound, Bob?"

"How much longer can I, sugar?" Everyone laughed at that.

"I've got security watch at eight, but I can certainly supervise the process." Ryan stood up and set his plate on the growing pile on the table.

Pete joined them. "Yeah, count me in, too."

At that, the rest of us got up and added our dishes. Ben and Tony had table clearing duty and started carrying everything into the house. Marietta had already gone in and started heating water for the dish-washing team, which was Rusty and Tara that night. We always tried to pair one of the older kids with one of the younger ones.

Mike and crew headed for the shed where they had left the inverters and controllers after testing them. The solar panels were set up to the side of the house facing south, but were not connected to anything electrical. That turned out to be a huge blessing, since the pulse could have fried everything, including the panels, if they had been connected to anything. We had read that a solar panel itself should be inherently resistant to an EMP to some extent. But, if damage occurs, it is likely due to the wires between the solar panel and either the solar charge controller or the inverters. And that's about the extent of my knowledge on that subject, which I overheard Mike telling Russ and Bob right after they had inspected the electrical components. I trusted the guys to get it working. I just wanted a functional fan and a shower.

**\*\*\*\***

Millie and Janet had gone out to the gardens, and they came back with their arms full of baskets with onions, carrots, radishes—yay!—and greens. They called out to the kids in the yard to come help them. Everyone gathered around the table to admire the haul.

"We should probably start putting some of this back. The onions we can just tie up and hang in the root cellar, and the radishes will keep down there for a bit. We'll can some of the carrots, but the greens I'm thinking we may dry some of for soups this winter." Millie seemed to be counting off a list in her head. "Not everyone likes greens, so we can add small amounts to our soups and stews. They won't even know they're in there. You can successfully can greens, but I think they are just so bland done that way—and it takes over an hour to process them. It's not worth burning up that much gas or wood."

I was inspecting the greens. "How will we dry them, Millie? We have no power for the dehydrators. Yet." Ever hopeful, that's me.

"The old-fashioned way. We lay them out on screens and let the sun do the work. Monroe made some up not too long ago, so I could try them out. They take longer than the dehydrator, especially this time of year when it's not so hot, but they work. Once they're dried we can put them in jars or plastic bags and use them whenever we want. In fact, I know a little trick I've been meaning to show you all. Follow me."

We followed her into the kitchen. She took out a zippered plastic bag and a bowl. She put water in the bowl and set it aside. Then she took a couple of leftover biscuits—yes, there were actually a couple of leftovers!—and put them in the bag. She zipped the bag almost closed, leaving about an inch open. Then she pushed the bag down into the water until the biscuits were below the surface. The bag closed around the bread just like we had used the vacuum sealer on it. She zipped the rest of it closed, pulled it out, and dried off the outside. Holding the bag up for us to see, Millie had a huge grin on her face.

"A little trick I learned from my preserving group at church. It doesn't get all the air out, but it definitely gets a bunch of it. Whatever we can do to make food last longer, right?"

This woman never ceased to impress me with her knowledge of alternative methods of doing things. She was better than an e-reader with a hundred books. We oohed and aahed over her results, then walked back outside. I hollered for the kids who were out there.

"Alright, gang, take that haul over to the pump and get it cleaned off. Leave it all out there when you're done, so it can dry a bit before we take it inside. Looks like we're canning tomorrow!"

The kids grabbed the veggies and took them to the pump. We were about to head back to the kitchen to check the dish-washing progress when Rusty came bursting out the back door with the radio in his hand.

"Mom! Dad! They're calling from the front! There's somebody at the gate asking for Uncle Monroe—well, they asked for the owner of the property. He said he was with the sheriff's office!"

Do what? Now what is this all about?

# Chapter 21

The sheriff is an elected official; he has to be reelected every term. His staff, on the other hand, are not. They are hired by the sheriff. If a new sheriff is elected, it is his choice whether or not to keep the deputies and office staff in place at the time of his service. Unless they present a huge problem, the sheriff will many times retain the services of the previous sheriff's staff, if for no other reason than they already know their jobs, and he doesn't have to take the time to find replacements and train them. Tim Miller was on his second sheriff.

When everything went down, Tim was in the office. When he tried to start his patrol car, he knew this was something big. No one else showed up for work, including the sheriff, who lived about twenty miles away. As the day wore on, people came into the sheriff's office, on foot for the most part, trying to find out what was going on. Tim had no idea, and told them as much. When the sun started going down, with no word from anyone, since the radios weren't working either, he knew this was going to last for a while. His place was ten miles away, and he wasn't in any hurry to get home, especially on foot, so he decided to spend the night there. The sheriff had a nice couch in his office. He locked the front door and headed to the back.

He had cleaned out all the leftover lunches in the fridge throughout the day. They weren't his, but the power was out and the food was going to spoil, so someone might as well eat it. There were chips, crackers, cookies, and candy bars in the vending machine. Those might last a little while. There were four five-gallon bottles of water for the dispenser, plus an almost full one already on it. There was a shower in the locker room, but he didn't know how long the water pressure would last. That would be a problem for the toilet as well. He could step out back to take a leak, but the other … Well, he'd have to think about that one.

The biggest thing the place had going for it was the gun racks. There were a half dozen shotguns, both tactical and standard, a couple of M4 carbines, and pistols in multiple calibers, multiple styles. It was almost like the city council had gotten them off the clearance rack somewhere, because there was no rhyme or reason to them. There were, however, many thousands of rounds of ammo for each caliber represented.

The more he thought about it, the more it made sense to him to stay in the sheriff's office. There were supplies in the basement, which was also an emergency shelter. Food, water, blankets, lanterns—everything he'd need to survive. If he rationed it right, he could probably stay there for months without having to leave—once he figured out that bathroom problem. He had nothing at home in the way of supplies. Maybe half a jar of peanut butter and a few slices of cold pizza that probably wasn't so cold now. Yes, he was much better off staying put.

He went down to the basement to see exactly what he had to work with. They hadn't even opened the crates when they were delivered. They'd moved them to the basement and forgotten about them. When he popped the top on the first one he found boxes of MREs. Hundreds of meals, just for him. In the next crate were cases of water in pouches like the kids' drink you stick the straw in. He kept opening the crates, pulling out things he wanted to try or might need soon, like blankets and lanterns, as well as a couple of the MREs. In the last crate, he found stacks of honey buckets—basically, a five-gallon bucket with a liner, a seat, and a lid. He grinned as he pulled one out. *So much for the bathroom problem.* There was a piece of paper with instructions on it inside the bucket. He started to toss it aside, but something caught his eye: "Odor Control & Maintenance." He decided to give it a look.

*In an emergency situation, you may have to use whatever materials you have at your disposal for odor control. The following items can be used:*

*Sawdust: After using the bucket, sprinkle a thin layer of sawdust. This will reduce the odor and still decompose.*

*Cedar Shavings: These work even better, and may provide a more pleasant smell. In a remote area, if sawdust or wood shavings are not available, even dry leaves may help reduce odors.*

*Wood Ash: If your home includes a woodstove, wood ashes can also be sprinkled over waste in the bucket.*

*Straw or Peat Moss: Other recommendations for a bucket additive to keep down odors include chopped straw or even peat moss to encourage the formation of a crust atop the waste.*

*Keep the lid tightly closed when not in use to prevent the spread of germs and disease.*

Tim found a nail sticking out of a board and stuck the note to it. He was pretty sure he wouldn't remember all of that, and he wasn't really sure where he could find any of it, outside of the wood ash. Oh well, he'd worry about that later. He could still use the toilet for now.

He went back upstairs to the sound of someone banging on the front door. Annoyed at the interruption, since he really wanted to try out one of those MREs, he dropped the items he had brought up with him in the break room and went around the corner. Standing at the door were Alan, Rich, and Steve. *Great. Just what I don't need. No way am I letting them in here. Those supplies are mine.* The survival instinct kicks in quickly when you need it.

He went to the door and spoke through the glass. "Hey, fellas. What's up?"

Alan looked at him like he had grown two heads. "What's up? Have you been asleep all day? The world has gone to hell. Let us in, so I don't have to yell through this door."

Tim was shaking his head. "Sorry, Alan, I can't do that. I'm under strict orders to keep this place locked down. Nobody in or out." Not entirely true, but they didn't know that. Or did they?

"Orders from who? Who gives a shit anyway? There's nobody in charge anymore. There's no laws, or cops. You are officially unemployed, Timmy. Now open the fucking door and let us in. I know you got guns in there. God only knows what other sweet stuff you have. We're gonna have some fun now!"

"What makes you think everything won't be back on in the morning? You don't know how long this is going to last, Al."

"Because it ain't just the power, dumbass. It's everything. Nothing modern works. I don't know what the hell it is, but it ain't gettin' fixed tonight, or next week, or next month. Now, are you going to let us in or not?"

Tim stood there weighing the consequences of whatever he was about to do. If he let them in, they would ransack the place, find the supplies in the basement, and take it all. They'd take all the guns and ammo. Sure, they'd probably take him with them, but did he want to go down the path they were heading? What if they were wrong, and things did turn around? He'd be out of a job, probably on the other side of the bars in a jail cell. No, he wasn't willing to take that chance. Not yet.

"I'm sorry, Alan, but I can't. You might be right about the situation, but you might be wrong, too. I need to keep this place secure, at least for a while, and see how everything goes. I need this job, man. Come back in a few days, see how everything is going then."

"Screw you, Tim! I hope you rot and die in your own filth in there! Yeah, we'll be back, *buddy*! Count on it!"

Alan slammed his hand against the door, then turned and stomped off. Rich and Steve had stood there silent the whole time. They looked at Tim, then at each other, shrugged their shoulders, and followed Alan to his truck.

Tim watched them until Alan fired his truck up and sped off. Why was his truck running? Maybe Al was right about what was happening, but Tim wasn't ready to test that theory just yet. No, he was staying put for now. *Al will calm down. Hell, he was probably high and will forget the whole thing when he sobers up. Everything will be back to normal by then.*

****

Tim had been holed up in the sheriff's office for weeks. No other employees showed, including the sheriff, so he had the place to himself. He was bored, since there was no TV or radio, but he had food and shelter, something a bunch of other people apparently didn't have. He stayed out of the front lobby area so no one would know he was there. Some folks came to the door in the first few days, banging and shouting for help. He hid in the back, away from the windows. He reasoned with himself that he couldn't help everyone, so he shouldn't help anyone. If people knew he had food in there, they'd try to get in to take it from him. The only people who knew about the emergency supplies were the ones who worked at the sheriff's department and the city council members who had requisitioned them. He hoped none of them remembered.

After about three weeks, Tim heard a new sound out front—the sound of a key in the door lock. He jumped up from the sofa he had been napping on in a T-shirt and boxers and rushed to the corner to see who was coming in. If they had a key to the door it had to be someone who worked there, or the mayor. It turned out to be both the sheriff and the mayor. He ran back and put his pants on. The boss had arrived.

****

Gary Burns had been the sheriff for over ten years. He was a good, fair man who always had time to listen to the people he served. Angie Hale had been mayor for almost eight years, due to her similar philosophy of listening to those who put her in office. She and Gary worked very well together. There were rumors around town that they had more than just a working relationship, but so what? He had been a widower for the last six years, and she had never married, choosing a career in local politics over family life. Together, they almost always put the people before themselves.

Gary unlocked the door and peered inside. He didn't see or hear anything out of the ordinary, so he proceeded into the lobby.

He turned to Angie. "Are you sure I can't talk you into staying out here until I get the place checked out?"

She nodded firmly. "Yes, Gary. I don't think I'll be any safer outside alone than inside with you. Lead the way."

He held the door for her, then closed and locked it from the inside. He pulled a flashlight from his belt and started toward his office. Just as he got to the corner, Tim stepped out into the light beam. Gary jumped in surprise; Angie screamed.

"You scared the hell out of us! What are you doing here, Tim? How long have you been here? Why were you hiding back here?" Gary peppered him with questions. Tim had answers.

"Hey, Sheriff! Man, am I glad to see you! It's crazy out there, ain't it. I've been here the whole time. I was here when everything went off, and I knew we had valuable stuff in here, like the guns and ammo, so I felt like it was my duty to ... you know ... guard the place. I was hiding because I didn't want anybody to know I was here. People were banging on the door at the beginning, looking for help, and I didn't feel like I had the authority to dispense the emergency supplies from the basement, so I just stayed out of sight. I've just been keeping the place secure, hoping you'd show up soon, and you're finally here! Where have you been all this time?"

While Tim was going through his speech, Gary kept walking through the offices, looking in to see the state of the place. When he got to the breakroom, he found piles of MREs sorted by meal. He looked at Tim with a raised eyebrow.

"I see you're not missing any meals while those people outside starve. Is that what you believed was the purpose of those supplies, Deputy?"

"No, Sheriff, but like I said, I didn't feel like I had the say so over them, so I just waited in here for someone to show up who did. Madam Mayor, I believe that's you."

Angie had remained silent during their conversation thus far. She replied, "Yes, that would be me, Deputy Miller. I would like an immediate tally of just what we have left in here that we can share with the community. There are people starving to death in their homes as we speak. There does not appear to be any help coming any time soon, so we need to bring the people together and help each other. It's past time these supplies were distributed to the community. If this isn't an emergency, I don't know what is."

"Yes, ma'am, it sure is an emergency. Have y'all been able to find out anything about what's going on? There's a wind-up radio in the stuff downstairs, but I didn't hear anything but static on it when I tried it out. Is there any news?"

Gary was still looking around as he spoke. "Yes, we know what happened, but we don't know who did it or why. The only information we've been able to get is from ham radios. Someone detonated a nuke in the atmosphere, which caused an EMP over pretty much the entire country."

"A *nuke*? Are we at war? Is there radiation out there? What's an EMP?" Tim sounded almost hysterical.

"Simmer down, Tim. It was high enough up that there appears to have been little to no radiation associated with it. To my knowledge, we are not at war—yet. We still don't know who's responsible. EMP stands for electromagnetic pulse. It's like a lightning strike hundreds of miles wide, and fries everything connected to the power grid, as well as anything with a computer chip in it. Pretty much nothing modern works now. Were there packing lists in with the supplies, that gave us a count of everything? Have you kept up with what you've used? I appreciate you keeping an eye on the place, Tim, but we need to get this stuff ready to hand out. I've spent the last couple of weeks just going from house to house, farm to farm, and seeing how people are holding up. Some of them are in pretty bad shape. The folks in the country are better, because they have gardens, and they know how to hunt and fish. City folks don't know any of that stuff."

"How have you been getting around, Sheriff? My patrol car is dead."

"I've got an old 1950 pickup I restored years ago. Had it stored in my garage. I'd run it once a month, just out on my property, so it was good to go."

"Then, why didn't you come into town, come here to check on things?"

"I was trying to every day. But every day someone else needed my help. I had to bury a whole lot of folks. Mr. Walker's pacemaker stopped. Mrs. Evans couldn't keep her insulin cold. The retirement home just outside of town was the worst. It took us a good week to get all those folks buried properly. I just hoped everything here was still secure, because I was too tired to come on in by the end of the day. I finally got to Angie—er, Mayor Hale's house two days ago. We checked on her neighbors and had to lay a couple more to rest. There was a young woman who was scheduled for dialysis the day of the pulse. She didn't make it. Another woman went into labor and hemorrhaged. She bled to death, and we found the baby beside her, a little boy. I'm guessing her husband was at work and never got home. It's been pure hell."

Tim looked shocked. "Man, Sheriff, that's awful. I guess you just don't think about all the ways we depend on electricity until you don't have it anymore."

"No, you don't, which is why we want to get these supplies out to the people who can use them. The folks outside of town, they seem to be faring much better. We should concentrate on the ones close by. We need to figure out a way to let everyone know we are going to be handing stuff out as soon as possible."

"Sheriff, I understand wanting to help people, but I gotta ask: do you have any idea how long this is going to last?"

"No, I don't. I'm thinking it could be months, possibly years. What difference does that make?"

"Well, if you hand this stuff out to whoever comes by, and everything isn't back on, what then? Did you just prolong the inevitable? This was enough supplies for a thousand people for a week. There's that many at least in town. So, what happens next week, and the week after that? Will it do any good now?"

Gary took in everything Tim said. He was surprised at the forethought the man had given the situation. Or was he hoping to keep the food for himself? One way to find out.

"So, do you have a plan as to the best way to utilize these items, Tim? Just keeping them stored here is not helping anyone. How do you suggest we proceed?"

Angie started to protest, but Gary held his hand up to her with a slight shake of his head, in a gesture that said "Let's see what he has to say."

Tim looked confident as he replied. "Well, Sheriff, I think we should just leave things the way they are for now. I mean, I've been keeping this place locked down—no one has gotten in until today. I can keep on staying here, keeping everything secure. Of course, I'll need supplies to do that …"

Angie blew up. "How did I know you'd respond with something like that, Deputy? Have you already done the math and figured out how long you can live off those rations by yourself? Gary, this is ridiculous. We have to get this stuff out to the townsfolk! Why are you even talking to him like he has a say in this matter? He doesn't! As far as I'm concerned, he has been paid in full for services rendered for the past three weeks with food, water, and shelter. That's more than most of those folks out there have had. He can have another week's worth in payment for helping get the supplies distributed, and the guns and ammo loaded in your truck. That's it. The rest belongs to the people!"

Tim looked at Gary. "Sheriff, I know what it sounds like, but there's more at stake here than just the food. Here, we can keep this place secure. We've got bulletproof glass out front, metal doors out back. The guns and ammo are locked up tight in the cage. Nobody is getting in there without a key or a big-ass truck. Plus, is there no law and order now? Is it every man for himself, and the bad guys get the run of the land? Are we not supposed to protect and serve, whether we get paid or not? I don't think we should just go home and hope somebody fixes everything before only the evil remain. No, someone needs to be here, to represent the law. I'm volunteering to do that. No one else showed up in all this time. I was here."

"You were here hoarding all these supplies for yourself! The only person you were serving was *you!*" Angie practically spat the words out as she pointed a finger at him.

Gary waited for her to get it out of her system, then nodded. "You're right, Angie, we do need to do something for the townsfolk, but he's right too. We need some kind of representation that there is still law enforcement. We need it now more than ever.

How many people have we talked to that told us they had been attacked, robbed, or beaten by gangs already? And this just got started. What's it going to look like in another month? Some people still had food, or were able to find some. The grocery stores have all been looted, there's nothing left. Now is when it gets really bad. Hungry people are desperate people. I'll take you to your place, with a week's worth of supplies, then I'll come back here and stay with Tim. We can go out on a rotation and check folks, maybe leave some stuff with the ones who are the worst off. We also need to see if there are any houses that haven't been checked that belonged to folks who never made it back. I know we saw some standing open, so that may be a pipe dream, but we can look. Unless you have a better idea."

Angie stared at him, then Tim, then back to Gary. Her expression softened a bit. "I do. I'm staying too. We can work together to come up with a plan to keep the town as stable as possible. You guys can bunk in the offices and I'll set up a cot in the basement."

"Angie, I don't think—" Gary started to protest, but she shook her head.

"No, Gary, you're not talking me out of this. This is the best plan. We have plenty of time to figure out how best to help the most people since we don't have anything else to do. Plus, we've only checked on the folks on my side of town. What about north and east? We need to know who needs help and where they are.

We also need to figure out something for the foreseeable future. We need to talk to the farmers—not the ones with the little quarter-acre gardens, but the big farms. We need food for a lot of people for the long term, and that's where it's going to come from. We'll have to come to some sort of agreement with them, something in exchange for the food. We can't expect them to feed everyone for free. The people who are able to will be expected to help work the fields in payment for some of the crops. We need to set up medical facilities, and figure out how to get the doctors and nurses to them. They can be paid in food. Money is worthless. We need to start bartering for services and commodities. We need to secure and protect our community and its inhabitants. Everyone is just sitting around waiting for everything to come back on; waiting for someone to fix this. We can help ourselves, but we need to get our butts in gear. It's spring. It's planting time. It's planning time, right now."

Angie had been talking non-stop, planning their future, the town's future, and it was easy to see it succeeding. She smiled to herself, and Gary saw it and grinned at her.

"Been planning this for a while then?"

"Actually, I just came up with that while I was saying it. And it sounds like a damn fine plan."

"And that's why you're the mayor." He gave her a nod and a wink. "Alright, I guess we have a plan then. Tim, let's get to rearranging in here. You can set up a cot in the break room. I'll take the sofa in my office. Unless you want us to haul it down to the basement for you, Angie."

"No, a cot is fine for me. You keep your couch."

"Great. Let's get busy."

Tim didn't look pleased. He turned away without a word and headed down to the basement. As he walked away, Angie looked at Gary. "Is he going to be a problem?"

"No. First sign of trouble, he's out the door, with nothing. He'll do what he's told or do without."

"I hope you're right, Sheriff."

Gary thought to himself, *Me, too.*

# Chapter 22

When the sheriff showed up at the gate, we were all concerned and curious. Was it a "just here to see how you folks are doing" visit, or a "we got some news from DC you need to hear" call, or the one we feared the most, a "you're going to have to give up all your stuff for the greater good" nightmare like we had heard about on the ham radio that night. None of us wanted to think that the sheriff, an elected official and the highest authority in the county, would capitulate to that mindset. Only one way to find out.

There was nothing that was going to keep most of us away, so we walked en masse to the gate. Millie stayed back with the kids. We armed ourselves with both sidearms and rifles, not knowing what to expect, but curious to see what the man had to say. Depending on what that was, this could be a long, interesting night.

****

Sheriff Burns knew where the Warren farm was located but had not been out that way intentionally looking for it in a couple of years. He was surprised at how well camouflaged the gate was now. He had been working his way down the road the better part of the afternoon. He found a few people still in their homes, but most of them were empty. The ones who were toughing it out had small farms with livestock and gardens. They reported being robbed of both, to the point that they had taken to guarding their properties day and night to try to stop the thefts. The Glass brothers' names came up more than once as the suspected culprits, as they had made the rounds in the area looking for "help." It was no coincidence they had shown up at their neighbors' doorsteps and then a day or so later the garden had been worked over, or some chickens or rabbits came up missing. He would definitely have to pay them a visit when he got back to town.

He stopped on the road and looked long and hard at the foliage. It was about fifteen minutes before he finally found the gate. *Good work, Monroe. Hopefully you and yours are safe inside.*

\*\*\*\*

The sheriff arrived at the gate and yelled out, "Hello! Anybody out there? It's Sheriff Burns, looking for Monroe Warren!"

Brian and Ryan were in the holes; Brian radioed in what the sheriff had said, but they did not acknowledge him, nor reveal their locations. Russ told them to hold tight; we were on our way.

We got to the gate and Monroe went through with Mike and Bob flanking him, as well as the dogs. The two biggest, the German Shepherd-Rottie mixes Max and Roxie, had taken it upon themselves to be alongside whoever went through the gate. The rest of us waited inside the perimeter, but in full view of the sheriff. Monroe walked up with his hand extended.

"Evening, Gary. What brings you out this way?"

Gary was visibly relieved to see Monroe, though he was looking cautiously at his security detail. He shook Monroe's hand. "Hey, Monroe. Good to see you, and good to see that you're well. Might I have the pleasure of being introduced to your companions?" He didn't seem intimidated, just curious.

"This is my nephew, Bob, and Mike is a friend. The rest back there are friends and family who are staying here for the duration. What can we do for you?"

"Glad to see you've brought a bunch of folks in to weather this storm together. I'm sure I don't have to tell you that everything has kind of gone crazy out there. Angie, Mayor Hale, thinks we need to bring the community together and help each other get through this mess. She's asked me to call on the farmers who have large pieces of land that can be farmed for a community food bank."

"Well, as you can see, we have a small community here now." He gestured behind himself, taking us all in. "We're feeding and housing over two dozen people, and actually looking to bring in another dozen or so. I'm not sure we'll have food to spare for feeding that many more people."

"Oh, I think you might have misunderstood me, Monroe. We're hoping you'll plant more crops than you already have, more than what you need to maintain your people here now. We're looking for new food sources, not any you're currently using. We'd like you to till up and sow as much of your land as possible."

"I'm not sure my people can work that much land. We're pretty busy taking care of all the day-to-day chores that need doing right now for us. I don't know how we'd be able to add more work to the load we already have, which includes security watches. We've already had trouble here, and at the Callen place. Not to sound petty or anything, but there doesn't seem to be anything in that situation that would benefit us."

Gary held his hands up. "No, no, that's not what I was asking for. Sorry, I'm not doing a very good job here. Let me lay it out. We need food to feed hundreds of people in town. You have the land. In town we have access to gas storage tanks, seed and fertilizers, and people to work the land. You provide the space and the instructions, we'll do the rest. We'll also want to figure out some kind of trade for some of your livestock. We already have a couple of butchers lined up. We're finding out who all has skills that could benefit the community, like sewing, blacksmithing, even cooking—you wouldn't believe how many young people can't actually cook. We are going to set up a medical area so we can have doctors and nurses there to offer care to those who need it. In exchange for your part, you will have access to the medical facility and probably anything else you may want or need. Does that sound like something you would be able to help us with?"

Monroe was quiet, mulling over what the sheriff had said. Mike leaned in and whispered something in his ear. Nodding, he replied, "I'm going to have to talk to my folks about this first, Gary. I don't know how I feel about a bunch of strangers traipsing through my place to work a garden, seeing everything we have, thinking they might want some of it, or all of it. We've spent a lot of time making this place invisible and securing it as much as we can. If you hadn't known where it was, would you have been able to find it?"

Gary shook his head. "No, sir, I sure wouldn't. But, I don't think—"

Monroe stopped him. "We ain't willin' to take any chances with the safety of our people. We've got too much at stake here. Come back in a couple of days. We'll talk more then."

"Can I come back to talk again tomorrow? Every day that goes by is another day someone goes without food in town. It's getting pretty desperate there. We have emergency rations in the shelter at the office, but that won't last long. We need to get moving on this right away if we can."

"Alright then, tomorrow. We'll talk tonight. You'll have my answer when you come back."

The men shook hands all around and Gary headed back to his truck. He started it up, waved at everybody, and headed back toward town. Monroe, Mike, and Bob came back inside and closed and locked the gate. As they were sinking the big post, Monroe kept walking toward the house. The rest of us followed.

"Group meeting up at the house. We need to talk about this right now."

****

Most people in this country are clueless as to how to survive without power, or grocery stores, or the internet. A hundred and fifty years ago there was no such thing as electricity. People used lamps and candles for lights, and fireplaces and wood-burning stoves to cook and heat their homes. They worked hard all day on crops and livestock for food, as well as barter items to get the things they couldn't or didn't grow, like flour and sugar. They hunted and butchered their meat themselves, preserving it with methods no longer in use today, for the most part. They made their own clothes or traded with someone who possessed that skill. There were general stores, but they held very little in the way of "prepared" food—maybe some jerky, or a few canned goods. The stores would trade with people for items they might not have were it not for their bartering, so they could offer those bartered items to other customers—say a bushel of apples for a bolt of cloth. Then someone would trade two dozen eggs for half a bushel of those apples. Yes, there was money, but there was quite possibly just as much purchased through barter as with gold or silver.

As far as knowledge and experience, people back then learned how to do the things they needed to do every day to exist, such as farming, cooking, hunting, or sewing, from their parents and grandparents. If someone wanted to learn a special trade, like boot making, they would work for a person who had that skill or craft, many times for room and board, just to learn how it was done. They could then use that skill to make goods they could use to barter for things like food, if they lived in a city and didn't have the means to grow it. They didn't look stuff up in books. They learned by doing, as part of living in that world.

While we didn't know how to do everything they did then, we did have the resources to learn it. If Millie or Monroe didn't know it, we could look it up in one of the hundreds of reference books I had saved on the e-readers. We had already started canning meats for the winter. Bill and Ryan proved to be above-average hunters and were good for at least a deer or a wild turkey a week. We had brought male and female together in the farm animals, so our herds and flocks would grow. We were turning a small "hobby" farm into a small business without even realizing it. We knew that places like ours would be an integral part of any rebuilding that happened in our little part of the world. Food was in the top three most-needed and valuable resources, and we had the capacity, knowledge, and manpower to produce quite a bit.

We didn't have a lot in the "need" category right then, but at some point we probably would. Fuel, candles, seeds—in case ours weren't viable for some reason—as well as clothes, shoes—or shoe repair at least; these things meant we weren't completely self-sufficient. Though we could probably learn how to do most things, being able to barter for them would save us the time of learning it, as well as the time it would take to do it. Surely there were people in town who had skills they could barter for food, besides actually working the land. Not everybody was physically able to do that kind of work, but they could possibly possess other skills or knowledge they could offer instead.

Still, the idea of letting the world know where we were, even our small part of the world, was a frightening thought. Letting people in our gate, to walk through the yard, with all of our buildings and gardens and livestock there in plain view, with no way to hide or disguise it? I, for one, was not on board with that. If that made me a shitheel, so be it. We had worked hard to get this place set up for us and the people we loved and trusted. It was hard enough to keep it all safe when people didn't know what we had. How much harder would it be when some of them found out?

I voiced all that at the meeting. "If there was a way to give them access to only the part that had the fields we were planting for them and nothing else, that would be one thing. The problem with that is if we cut a new road or entrance for that purpose, then we have a new security problem. Right, Mike?"

He nodded in my direction. "Yep. You nailed it, Anne. We were talking about the exact same thing on the way back from the meeting with the sheriff. The only way this can work without anyone seeing this place is with a new entrance. Even then, we'd want the fields they were working as far from this section as possible. I haven't been much further back than the other wood shed. How far away could we plant and keep the workers from seeing the place, Monroe?"

"This property is a long tract. We've got about four hundred feet across and about two thousand feet front to back. We lose probably a hundred to a hundred and fifty feet of that in the foliage we've let grow up. We use about four to five acres for everything up here. That would leave us with a good ten acres to play with for this project. The upside is there's a rise that would keep anyone from seeing all this from back there. The downside is there's nothing to stop any of them from walking up the rise."

"Could we put up a fence?" Russ asked. "I know fences only keep honest men honest, but is it an option? Four strands of barbed wire could be a deterrent."

"We could, but then we are going to have to keep an eye on that area as well. What else could we do?"

Mike had a question. "Who owns the land just east of this?"

"That'd be Matt and Nick's family. Why? What you got in mind?"

"You think they'd let us use their property to cut the access?"

"I don't think they'd mind at all, since we're keeping their kids safe and fed." Monroe laughed at his own comment, and the rest of us joined him. Reasons to laugh had been in short supply the last few days.

"Okay, here's what I'm thinking," Mike continued. "We come in from their property, as far back as possible. No one can see this place through the tree line. I know, I've walked it. We cut the access road in back there. Yes, Russ, we need to start immediately on a cross section of fence, just on the other side of the ridge there. Then, we drag the trees we cut down for the road up and pile them up against that side of the fence. Another deterrent, and it hides the fence and makes it look like the trees were just dropped from other land clearing. I don't know that it will keep anybody out who really wants through, but it'd be a lot of work for someone who should already be drag-ass tired from working the fields. What do you guys think?"

Nods, smiles, and thumbs up from the group were the answer. Monroe called for quiet. "Everybody here has a vested interest in this place, so everybody has a right to speak. Does anybody have any opposition to us helping out the folks in town this way? I know some of you have felt guilty for being here safe and fed while other people have been going without." He glanced at Sara, who gave him a slight smile in return. "This is something we can do to help, without putting our people or this place in jeopardy—hopefully. Is there anything we've missed or forgotten that you can think of? Now's the time to speak up."

Everyone was looking at each other, but no one had anything more to add until Luke raised his hand.

"I would suggest when we get some more campers in here, we kind of line them up on this side of the rise. That would block the view from that side as well."

Mike grinned at him. "Excellent idea, man. Make it look like a trailer park on this side. Much harder to see around. I love it."

Monroe stood up. "Then we're all in agreement. We'll get started first thing tomorrow."

# Chapter 23

Jim Dotson had hurried back to his family to share with them what Monroe had proposed. The more he thought about what they had discussed, the more sense it made to him—and the angrier he got. The idea that someone might try to take or harm one of his girls made him so mad he saw red. He ran up the steps and into the house. He dropped the rabbits on the kitchen table and called for his wife.

"Charlotte, honey? You in here? Where is everybody?" He looked around and was immediately concerned when he didn't see or hear any of his family. He raced to each bedroom, calling out their names. He was just about to go into full-on panic mode when he heard talking coming up from the basement. He rounded the corner to see his wife, daughters, and granddaughter coming through the basement door, the girls' arms loaded with home-canned goods.

"Jim? Is that you running around up here? What's the matter?"

Jim ran to his family and wrapped them in a group hug before stepping back and scolding them. "Why wasn't anyone watching the front? The door was unlocked. Anybody could have just walked

259

in here! And what were you doing going down those stairs, honey? You could have tripped, fallen, and broken your neck."

Charlotte told the girls to set their jars down on the table next to the rabbits and put her left hand on her hip while the right steadied her on a cane.

"I wanted them to bring a few things up so we don't have to keep going up and down the stairs. I'm sorry about the front not being guarded, but we were only down there about ten minutes, Jim. What could happen that fast?"

"I'll show you. Follow me. Everybody."

Jim walked to the door, took his watch off, and handed it to Shannon. "Once I get on the other side of the gate, start timing me. Y'all wait here."

He walked down the driveway to the gate. He wanted to show them exactly how it would happen, so he climbed the fence. Once there, he yelled back to the house, "Okay, darlin', start timing!"

He climbed the fence and walked back toward them. The driveway was about five hundred feet long. He walked at a pretty brisk pace, but not running. When he stepped up on the porch, he hollered, "Time!"

Shannon looked at the watch, then back to her grandfather. "Two minutes, Grandpa."

He looked at his wife. "Two minutes, honey. Had I been running, like someone who was trying to get here as quickly as possible, maybe one minute or less. In the remaining seven or eight minutes they would have walked through the front door, found you all together in the basement, and I don't even want to think about what could have transpired before I got here. Bad things happen fast. We can't stop being vigilant for a second."

Carrie put her arm around her mother's shoulder. "I was supposed to be on watch. It's my fault. I'm sorry, Dad. It won't happen again. It's just really hard to keep an eye on everything, and get the things done in here we need to do …"

Jim nodded. "Yes, sweetie, it's very hard for just the five of us to take care of and secure this place. Honestly, it's impossible. Let's go inside. We need to talk about what happened while I was out hunting."

Jim had pretty much made up his mind while he was walking home that they needed to take Monroe up on his offer. Since he had gotten back, events had sealed the deal for him. Now he just needed to talk his wife and daughters into leaving their home. *Good luck with that, buddy.*

\*\*\*\*

After hours of talking, arguing, crying, and finally planning, they decided as a family that moving to the farm was indeed the best option for them for the foreseeable future. The girls were devastated at the thought of leaving their home, but Jim assured them that he could get back on foot in about thirty minutes if needed. He was relatively sure that once they left the house it would be open season on whatever they left behind for the scavengers, so he told his family to take anything they didn't want to lose. They spent the rest of the evening packing clothes into anything they could find—Jim reminded them to take the winter stuff as well, just in case—as well as all the canned goods they had put up, and loading it all into the motorhome. When that was done, they went to the garden and pulled everything that was ready, loading it into baskets which also went into the camper. When they had finished, there was barely any open space in the motorhome.

"Jim, how is this going to work? We have so much stuff in here, there's no place to sit, much less sleep. Do we have to take all of it now? Our house isn't far from the Warrens—surely we could use someone's truck to come back if we needed some of this stuff. Winter clothes? It's May. We won't need winter stuff for at least five or six months. Surely things will be back to normal by then. I really think we should leave most of this stuff here and just come back if we need it."

Jim shook his head. "Char, you need to look at this like we may never come back here. Once we leave, there's no one to watch the place, so anybody can come in here, see we've left, and take the place apart looking for anything of value we might have left behind. They could burn it to the ground out of spite. It won't be safe to come back here for anything, and there's no guarantee anything would still be here if we did. Monroe has lots of storage space—barns, sheds, garages—so we'll have places to put the things we aren't using when we get there. The food will go into their food stores. They cook for the group, so we don't even have to worry about keeping those supplies in the camper. This will just be for sleeping, and if we need to get away for some quiet time. They have a small community set up and they want to expand and bring in more people. It will be much safer there, especially for you and the girls."

"Why are you so worried about us? Did you hear something you haven't told us?"

Jim had intentionally left out the story about the attempted abduction of Casey Callen, hoping to shield them from some of the ugliness this new world was serving up. He could see he would have to tell them now, so they would understand his urgency to get them relocated to a safer place. Once he had related the horror of that situation to his family, he could tell by the shocked looks on their faces that despicable acts like the ones already being perpetrated had not crossed their minds. Normal people don't go out of their way to hurt others. Living in the country had sheltered them from the ugliest scenarios the pulse had caused.

Knowing what the world was like now gave them a sense of urgency to get moving that they hadn't had before. They spent the rest of the evening finalizing their packing. More than once

Charlotte broke down at the thought of leaving her home. They had bought the place right after they got married and had the house built custom for them.

"I can't believe we might never see it again. This is the only home our girls have ever known. Are you sure this is the best way to go?"

"Yes, honey, I'm sure. After what Monroe told me, we've been damn lucky to have not had any more trouble than we have so far. The Glass brothers are angels compared to the guys they ran into at the Callen place. We need the safety of their numbers. Things are going to get worse. Much worse. We need them. They need us. We need to do this."

Charlotte nodded reluctantly and dried her eyes. "Okay then. No more boo-hooing. First thing in the morning, go let them know that we're moving in. It will be good to see Millie and Monroe again. I just hope we can make it work."

"We'll make it work. We have to make it work. Our girls' lives depend on it."

\*\*\*\*

The tractor was able to pull the motorhome, but it was very slow going. By the time they got it back the next day, it was well into the afternoon. Everyone was exhausted once we'd finished stowing the food they'd brought in the root cellar—which was definitely at maximum capacity at this point—and the extra clothing and personal supplies in one of the trailers we'd brought. With everything out, there was less weight, and Pete was able to push the camper where Monroe had designated for them—close to the outhouse, but not too close. With a portable tank for their black water that could be hauled to the outhouse to empty, Charlotte and the girls were given the privacy of their own bathroom.

The arrival of two available women caused a bit of excitement among the single men. Almost immediately it seemed they weren't as scruffy or gamey as they had been the day before. Even the younger boys appeared to be a bit cleaner, what with a teenage girl in the place. Ben and Rusty actually asked Janet to cut their hair, and when the Thompson boys heard there was a potential barber, they requested a trim as well. When Mike, Bill, and Ryan lined up, Bob started teasing the lot of them.

"Well, look at all you fellas wantin' to get beautified all of a sudden. You'd think there was a Sadie Hawkins dance coming up or somethin'. You do know the world has gone to shit, right? Why you all so worried about what you look like? It couldn't have anything to do with our new arrivals, now could it? Y'all are pathetic. You'd think you never saw a gal before."

Janet gave him the stink eye. "You might think about some personal grooming yourself, dear. Your hair is getting a bit long, and apparently you've lost your razor in the move."

"Honey, it's the end of the world. No one shaves in the end of the world. They do good to wash up from time to time. We've got more important things to worry about than shaving."

Janet looked at the three clean-shaven men waiting for a haircut. "Apparently that doesn't apply to everyone. Only married men."

Monroe rounded the corner just then, clean shaven as well. Janet looked at her uncle, then her husband. "Apparently it only applies to you, then."

The haircut crew laughed, Monroe looked confused, and Bob just got in line behind Ryan. Ryan turned to him with a smirk. Bob shot him a look that could have taken out a small town.

"Don't say one damn word, Lawton."

They all lost it then, and the three men all held up their pinky fingers in Bob's direction. Bob responded with his own finger gesture.

Even though he didn't know what was going on, Monroe grinned at them. "When you fellas are done getting purty we need to work the Dotsons into the security schedule, Mike. Not Charlotte or the girl, but Jim and his daughters are all excellent shooters. They're almost enough for another team by themselves. They brought food that would have lasted them damn near a year, so we don't even have to worry about planting anything else just yet. Jim, Ashley, and Carrie will help with the hunting, too." The last comment was directed at the Lawtons, since they had pretty much assumed the hunting duties, leaving others free to perform other tasks. Ryan perked up and a huge grin spread across his face.

"They hunt, too? Oh man, I know I'm falling in love now."

"Easy, little brother. Getting a haircut ain't gonna make you pretty. Your face still looks like you're getting over the chicken pox. You might scare the hell out of them."

"Pfft. Just gives me character. Makes me look bad ass."

Bob put in, "If by 'bad ass' you mean it looks bad and you're an ass, then yes, yes it does."

"Whatever, Pinky."

Ryan turned his back on Bob as the rest of the men, including Monroe, busted out laughing again. Janet had not yet heard her husband referred to by the new nickname and looked questioningly at him. He just shook his head vigorously, as if to say, "Drop it, honey. Don't ask."

Mike got control of himself. "I'll give them a couple of days to get settled, then we'll move them into the rotation. Do they have a preference of whether they are together or not? I really think Carrie should stay back. I don't want to risk anything happening to our new nurse."

"Me either, and I've tried to tell her that myself, but she's adamant. I think they're worried about earning their keep here, which is horse shit and I've told them that, too. Maybe we could come up with a new addition to the detail that keeps her, Kate, and Millie close to the house. Maybe watching the new fence line the guys are putting up. Yeah, while you fellas are getting all trimmed up, Russ and the rest of them are running new fence. I reckon you're allowed a bye, since most of you just came off watch, but make sure you go check to see if they need any help when you're done. Pete is on the tractor cutting the new path behind the Thompson place where you marked it, so you should probably go check his progress as well. Matt, since she's about done with you, you hustle back there and check on him. I didn't want him to go without a bodyguard, but he said he wanted to get started on it before it got dark, and already had the tractor out from moving the motorhome in, so he went on."

Mike looked concerned. "No, he should not have gone without someone to watch his back. Janet, I'll catch up with you later on the haircut. I don't want him alone. He's barely learned to fire a gun, and he sure wouldn't hear anybody coming in on him over that tractor."

With that, Mike headed toward the house. Bill stepped out of line and followed him. "Wait up, Mike. I'll go with you. I'm sure there's nothing to worry about, but just in case …"

"Okay, I'll meet you at the new fence. Let me get my stuff."

Ryan called after them, "You guys need me to come with you?"

Mike shook his head. "Nah, I think we can handle it. You need to stay here and let Janet see what she can do about making you not so scary looking. I'm sure she does great cutting hair, but the rest of you … Well, she won't have much to work with."

Bill slapped him on the back and snickered. Ryan picked up a dirt clod and hurled it after them. They side-stepped it and kept going. Ryan mumbled under his breath, "Assholes. No brotherly love here." Then he yelled after them, "I don't have to take this kind of abuse! You're gonna miss me when I'm gone! Someday!"

Bill turned and walked backward, antagonizing his little brother as he went. "How can I miss you when you won't leave?"

He laughed, and turned back toward the bunkhouse to grab his guns and pack. They weren't expecting any trouble, but they wanted to be ready, just in case.

They weren't ready.

# Chapter 24

Clay and Jay Glass had done alright hitting up the people in the area for help. While not everyone had donated to their food fund, a lot had, and some had been good for more than one round of supplies. Two times was pretty much the limit of the neighbors' generosity, however. After that, they got comments like "maybe you fellas should try hunting or fishing." Jay was open to that. He had even talked to more than one person about them possibly teaching the guys how to clean game. Clay, on the other hand, was more interested in what he could get without that much work.

The Glass family was the result of a system that rewarded individuals for not being productive members of society. Rhonda Glass had been "disabled" after a stack of cases of plastic bowls toppled over on her two years earlier at a warehouse store. That just happened to coincide with the government assistance she was receiving for being a single mother running out, as Jay was just about to turn eighteen. She had never worked a regular job and nor had her sons. They didn't know how to take care of themselves because they had never had to do it. Uncle Sam had provided their income.

They lived in a small trailer park where the rent was cheap. The owner, Keith Bilton, had been harassing Rhonda for the rent money for two weeks. She had told him more than once that she couldn't pay him until she got her disability check, and with everything shut down she had no idea when that would be. He told her she had until the end of the month, then she was out unless she figured out some way to pay. So now, besides trying to get food, they needed to get their hands on some money as well. None of them realized yet that paper money had no value anymore.

Clay had been scoping out houses where there had been no answer from inside when they knocked asking for food. He hadn't had to break into any yet, though he chose to try at the Dotson home, only because he knew they were sitting on a buttload of food they were being stingy with. He was sure the Warren place was a goldmine of supplies, but there were just too many of them with guns in there. There was no way just he and his brother could get in and out of there. Plus, it would have been a lot of work. No, they would work the empty houses first.

They starting breaking into any house where no one answered their knock. They took all the food they could find. Then they rummaged through closets, drawers, and medicine cabinets, looking for valuables and prescription meds. They were rewarded with some cash but mostly a whole lot of guns and ammo. They took it all without knowing that was one of the new currencies.

They siphoned gas out of any vehicle they found sitting; they had five-gallon cans piled up under their trailer.

Keith had let them use his old pickup, which was still running, in exchange for them keeping gas in it and a percentage of whatever they looted. They gave him half the cash, about a quarter of the food, all the live animals they had stolen—since he knew how to clean them and they didn't—but none of the weapons. Even Clay had figured out that, at some point, they were going to have to start taking from people who refused to share what they had with their neighbors. They'd need the guns for that. In a world where there was no longer government assistance, or factories making food and clothes, it was the strongest and smartest who would survive. Those who were willing to do whatever they had to in order to get what they needed. Clay intended to be a survivor. His brother had no choice but to be one as well. Their momma had taken care of them their whole lives; they'd take care of her now, no matter what they had to do to make that happen.

****

It was purely a coincidence that the Glass brothers ran into Alan and his crew, and it was ironic that it happened at the Dotson house. Over Jay's objections, Clay had wanted to scope the place out, to see if there was a way to breach the house, or at least the basement, without being seen.

"Jay, I'm telling you, they are sitting on a mountain of food in there. That old lady can cook, and she can put up what she cooks and grows. It ain't fair, them havin' all that and not sharin' with others. It ain't neighborly. Plus, I guarantee they got piles of guns and ammo. Old man Dotson is known all over the county for his huntin' skills. We've about run through all the empty places out here. We're gonna have to start makin' folks share with us."

"That ain't right, Clay. Why should they give us their stuff? They gotta eat too. Why don't we try huntin', or fishin'? I know how to fish and how to clean 'em."

"Because Momma hates fish, or have you forgotten that? If you want to eat it, that's fine, but we still need meat for her. And that home-canned venison old lady Dotson gave us was awesome. She wouldn't have given us that if she didn't have a whole bunch more stored up. Now c'mon, let's check the place out."

Jay followed his brother up to the gate. Clay had gotten his hands on a nice set of binoculars on one of his "supply runs," which he pulled out to get a better look at the house. He didn't see any movement outside, but it was just getting daylight, so it was hard to see that far. He was just about to climb the fence when Jay whispered, "Do you hear something? I think I hear a truck or something."

Clay picked up on the sound his brother had heard. Just as he was about to tell Jay to hide, a truck rounded the corner and caught them in its headlights. Rich Hawkins jumped out of the passenger side with a pistol pointed at them while Alan was screeching to a halt.

"Hold it right there, fellas. Keep those hands where we can see them. What you boys doin' out here so early?"

Clay counted two more in the truck, getting out through both doors, armed as well; they were outnumbered. He held his hands out to the sides of his body. Jay mimicked his brother's stance.

"Just checking this place out to see if there's anyone living there. We've run out of food, and most of the houses out here have already been picked over. This was the next one in line for us. How 'bout you guys? What brings you out this way?"

By then, Alan had gotten out and walked up to take over. "Same thing. We need supplies. So, you live around here? You know the folks that live up there?" He motioned toward the house with his head.

"We live the other side of town. We know them by name, ya know, just to say hi in passin' if we see them in town. You fellas live around here? I don't reckon I've seen you around before."

"We're staying with some friends that live out this way, the Callens. Actually, they aren't there. Not sure where they were when it all went down, but we knew them before so we didn't figure they'd mind if we crashed at their place. So, if you know these folks, any idea if they're home, or what they might have up there? We're running low on food where we're staying."

"Well, old lady—I mean, Mrs. Dotson—she's crippled, so she don't get out much, but she has a nice garden every year, and Mr. Dotson is a big hunter. She cans all kinds of stuff, so we figured if they ain't home we might be able to get some food here. You fellas are more than welcome to come up with us to check. I'm sure there'd be plenty to share, cuz that's what folks should be doin' now, ain't it? Sharin' with their neighbors."

"Yes, yes they should. What's your name, buddy?"

"Clay. This is my brother, Jay. What's yours?"

"I'm Alan. This is Rich and Steve. Pleased to meet you boys. Let's go up and check this place out, together. Who knows what we might find?"

Clay nodded and started to climb the fence. Alan stopped him.

"No need to climb, Clay. We have a key." He motioned to Steve, who ran to the truck and came back with a pair of bolt cutters. He cut the chain, and as it was falling to the ground, Alan opened the gate and gestured for Clay and Jay to go through first.

"After you, friends. Let's go see what these folks might have to help out a neighbor."

\*\*\*\*

Clay didn't bother telling their new acquaintances they already had a pretty good idea what was up at the house, since they had already been there, but having other guys around to help if things went bad was a plus. Old man Dotson was going to be in for a rude awakening if he came after them with a shotgun this time.

When they got to the house and found it abandoned, Clay was slightly disappointed. He would have loved to see the look on Jim Dotson's face when five of them showed up at his door. *Bet he wouldn't be so apt to not share what he had then.* He was even more disappointed to find that they had taken all their food and supplies with them. He came running up from the basement as Alan was slamming cupboard doors open.

"Nobody's here, and there's nothing left. No food, no guns—nothing. They even took their clothes. Where would they go? How could they get there? His truck's in the driveway, and probably won't run anyway, cuz it's too new."

Alan raised an eyebrow at Clay. "You were looking for guns?"

Clay stammered, "Well, uh, you know you can always use a gun for hunting, and, um, you never know when you might need to protect yourself. I mean, who knows, with everything gone to shit like it is, when you might, you know, run into some assholes on the road... not that you guys are assholes, but, you know ..."

"Yeah, I do know. Shut up. Did they have any other vehicles they might have left in? Anything older that could still be running?"

"Not that I know of. Hang on a sec."

Clay went out the back door; it only took him a minute to check, and he headed back in. "They had a motorhome parked out back. It's gone. But I don't know how they could have used it to leave. It shouldn't be running either. It wasn't that old."

"Anybody else live out here they might have moved their motorhome to, if they figured out how to move it?"

Clay stood there thinking. Jay finally spoke—it was the first time since being confronted by Alan and his crew. "The Warren place is only about a mile or so away as the crow flies. Their place is big. They could have gone over there, I guess."

Alan looked at Jay. "This Warren place—where is it exactly?"

"Well, from here, you go out to the main road, turn right, go about a mile, turn right again, then go about two miles. It's on the left, but it's not easy to find these days. They've got the gate hidden and you can't see in the place from the outside anywhere."

At the words "gate hidden," Alan looked to Rich and Steve, who were both listening intently to Jay's description. He turned to Jay. "Do you know how many people are at that farm … What was it, the Warren place?"

Jay backed up a step, coming into contact with one of the kitchen chairs. "Um, well, there used to only be the Warrens, which was two people. But we ran into them a while back on the road out in front of their place, and they had some other guys with them we didn't know. So, no, no idea how many's in there now, but I do know it's a lot more than two."

"Give us a minute, would ya, fellas? I need to talk to my buddies about something."

Clay saw his opportunity to get Alan's attention again. "Sure thing, Alan. We'll just wait out on the porch. C'mon, Jay."

****

As the Glass brothers went out the door, Alan looked again at Rich and Steve. "Well, guys, we were needing some more men to help us take that place. These two might be a good addition. They know this area and the folks who live here pretty good, so it seems. They may be able to get them to open the gate and let us walk in. What do you think?"

Not wanting to incur the wrath of their slightly psychotic friend, they both nodded and smiled. Rich replied, "Sure, Alan. Sounds like a great plan. But, what if they don't want to join us?"

Alan headed toward the door to bring in his new recruits. "You say that like they have a choice."

# Chapter 25

I was walking up to the new fence line with a jug of water and cups when I ran into Mike and Bill. Mike was ranting as he and Bill quickly headed toward the spot Pete was clearing. "I can't believe Pete went off alone with no backup. How many times do we have to go over safety protocols?"

Bill shrugged. "I hear ya, but some people just don't get how unstable and dangerous things are right now. Do you know if he at least has a sidearm with him?"

"He had one on earlier when we went to get the Dotsons. I just hope he kept it with him."

We got to the spot where Russ and his crew were working. Russ saw the look on Mike's face. "What's up? Has something happened?"

Mike stopped long enough to relate the story to Russ. Russ shook his head, frustrated as well. "I truly hope it doesn't take someone getting hurt, or worse, possibly killed, to get the message across that it is a very unsafe world we are living in right now. No one should go anywhere alone, even within the relative safety of this place. You want any help? These guys can handle this without me. I'm pretty sure Matt and Nick have strung more fence than all of us put together."

At the sound of their names, the Thompson brothers looked up and grinned around the barbed wire staples in their mouths. I almost tripped over a root, laughing at their antics. They looked like something out of a bad B-rated horror movie. When I finally got control of myself I asked if anyone wanted a cool drink. I held back from Matt and Nick.

"You boys might want to pass. We wouldn't want your new teeth to rust."

Matt spoke around the staples. "It's alright, Miss Anne. They're galvanized."

At that, we all had a good laugh. However, that came to an abrupt halt when we heard what sounded like gunfire coming from the direction Pete was working. We all dropped everything, picked up our rifles, and ran toward the sound.

****

Alan had taken the route Jay told them about to within a half-mile of the farm's gate. They got out of the truck and walked along the road, looking for any weak points. They found none.

Clay had been nervous since they had been "invited" to join the crew, but was trying to be nonchalant about it. "So, what are we looking for out here anyway?"

Alan turned to him. "Simple. A way in."

Clay's eyes got wide. "Man, we can't go in there. They've got I don't know how many people in there. I just know it's a hell of a lot more than the five of us. And I think they have guards or something. When we were out here before, a bunch of them came out of the gate to run us off."

Alan had already partaken of the meth again, and had a wild look on his face. "Then we won't use the gate. Who lives there?"

Clay pointed to Matt and Nick's house. "That's the Thompson place. We ain't seen nobody over there, and no one answered the door when we knocked a week or so ago. I don't reckon they were home when everything went off."

Alan grinned at him. "Well, then, let's go see if there's another way into this place. I'm sure the Thompsons won't mind if we cut across their yard."

As they started down the tree line, they heard what sounded like an engine running. Rich looked toward the sound. "Is that a tractor?"

Alan leered at his crew. "That's exactly what that is. Let's go introduce ourselves to the neighbors."

****

Pete had been working the tree line from our side of the property. He pulled down trees and cleared brush up to the fence. Since the livestock weren't allowed free range of the property, it wasn't a problem to cut the fence back there. Once he had a few sections of it cut away, he climbed back on the tractor and continued with the clearing on the other side, pushing over the posts as he went.

He had really gotten the hang of handling the big machine and was about to declare the path cleared when he felt something hit him in the back. A sharp, burning pain emanated from the spot. He reached back and felt something wet, and when he brought his hand back in front, it was covered in blood. He realized he had been shot, but he would have thought it would hurt more than that. He reached down to turn the tractor off and felt another bullet hit him in the shoulder. That one hurt a lot more. He yelped in pain as a third flew over his head. He slumped forward in the seat, the tractor jolting and stopping when his foot came off the clutch. It seemed like time had slowed down, or he was in some kind of slow motion. Every attempt at movement felt like how he imagined being in quicksand would feel.

When the final bullet hit him in the neck, he closed his eyes and thought of his wife and son. He prayed they would stay safe in this horrible new world. Hopefully the people here could protect them for him, since he wouldn't be there to do it himself. He was gone before anyone got to him.

**\*\*\*\***

"Oh my God, you shot him! You just shot him!" Jay had a look of shock on his face as Alan lowered the rifle and ejected the spent casing. He turned to the group of men with him and saw a mixture of shock, disgust, and downright fear. Rich and Steve were no strangers to murder, but Alan had done most of the killing in their trek across the county. Moreover, those people had been an immediate threat to the men as they took their homes, supplies, children, and wives. This man never even knew they were there.

Alan became indignant at the accusing stares. "What? Did you think we were just gonna go knock on the door and ask for their supplies? One down, that's how I see it. And look—he was nice enough to open the back door for us."

Jay was backing away, tugging on his brother's arm. "C'mon, Clay. This ain't us. We don't murder people. We might steal stuff, but we ain't killed nobody, and I ain't ready to start."

Alan pulled the rifle back up and pointed it at Jay. "You ain't goin' nowhere, asshole, 'til I say you do. You're just as guilty as the rest of us by being here, so you might as well go all the way now. Anyone who tries to leave ends up like that guy."

He motioned with his head toward the body. Jay stopped his backward movement, but didn't come any closer to Alan. He looked at his brother, who appeared to be in some kind of state of shock, as he wasn't talking, wasn't moving, wasn't doing anything except staring at the dead man. Clay turned to face Alan, nodding slowly.

"Sure, Alan. Let's do this. Lead the way."

Jay looked at his brother like he'd lost his mind. "Clay, you can't be serious. We can't do this!"

Clay shook his head. "We're in it now, little brother. Might as well go for the gold—or whatever they're hiding in there."

Alan grinned. "Now that's more like it. Let's go see what they *are* hiding in there."

Alan headed toward the tractor, hugging the tree line, focused on getting inside the place to see what they were protecting so fiercely. As he walked, Clay held back a bit and grabbed Jay. He spoke quietly, but not quietly enough. "Play along. First chance we get we're outta here. We ain't murderers."

Alan sneered. Whatever. He'd deal with them later.

****

We ran nonstop to where Pete had been working. Mike got there first, saw that Pete was down, crouched low, and held up his fist in the motion that meant freeze; he had been teaching us tactical hand signals during our training. We all stopped in our tracks. He then moved his hand down toward the ground in the crouch signal. We all got low. He crept up toward the tractor, checking the area through the scope of his rifle. The rest of us were within the tree line, watching his every move. He turned and pointed to Russ and Bill to come to him, staying low. Bill headed that way. Russ looked at me.

"Anne, please go back. I can't do this if I'm worried about you. We need Kate to get ready for Pete, if he's still alive. You need to let her know."

I shook my head forcefully as tears ran down my face. "Hell no. I'm not leaving you. Pete looks dead, and I can't bear the thought of that happening to you. No, I'm staying. I've got your back. I love you, Russ Matthews. Keep your head down, dammit."

He nodded and sighed, kissed me, and headed toward Mike. I turned to Matt and Nick, who were right behind me. "Nick, go find Monroe. Tell him to put the front guard on high alert, that we have shots fired. They probably didn't hear them, since we barely did over the tractor. *Don't* tell Sara anything until we know what shape Pete is in. Have Millie get the kids to the basement. Everybody goes into lockdown mode. We've drilled on it. This is why. Stay down, but hurry. Now *go!*"

After the first encounter with the Glass brothers, we had worked up a protocol of sorts as to what to do when the alarm was raised for any reason. Millie was in charge of getting the little kids to the basement, with Sara's help since she was still apprehensive about using a gun. She could, she just wasn't comfortable with it yet. Everyone else had an assigned post. No matter who was on security watch, those positions would change to Brian and Ryan in the holes, with Marietta, who had turned out to be quite the sniper, in the treehouse. Bob was ground patrol, along with Mike. Since Mike was with us, Sean would take the area around the house and buildings. Janet and Kate held positions inside the house, along with Ben and Rusty. Monroe was pretty much the foreman, overseeing all of it and manning the radio we normally kept in the kitchen. Once we went into lockdown, the ones in the basement were to stay there until the phrase "Freedom comes with a price" was spoken through the door. If anything other than that phrase was delivered, Millie would fill the doorway with double-ought buckshot. We hadn't had to test that scenario yet, and I truly hoped now wasn't the time.

Nick took off for the house. Matt watched his brother run off, then turned back to me. "Is Pete dead, Anne?"

With tears streaming down my face, I looked at him. "I don't know, honey. I hope and pray he's just hurt. Stay down."

Mike pulled the rifle down and held up five fingers. Five bad guys. Holy shit. He was positioned on the far side of the tractor, with the engine block between him and the shooters. He was beside Pete, who was still slumped over the steering wheel. He reached up with two fingers and placed them against Pete's neck. After a moment, he brought his hand down. With a look that was a mix of sheer agony and anger, he turned to us and shook his head. Matt lowered his gaze, sobbing quietly. I wrapped my arms around him and we cried together.

The day we had hoped wouldn't come was here. We'd lost one of our people. Someone with whom we had shared a meal and a laugh. Someone whom we had worked alongside to make our new home better and safer. But it wasn't safe enough. We knew that now. Now that it was too late for Pete.

Bill was enraged. He stood up and screamed, "You assholes are dead!" He started firing his Henry Big Boy rifle as fast as he could. The murderers—yes, I could call them that, because that was most assuredly how I thought of them now—returned fire. Mike and Russ were trying to get Bill under control, but he shook them off and kept firing. It didn't look like he was really aiming at anyone in particular, just shooting repeatedly in their vicinity. He spent all ten rounds and stopped to reload. He didn't take cover. He stood there in the open from the chest up. Mike grabbed him around the waist.

"Bill, get *down* before you get shot!" As Mike was dragging him to the ground, a bullet glanced off the tractor hood and ricocheted into Bill's eye. His other eye went wide, then dull as the life left his body.

"*No!*" I didn't even realize I was screaming. I ran and knelt down beside Bill, took his head in my hands, and laid it in my lap. I was crying hysterically. Russ tried to pull me away, to get to me to safety, but I wouldn't leave. I looked from Bill to Pete, back and forth, trying to figure out what I could do to help them.

We had planned for all kinds of medical emergencies. We had prepped supplies, taken classes, read instructional books. Weren't we ready for a situation like this? The cold hard truth was no, we absolutely weren't. We had gotten lucky when our people got into it with the scavengers. None of ours had been hurt bad, not that a gunshot wound is ever good, but none of the injuries had been life threatening. In the span of just a few minutes, two lives had been lost.

I didn't know how we were going to tell Sara and Ryan their loved ones were gone. It turned out we would only have to tell Sara; as I was trying to figure out what I would say, Ryan and Bob ran up. Ryan stopped dead in his tracks when he saw me on the ground with his brother's head in my lap, covered in his blood. His normally happy-go-lucky demeanor turned dark with pain and rage. He dropped down beside me and lightly touched Bill's head. He didn't have to ask—he knew his brother was gone. He leaned down and said something in Bill's ear which none of us could hear. Without saying a word to anyone, he stood up, unslung his .30-06 deer rifle from his back, and laid it across the tractor hood. He looked through the scope toward the tree line, and pulled the trigger.

Ryan looked over his shoulder to the body of his lifelong best friend. With silent tears running down his face, he tenderly said, "I got one for ya, bubba."

****

As they were walking toward the tractor, Alan was extremely cocky. "You see him go down? That's what happens to people that fuck with me. You don't show me respect, you're dead to me. Literally."

Rich was trailing Alan, putting more and more distance between them. "Man, you shouldn't have done that. We still don't know how many people they have in there. We don't know where they all are. This is going to get bad, real bad, and probably real fast. They could come swarmin' out of there with thirty people any second. We should go while we still can."

"Go? You mean away? The only place we're going is right through that spot the dead guy cleared out so nice for us. This is a sign, my man. They just happen to be cuttin' a new entrance when we just happened to be checking the place out? It's meant to be. Besides, if they had thirty people, why was he out here alone, with no backup? I bet they barely have enough to keep the place goin'. C'mon, I want to get a look inside, see what they're protectin' so hard."

Steve was keeping pace with Alan. "Al, Rich is right. Just cuz we can't see anybody don't mean they ain't in there. We need to hightail it out of here, come back later when we get more guys. I thought that was the plan, to get more guys."

"We got more guys! Dumb and Dumber over there—that's two more guys. How many more do you think we need?"

Rich replied under his breath, "A lot more."

Al was turning to give Rich a mouthful when the shots started. They all dove for the tree line, a couple of near misses for Al and Steve in the front. Al crouched down, swearing.

"Son of a bitch! There *is* someone else out there. And the assholes are shooting at us!" Al and Steve returned fire from the cover of the trees. After a minute or so, the shooting from the tractor stopped. Al turned to his crew and found Rich on the ground, holding the side of his head, blood running down his arm. With all the gunfire, they hadn't heard him screaming until it stopped.

"Oh my God, he shot my ear off! Oh my God, oh my God! Al, Steve, help me, I'm dyin'!"

Jay stood up with his .22 rifle in hand and yelled from about twenty feet away. "What did you expect? You killed one of their people! You're crazy, man! Clay, we need to go—this psycho fucker is going to get us killed!"

Alan had started to stand to have it out with Jay when he heard the bullet go by. It hit Jay in the center of his forehead, and

290

his head snapped back as the blood sprayed over his brother below him. He crumpled to the ground beside Clay, who stared at his brother's lifeless body. He reached out to touch Jay's arm, shaking him, trying in vain to bring him back.

"Jay? Jay! *Jay!*" He turned on Alan. "You stupid son of a bitch! Look what you did! They killed my brother because of you! This is all your fault!" Clay reached for Jay's rifle, and Alan brought his own to bear on Clay. Alan spoke softly, but with a voice full of malice.

"You want your momma to bury both of her idiot sons today? Don't be stupid, boy. Put that rifle down, before I put you down."

Clay was staring at him. "Yeah, you're right. I've got my momma to take care of. What now?"

Alan smirked at him. "Now, you carry your brother home so you can bury him where your momma can say goodbye. We're outta here."

Clay looked incredulous. "I can't carry him by myself! I need you guys to help me. I can go get the truck and bring it here ..."

Alan was shaking his head and turning away. "Nah, we gotta go, before those assholes get here. We're two men down now. We're gonna need more guys before we head through that hole over there."

He motioned to the cleared spot, then reached down to pull Rich to his feet. "C'mon, Van Gogh. Let's go wrap that ugly head of yours up. By the way, you're riding in the back of the truck. No way you're gettin' in front to bleed all over my upholstery."

The three men headed back the way they had come.

**\*\*\*\***

Clay stood there with his brother's body, unsure of what to do next. The sound of the tractor starting kicked him into motion, and he took off across the yard, heading for the field that would take him back to the Dotson place via the shortest route. Alan had been adamant they ride in his truck there, probably to keep the Glass brothers from taking off and leaving them. Now, Alan was leaving him to find his own way back.

As he headed back to retrieve his truck, a thought dawned on him. *The people at the Warren farm might come out to investigate, to see if they did any damage. What if they take Jay? What would I tell Momma?* There was nothing else to be done, though. He couldn't carry him alone, and his truck was a couple of miles away. He'd have to take the chance.

He picked up his pace. He needed to get his truck, get back to Jay without being seen, and get his brother's body loaded up to take home. He wasn't sure how he was going to get that middle part done—the not being seen—but he'd cross that bridge when he got to it.

As he headed further across the field, he heard another truck, not Alan's. He turned and squatted down in the tall grass to see who it was. The truck stopped at the gate to the farm. When the door opened, he almost peed himself.

The sheriff was here.

# Chapter 26

We loaded Pete's and Bill's bodies onto the scoop attached to the tractor. Ryan wanted to carry his brother himself, but we were able to convince him this would get them back the quickest. We were all in shock, but Ryan was falling into a black abyss right before our eyes. It was there in his face, in his demeanor, and it seemed to be enveloping his heart and soul. They had shared with us that he and Bill had been close growing up, despite the four-year age gap, but when their parents died in a freak car accident, twenty-year-old Bill took over raising his sixteen-year-old brother. Bill made sure he finished school, taught him a good work ethic, and showed him, through his own actions, how to be a good man. Neither had ever married, though there had been some close calls. Ryan fell in love easily; Bill, much more cautious, was always looking for the right woman. At thirty-two, he still hadn't found her. Now he never would.

Mike watched the remaining marauders slink off to wherever they came from through his minis, desperate to finish them off, but not wanting to take the chance we might lose any more of our people. No matter. He'd seen them, and confirmed their identity with Russ. The shitheels from the Callens', and the Glass brothers—at least one of them. I was surprised at the Glass boys being a part of this. We'd known they'd show their faces again, but figured it to be in more of a pain-in-the-ass way, with us firing shots over their heads to run them off, not this. We'd find them and make them pay for what they had done.

Bob drove the tractor and the rest of us followed behind, with Russ walking in front taking point and Mike at the rear watching for any more trouble. Matt and I were holding each other, sobbing uncontrollably. He had not seen a person die before, much less someone he knew. It was all I could do to hold myself together for his sake. I kept thinking about Sara and Tony. They didn't know yet that Pete was gone. I tried to put myself in Sara's place and went into another hysterical rage inside. If it had been Russ, I would have wanted to die too. But I wouldn't be able to just quit, like my heart would want to do. I had a son who would need a parent, especially if he only had one left. Sara would have to do that now, not quit; she'd have to be there for her son. Which meant we'd have to be there for her, to make sure she kept going.

As we were coming to the rise where the new fence had been going up, we saw Monroe and Brian hurrying toward us, followed by Nick. When they saw the bodies in the scoop, I could see their eyes quickly doing a roll call to see who was missing. They knew if Bob was driving, Pete was hurt bad or dead. Nick broke into a dead run for his brother and Matt met him on the way. For two kids who could fight like feral cats, they also knew the chances were pretty good that they were all they had left for family—blood family anyway. They hugged each other fiercely and walked on with their arms around each other.

Monroe and Brian reached the tractor and saw Pete and Bill. They looked at each of us one by one, then Brian finally spoke. "What happened?"

We told them what we had seen and heard and what had happened after we got there. Monroe was beside himself. "Who was it? Did you see them? Did you finish them?"

Mike filled them in. "I think we took one of them down. It looked like they left a body out there. We can go find out for sure, but we need to take care of this first." He gestured to the scoop, and Monroe nodded grimly.

"You're right. We'll take care of them. Don't dare think we won't. But we've got some mourning and grieving to handle first. We don't need to go after them all emotional and out of control. We need to find them, plan it out, then take 'em out."

I'd never heard Monroe talk like that before. He was such a fun-loving guy, always giving people a hard time, then laughing at his own jokes or digs. This was a different side I hadn't yet seen. But then again, we were all about to see another side of ourselves and each other. Death had touched us; we were not immune.

We went on to the house and Bob parked the tractor under the trees. We stood there a moment before I asked, "How do we do this? We need to tell Sara before she sees Pete. What do we do about the kids? Do we let them see this? Dead bodies?" My voice broke at those last two words, because I still couldn't handle the thought that two of our people were gone.

Surprisingly, Brian offered a suggestion, and a good one at that. "Call for Kate and Sara. Tell the rest to wait. Sara won't get hysterical if Kate comes at the same time, since she'll think Pete is hurt and that's why we need Kate. Let Sara deal with it by herself first. She doesn't need to have to worry about Tony right this second."

We agreed that was the way to go. Monroe offered to go get them, so Millie would know he was okay as well. He went to the back door of the house while we waited outside. What I know was just a minute or so seemed like an hour. Brian offered to go to the front and get the rest of our people. Yes, it would leave the gate unmanned, but we needed to be together at this moment. He looked to Mike for confirmation. A quick nod from our head of security sent him off at a run.

When Monroe came back with Sara and Kate in tow, Kate had a bag with her to treat any immediate injuries she could, since she didn't know what she would be dealing with when she got out there. She knew as soon as she saw our faces her services would not be required; I watched as the tears started to form in her eyes.

Sara hurried toward us. When she saw the bodies in the scoop, she stopped in her tracks, looking around feverishly for Pete. She raised a trembling hand to her mouth and started slowly shaking her head. Her knees began to buckle and Kate grabbed her to support her. Monroe was at her other side in an instant. They held her up and helped her continue toward us. She had to do it. She had to see him. She had to deal with it, now. We didn't have the luxury of time in dealing with death anymore. Dead bodies with no embalming would start to decay almost immediately, and no one wants or needs to actually see that happen to a loved one. Since their deaths were caused by trauma, and not disease, there was little to no risk of us contracting anything from them, but we did have to be careful where we buried them, so that the bodies wouldn't come into contact with any of our water sources. And we needed to bury them pretty quick; it was heating up, with summer coming on.

Sara was crying so hard she couldn't speak. She fell to her knees beside her husband, leaning on his body with great heaving sobs. She raised her head and released a wail so full of pain it cut me to the core. I joined her in her grief and Russ had to support me to keep me from collapsing as well. This just couldn't be happening. And yet it was.

We waited for her to get through her initial shock. No one was going to rush her. We were on her schedule for the moment. After about five minutes, she looked up at Mike. In a voice consumed with pain, she spoke. "Did you kill the piece of shit who murdered my husband?"

Mike knelt beside her. "Not yet. We wanted to get him back to you as quick as we could. But I will. Count on it."

She nodded to him without saying anything else. She looked back at Pete and leaned over and kissed his lips. There was blood on his face from the neck wound. She pulled a tissue out of her pocket and tried to wipe it off.

"I can't let Tony see him like this. I need to clean him up. I need some water ... something ..."

Kate stepped up and pulled some alcohol wipes out of her bag. "Here, Sara. Use these. I'll help you."

Working together, they got his face mostly clear of the blood. She looked at his shirt, seeing more blood from the other gunshot wounds.

"Can we change his shirt? Or cover him up with something? I really don't want Tony's last memories of his father to be this." She gestured to her husband's body, and her voice caught at the end. She closed her eyes, took a deep breath, and looked at me. "Anne, is there a spare sheet we can cover him with? Surely you understand; you wouldn't want Rusty to see Russ like this."

Just when I thought I had gotten control of myself, she said that to me. The thing I had been thinking since we found Pete. I lost it again. After a moment, I got myself composed enough to get out, "Of course, Sara. We wouldn't bury them without covering them with something. We've got extra sheets in one of the trailers."

"I'll get them. I know where they are." Bob took off at a jog toward the shed.

Brian came back with Marietta, Sean, Lee, and Jim. I had forgotten Jim was on duty, the Dotsons having been added to the security rotation immediately. Jim hurried over to us, specifically to speak to Monroe. Brian had told them what had happened, so he was not surprised at the bodies, but he looked shaken up when he actually saw them.

"Monroe, I know this is a bad time, but Sheriff Burns is at the gate. Said he was sorry he was late, that he was supposed to stop by this morning to get your answer on the extra fields but he got held up in town. Wanted to know if you could talk now."

"Well, I think now is a damn fine time to talk to the sheriff. We can tell him all about the lawlessness runnin' rampant out here in the county from thievin', murderin' pieces of shit. Let's go, Jim. Russ, you come with us."

They headed toward the gate. Bob returned with the sheets. Ryan had been silent the whole time. When Bob started to cover Bill's body, Ryan stepped up to him and held his hands out. "I'll do it. He's my brother."

Bob handed him one of the sheets and Sara the other. While Ryan covered Bill's entire body, including his face, Sara left Pete's face exposed as she covered his body with trembling hands. She looked to us when she had finished.

"Tony will need to see his face. He'll need that to believe it's his dad and that he's gone. I just want to cover up the blood and the wounds."

She ran her hand through his hair, stood up, and turned toward the house. She'd started to walk back when Bob touched her arm. "Hey, let me go get him. As soon as he sees your face, he'll know something bad has happened. It'll freak him out, and that will probably radiate through all the kids. Let's get him out here first, then we can tell the rest of them. He needs to be able to do this without a bunch of folks watching."

Sara looked at him and nodded, with just a hint of a smile on her lips. "That's a good idea. Thank you, Bob. I'll just wait here with Pete."

Bob went to the house to get Tony and was met by Ben and Rusty at the door. They had both been crying. We had forgotten they were upstairs. They would have seen everything from up there. Bob hugged them both and told them to go back upstairs; we'd come get them in a few minutes. He called to Millie in the basement and asked her to send Tony up, but keep the rest of the kids down there for just a bit longer. Millie and Janet must have figured out something was tragically wrong, and now they would know for sure it involved Pete. Tony looked confused and concerned as he walked out of the house toward us. Kids aren't stupid. They know when something's wrong. They just don't normally assume it involves their parents. Unfortunately, "normal" had been gone for everyone since the pulse.

When he saw his mother's face, it was clear Tony knew. His dad was gone. Without even seeing him, or perhaps because he didn't see him, he knew their worst nightmare had come to life. He ran to his mother, who opened her arms to receive her son. He looked around her waist and saw his dad's body.

"Nooo! Dad! Dad, no!" Over and over, in a voice filled with anguish, he tried to deny what his eyes told him. Sara held him tightly as the rest of us backed away to give them a modicum of privacy, except for Ryan. Still dealing with his own loss, he went to the small family—smaller now—and wrapped his arms around them both. They returned the gesture, all needing comfort and sympathy for their loss and knowing that, at that moment, the three of them understood it more than the rest of us could.

****

Gary watched as Monroe and the guys pushed the fake foliage aside so they could see each other, taking care to not get into the razor wire on top. When he saw the somber looks on their faces, he knew something was up.

"Hey, Monroe, fellas. Everything okay?"

"No, Gary, it isn't. We just had a run-in with some assholes, and they killed two of our people while we were working to get things ready for the townsfolk to start a garden. Ironic, ain't it—we're trying to help folks and lose some of ours in the process!"

The sheriff was taken aback at the forcefulness of Monroe's remarks, as well as the words he had spoken. "What? What happened? Can I do anything to help?"

"It's too late to help the ones we lost. The fellas think Ryan took one of them down, and that he's laying outside the fence over there on the Thompsons' side. If you want to go take a look, see who did this, we'll meet ya over there. We've got a way to get there through the fence. I'm sure you can understand why we wouldn't want to open the gate."

"Sure thing, Monroe. I'll meet y'all over there."

Gary went back to his truck, where Tim was waiting for him. They had decided to come out together so that, more than anything else, Tim could see what had been going on while he was safe and sound in the sheriff's office. While Gary didn't fault him for it, he was disappointed that Tim hadn't cared enough about anyone but himself to have at least checked on some of the folks in town to see if he could do anything to help. But that was the difference between doing a job because you loved it and were committed to your community, or doing it for a paycheck. Tim was definitely in the latter group, and since he wasn't getting a check anytime soon, he took his pay however he could get it.

Gary told Tim what Monroe had relayed to him, and that they were going to go see who had been left behind, to see if it was someone they knew. They had seen some unfamiliar faces in town that day, and Gary had surmised that people were making their way further into the country, trying to escape what had to be horrendous conditions in the cities by now. He knew why, but that didn't stop him from worrying about the path they would be going down very soon. With limited resources already, he didn't see how they could handle feeding more folks than they already had. It was something he would have to talk to the mayor about when he got back. Right now, they needed to deal with this situation.

****

Clay was freaking out. How could he get over there and get Jay with the sheriff around? He'd ask questions about how this happened. What would Clay say? How could he explain how horribly wrong everything had gone today? All they were trying to do was get by. Yeah, they had planned on breaking into some houses, but only those owned by people who weren't there and wouldn't need the supplies. Yeah, he had tried to break into the Dotson house before, but he had learned his lesson on that one: don't screw with people who are really good hunters, because there's a really good chance they have guns that they are really good at using.

It didn't matter. He had to go and get his brother. The sheriff knew who they were and would be coming around asking questions at home. *It's gonna be hard enough to explain to Momma that Jay's dead. I don't need the sheriff there making it worse.*

He pulled in the drive as the sheriff was coming in from the other direction. He was heading to the spot where he'd left the body. The sheriff pulled in behind him and followed. *Might as well get this over with*, Clay thought. *Looks like I'll have some help getting Jay in the truck after all.*

He stopped at the spot where his brother's body lay and got out. He thought it looked like Jay was sleeping, except for the hole in his forehead. The sheriff stopped behind him, effectively blocking Clay from leaving. He and the deputy joined Clay beside Jay's body.

"Looks like you've had some trouble this morning, son. Want to tell me about it?"

Clay slowly nodded and began to tell them what had happened. When he finished, the sheriff looked at Jay, then back to Clay. "Pretty high price your family paid today. Was it worth it?"

Clay became indignant. "Well, what are we supposed to do, Sheriff? Sit home and starve? Ain't no stores selling food. EBT cards don't work anymore. How are we gonna eat? How are we gonna live?"

"Like everybody else, Clay. You work for it. Do you know why that man you boys killed—the one on the tractor—was out there

305

today? He was clearing land and a path in for people who don't have yards, or seed, or tractors, or the know-how to grow food. Monroe Warren was opening up a section of his place to help folks like that. People who work the land will get a portion of the food for their families. You say you don't know anything about hunting? There are people who do know and can show you, teach you how to hunt, how to clean the game. But now, two of their people are dead. Do you think they'll still be willing to help anybody else out?"

Just as the sheriff was finishing his speech, Monroe Warren appeared with a group of men. When Monroe saw Clay, Clay saw Monroe's face turn red with anger. "The answer to that would be hell no! How did I know you would be one of the ones involved in this, Clay Glass? You can't shoot a squirrel or a rabbit, but you can kill a man who's trying to help other folks out? That man had a family—a wife and a young son. The other man you killed was the only blood family one of our folks had. Sheriff, I want him locked up. We need some kind of trial, a speedy one, so we can hang his ass in the town square."

Clay shrank back at Monroe's rage. "No, Mr. Warren, it wasn't me; it wasn't me or Jay. They made us come with them! They made us show them this place. We weren't shooting at your people! We tried to get them to stop. They wouldn't listen to us, even threatened to shoot us, too. We didn't, we wouldn't—"

"Don't lie to me, boy!" Monroe snapped. "You threatened to come back to my place shootin' just a few days ago! You may not have this time, but I believe you could and would do it. What are you gonna do about this, Gary?"

Sheriff Burns looked to be doing some serious contemplating. He finally looked at Monroe. "Honestly, Monroe, I don't know what we should do here. As far as I can tell, there isn't really any 'government' to speak of right now. I can't house prisoners in the jail—I can't feed them. I don't know what my authority is right now."

"I'll tell you what your authority is, Sheriff. The sheriff is the supreme law in the county. He outranks state and federal forces. The state and the Feds seem to have forgotten that. With no other law enforcement, it falls on you to keep the peace. Since you can't feed him, we need a speedy trial, just like in the Old West days, with a quick commuting of the sentence. All we need is a judge and a couple of lawyers. Surely there's someone in town to fill those seats."

The sheriff nodded firmly. He turned to Clay. "Son, I'm gonna have to take you in. I'll help you get your brother's body home to your momma, but then you're gonna have to come with me. Tim, you drive his truck once we get Jay in it. Clay will ride in mine."

Clay started crying. "No, no, please! I didn't do anything! I can't go to jail! Who'll take care of Momma?"

The expression on Monroe's face was emotionless. "You should have thought about that before you took up with them murderous thugs, boy."

# Chapter 27

We laid Pete and Bill to rest the next day on the hill next to the spot Monroe had set aside for him and Millie. Monroe read a passage from the Bible, very fitting to the situation.

"The righteous man perishes, and no one lays it to heart; devout men are taken away, while no one understands. For the righteous man is taken away from calamity; he enters into peace; they rest in their beds who walk in their uprightness." Isaiah 57:1-2.

Sara and Tony were supporting each other in their grief. To me, this was normal and healthy. It is never good to try holding all that pain inside. That was the very reason we were concerned for Ryan. The joking, grinning, fun-loving young man we had come to know had left us. In his place was a silent, brooding, dangerous-looking guy. Every effort we made to sympathize with him was gently but firmly rebuffed. He sought solitude rather than family.

As we headed back to the house, I pulled Russ and Mike aside and let the rest of our group go on. When I thought we were out of earshot of Ryan, at least, I shared my concerns with them.

"I'm really worried about Ryan. He doesn't talk to anyone unless they point blank address him, and then it's the bare minimum he can get away with for a response. He hasn't eaten a thing since yesterday, before it all happened. He insisted on taking his regular watch schedule this morning when we tried to substitute Carrie in his place. I don't know what we can or need to do for him, but I feel like we should keep an eye on him."

"I hear you, Anne, and I have been trying to keep up with him without being too obvious." Mike's face was grim as he continued. "He's in a bad place right now, and he's got to get through this in the way that's best for him. All we can do is let him know we're here for him if or when he needs us and give him space. I saw this when I served, when we lost men. Their best friends, brothers-in-arms, wanted nothing more than to make those responsible pay for the pain they were feeling. I think that's where Ryan is right now. He's hurting so bad and he wants those men to feel his pain. The best thing we can do is keep him from doing something stupid."

We were so wrapped up in our conversation we hadn't realized Ryan had come up behind us. I physically jumped when he spoke. "I appreciate you guys worrying about me, I really do. I know you love me and consider me family. I feel the same. And yes, that's exactly what I want: I want those fuckers *dead*. But I'm not going to go off half-cocked trying to take them out by myself. Just promise me, Mike, that when the time is right, we find them and end them. I can't stand the thought of them walking around, breathing, eating, laughing, or anything else when I just put my brother in the ground."

He looked back up the hill to the spot we'd just left. The night before, Lee had made some really nice markers, waterproofed and sealed, and the morning sun was glinting off of the shiny surfaces that were the result of his hard work. Mike laid a hand on Ryan's shoulder as we continued walking back toward the house.

"We will, brother, you have my word. Just not right now, not yet. We need to do some healing. We need to beef up security. We need to retrain everybody on protocols—*no one* goes *anywhere* alone again. *Everyone* we don't know is a potential threat. We're going to have to rethink how to keep our security in place and keep our people safe if we decide to go through with this plan to let folks from town in to work that land back there."

We had caught up to the rest of the group and Monroe heard that last part. "I already told the sheriff I didn't know if we were gonna go through with it. I absolutely am not comfortable with anybody being on our land that's not a part of our group now."

Millie, who almost always deferred to whatever the rest of us thought, felt, or said, surprised us all. "Monroe, would you condemn all the people in town we could help with this new garden on the actions of a few bad men? I'm almost positive those men are not from town. I would think the ones who could be helped would be willing to provide security for the land that holds the garden, as well as the area between there and here, for themselves and us.

Surely you can make that part of the deal? I'm sure Gary would agree with those terms. If not, then we close it back up, just take care of our own."

Monroe leaned over and kissed his wife on the cheek. "Alright, Millie darlin'. We'll try it your way. Gary'll be back in a day or so. I think he wanted to give us time to take care of our business and simmer down some—not that it's likely we'll do that anytime soon. Plus, he has to figure out how to deal with that Glass boy *and* try to find those assholes who did this to our people. We've all got stuff to do for now."

Sara walked up to Mike, tears still glistening in her eyes. "I want you to teach me and Tony how to shoot. I don't mean the target practice stuff I've been doing. I mean pistols, shotguns, rifles—all of it. I want both of us to be as comfortable with any kind of gun as you are. I was stupid to think we could go on the way things used to be, helping those less fortunate than us. All that got us was pain and loss. No more, Mike. Pete wanted to spend more time with you on gun training and I talked him out of it. I told him we were safe here, that it wasn't like being out on the road and there were plenty of other people here who could handle that part. I was wrong—so, so very wrong. I was scared of guns; I still am. But I don't want to be, not anymore. I've already lost my husband. No one is taking my son from me."

Mike didn't say anything, just nodded back at her. Sara then addressed the rest of us.

"I owe you all an apology. I was blind to what the world is becoming. I didn't want to see it for what it is: a place where no one is safe any longer. I see that now, though it's too late for my husband. I hold a degree of responsibility for his death. I told him it couldn't be as bad out there as you all were making it out to be. I told him *we* didn't have to resort to violence, that we were better than that. Again, I was very, very mistaken. If we never help anyone outside of the people here now, I'm fine with that. You are the only ones I care about now. I will fight by your side to keep us all safe from harm."

I was speechless; I think we all were. Honestly, I had expected Sara to go in the opposite direction. You know, "See how dangerous guns are? No one should have them!" The path many people mistakenly take after an event like this, without considering that the bad guys would never give their guns up. Yet here she was, eyes wide open, dots connected, seeing the world for what it was becoming—a scary, dangerous place.

Russ gave Sara a small smile. "No apology needed, Sara. None of us wants to think about what the world out there is becoming, but we have no choice. We can try to plan for the worst possible situations, and we still won't be ready for them. This is a perfect example. We were probably all too complacent, feeling a false sense of security. We couldn't see the world outside the farm, so we thought it couldn't see us. We were wrong. Starting today, we will prepare for the inevitable: people are going to die trying to survive.

We don't want any of those people to be one of us again. We will remain vigilant. We will take nothing for granted."

"It's going to get worse, folks." Mike said. "We're far enough into this now that many people have died from illness and starvation. The scavengers have already been through all the empty houses. They'll be starting on the ones that have people in them and taking by force whatever those people have left, which probably isn't much. As the population dwindles down, we are going to be left with pretty much three factions. Good folks like us, trying to eke out a life, working together for the common good, not bothering anybody else but willing to do what we have to do to ensure our safety and keep our supplies, and assholes like the ones who killed our people, trying to eke out a life by taking from others. By the way, those people will start forming gangs, to increase their numbers, in turn increasing their level of force. Problem is, the more mouths they have to feed, the more violent they will become to get what they need to survive. They will be our most imminent threat."

"What's the third faction?" Sean asked.

"Unfortunately, due to what we've heard on the radio, that will be our own government, trying to 'help.' Their whole 'for the greater good' philosophy would see us stripped of everything we have here, to be dispersed among everyone in this area."

"Oh, *hell* no!" Monroe exclaimed.

"I don't think so!" Bob added.

Mike nodded grimly. "Agreed. I'm not sure what to expect on that front. They will have us out-gunned, possibly out-manned—just depends on how many police and UN troops they bring with them. I truly don't think any US service men or women will bear arms against law-abiding citizens. I hope local law enforcement doesn't either. UN troops will have no such loyalty. Right now, though, our biggest threat is civilians."

Russ looked at all of us. "I told you when we got here that bad people were coming. I hate that I was right, and more so that it was this soon. We'll do what we have to do to keep our family safe. Let's get busy doing that."

# Acknowledgments

I'll start off by saying this again: thank you for purchasing this novel. The success of the first one was more than I dreamed possible. This installment has some pretty big shoes to fill.

I want to take a moment to thank all of you who left a review for the first book. I read every one of them, and some of them more than once. I received messages on Facebook, and email messages from my website. While not all of the above were positive, I understand where some of the negative comes from as well. This is a very scary idea, perhaps even more because it, or something like it, could actually happen. Everybody has their own ideas as to how a scenario like this would play out. I did take to heart some of the thoughts that were shared with me and incorporated them into this volume. If you see something you messaged me about at some point, give yourself a pat on the back, including my dad and my sister.

For any of you who are offended by the swear words, I'm sorry, but I'm pretty sure it would be a whole lot worse than that if this really happened. I try to keep them situation and character appropriate.

I have been called to task for situating the women in traditional homemaking roles. Here's the thing: if I'm a better cook than my husband, and he's a better fence stringer than me, why wouldn't we play to our strengths? Yes, this is the twenty-first century, and yes, women are taking on more positions formerly male dominated, but when you are thrust back to the nineteenth century technologically, are you going to fight over women's rights, or what you perceive as his and hers roles, or are you going to do whatever you are best at to help everyone get by, survive, and thrive? Regarding all my references to coffee making and coffee drinking: if SHTF and I couldn't get it anymore, that would be one of the things I would miss the most. I might need to buy some more for my preps, now that I think about it.

It's easy to sit back and read a book and think, "This guy's an idiot. It would never happen like that." Believe me, I know. I've done it as well. Having now been on the other side of the page, what my imagination came up with may not be what someone else's sees, and that's okay. I'm a glass-is-half-full kind of gal, so I want to see positive, good things in people. My husband is my alter ego, and helps keep me in the middle of the path.

This book series is based on something that could happen. It isn't like outer space science fiction we can read and enjoy, knowing it probably won't happen, at least not in our lifetime. We read books about mythical creatures, not expecting them to ever come to life, so we can immerse ourselves in the story without being bothered by "what if." This book is fiction. While I have based some of the characters' personalities and histories on people in my life, it is ultimately a story I dreamed up one day and decided to try to write. Forgive my ideas and ideals as to the way the events might happen. I want the books to make you think, but it isn't a true story and it hasn't happened—yet.

Now, to the thank yous. I have to again thank my husband, Jim, for his help in this whole endeavor. He helped me with quite a few sections in this book as to how to describe what the people were doing or building. On pretty much every trip we've taken this summer, he took on almost all the driving so I could write on the road. He keeps my mailing list completely up to date and did the first versions of the covers for both books. He's my number one fan and keeps me both grounded and over the moon. Thank you again, baby.

My circle is small, so again I thank my aunt, Carol, for her reading of my work-in-progress and input along the way. She never failed to message me to tell me how much she loved the most current version she had been reading and couldn't wait to get the next part of the story. My number two fan, right behind my hubby, with her own full plate, she made time to help me put out a good story. Thank you again, sweet aunt.

Thank you to all the followers on my social media pages. Your loyalty and enthusiasm are not something I will ever forget. I feel as if some of you are old friends. I wouldn't change that for anything.

Last, but certainly not least, I give the glory to God that he blessed me with a gift I didn't know I had, to share with others. I don't think I can say it any better than I did in the first book's acknowledgments: I placed my life in His hands and all I have is because of Him. Thank you, Lord, for the many blessings you bestow upon me every day.

Keep an eye out for the next installment in the *A Powerless World* series. Coming soon!

Find us on the web!

The website is always updating, so keep coming back for more info. Want to stay up to date on all our latest news? Join our mailing list for updates giveaways and events!

www.paglaspy.com

Facebook: facebook.com/paglaspy

Twitter: @paglaspy

Goodreads: P.A. Glaspy

Bookhub: P.A. Glaspy

34065202R00200

Made in the USA
San Bernardino, CA
29 April 2019